DATE DUE

APR 1 0 2015			
MAY 1 4 2015			
JUN 0 1 2017			
APR 1 6 2018			
12-22-18			
		PRINTED IN U.S.A.	

Last Bite

ALSO BY NANCY VERDE BARR

We Called It Macaroni: An American Heritage
of Southern Italian Cooking

Make It Italian: The Taste and Technique
of Italian Home Cooking

In Julia's Kitchen with Master Chefs
(with Julia Child)

Last Bite

A NOVEL

Nancy Verde Barr

ALGONQUIN BOOKS OF CHAPEL HILL　2006

Published by
ALGONQUIN BOOKS OF CHAPEL HILL
Post Office Box 2225
Chapel Hill, North Carolina 27515-2225

a division of
WORKMAN PUBLISHING
708 Broadway
New York, New York 10003

Library of Congress Cataloging-in-Publication Data
Barr, Nancy Verde.
     Last bite : a novel / Nancy Verde Barr.—1st ed.
        p. cm.
     ISBN-13: 978-1-56512-495-0; ISBN-10: 1-56512-495-2
     1. Women cooks—Fiction.   2. Rejection (Psychology)—Fiction.
3. Americans—Italy—Fiction.   4. New York (N.Y.)—Fiction.
5. Cookery—Fiction.   6. Italy—Fiction.   I. Title.
PS3602.A77744L37 2006
813'.6—dc22   2005053073

10 9 8 7 6 5 4 3 2 1
First Edition

For Roy

"Anybody can make you enjoy the first bite of a dish, but only a real chef can make you enjoy the last."

—François Minot, editor of *Guide Michelin*

Last Bite

Chapter 1

I've always been crazy but it's kept me from
going insane. —*Waylon Jennings*

They say insanity is repeating the same behavior
again and again and expecting different results.
I think real insanity is knowing the results will
be the same and repeating the behavior anyway. When my
most recent romance ended, I bought a gerbil and named him
Insanity. He's pretty innocuous and probably doesn't deserve
the name, but when he engages in that incessant wheel spinning
that leads nowhere, he reminds me that, when it comes to love,
I am prone to the same behavior. He also reminds me that the
last man in my life turned out to be a rodent. So from now on
it's just Insanity and me—and my job, which I love.

I work for *Morning in America,* a newsmagazine show on
national TV that airs from seven to nine in the morning. When
the credits run, I roll by as "Executive Chef, K. C. Costello."
The K. C. is for Katherine Conti, but I've been called Casey
since fifth grade. "Executive Chef" means that I arrive at the
studio sometime around five-thirty to oversee the preparation
of ingredients and backup dishes for the cooking segments.
Mostly I work with Sally Woods, the grand old dame of food

television and our regular on-air cook, but I also prep for guest chefs, cooking teachers, and celebrities who come on the show to demonstrate their talents or plug their new cookbooks. When you watch a food show and see all those little bowls of measured-out ingredients, when the chef puts raw ingredients into one pan and then turns to a twin pan with the ingredients all cooked, and when a finished dish miraculously appears from under the counter, that's because someone like me is backstage getting it all together. Preparing and cooking the food is the easy part, especially since I have a great assistant who is fast and efficient. What's tricky is knowing when to make the swaps from raw to partially cooked to fully cooked so that it all works out in the time allotted.

Occasionally, the show sends Sally on location to tape week-long food specials, and sometimes they send me along to do what I do. About two months ago, the executive producer told us that we would be spending a week taping food segments in several Italian cities. That is what led to the demise of my last stab at romance. I wanted Richard, my then-boyfriend, aka rodent, to meet me at the end of the shoot and spend a few days together in *bella Italia*. My vision was of him whisking me around on a Vespa scooter á la Audrey Hepburn and Gregory Peck in *Roman Holiday*.

Richard Payne is a dentist. (He really should have changed his name.) I met him when he appeared in a health segment on our show to discuss implant surgery. His six-foot-two frame is workout fit, and that morning I was getting excited just picturing him in his white dentist's jacket. I liked the six foot two because I'm five foot ten, and I know from experience that staring up into a man's eyes is more romantic than looking down. I was twenty-nine; he told the audience he was thirty-two. Seemed perfect.

After his segment, I went out on the set to chat; in other

words, to drop hints that I was single and would love to see him again. I'm not shy about being obvious but I am traditional about wanting the man to do the asking out. He didn't ask, so I told him that I would like him to be my dentist. I thought that was fairly obvious, but he just gave me his office number. After one appointment for a cleaning and general checkup and another for teeth whitening, I had to deep-six my principles and ask him out. Under other circumstances, I would have been more patient, but the office visits were expensive. He said he was planning on asking me out, but you just have to wonder what he was waiting for. We began dating, and after a few months, I more or less moved in with him. On one level, it was a matter of convenience. He lived near the studio; I was temporarily living back with my parents in New Rochelle, a forty-minute trip from the city. The distance makes a difference at night when you have to end a date in time to catch the train. It's huge at five in the morning.

On another level, I thought the relationship might be "it." We really enjoyed being together and mostly liked the same things. But, after seven and a half months together, I couldn't shake off a nagging feeling that something major was missing. When I asked him to meet me in Italy, he began to twitch. Then he frowned as though I'd asked him to come up with the formula for gene therapy.

"You know I can't leave my office on such short notice."

"But it's over two months away! You have a partner. You have a secretary who can reschedule your patients. You have a passport. You've never been to Italy."

"Here we go again," he said, throwing his head to the side in an exasperated gesture.

"What's that supposed to mean?"

"We go through this every time one of these trips comes up, Casey. You ask me to go somewhere and I can't. I explain why I can't. You start to swear at me in Italian and then you storm out."

"So, what's your point?"

"The point is that I would love to take a trip with you but I want to do it when we have the time to plan. Research the place, look at brochures, and talk to people who have been there. Find the best rates."

I put a little more pleading in my voice. "Just once, can't you be a little spontaneous?"

"No. I can't. I don't like to do things that just come up. I never have and I never will. You know that." And, there it was. I did know that, yet I kept expecting it to turn out differently. Obviously I am only a few brain cells away from insanity.

"This isn't working, is it, Richard?"

"I think we need a break."

"You want to break up? Just like that. No discussion?"

"I said 'break' not 'break up.' I can't discuss it with you when you're angry."

"We're arguing! I'm supposed to be angry."

"Well, it makes it hard for me to think," he said, in the even, measured tone that he used when we'd argue. Unfortunately neither the Irish side nor the Italian side of my heritage has ever grasped the concept of arguing in even, measured tones, so I began to yell at him in Neapolitan gutter language.

"*Mannaggia! Tu sei patzo,*" I sputtered before heading for the front door. I yanked it open and then slammed it behind me, shouting *"Vaffanculo"* at the molar-shaped door knocker. I didn't start to cry until I was halfway to my parents' house in New Rochelle.

WHEN I WALKED IN, my parents were in the den yelling at the TV. *Wheel of Fortune* was on and they were begging a contestant to choose a *C*. The player ignored them and chose a *B* instead.

"Oh. I can't believe it! It's so obvious," my mother groaned. "Who ever heard of a 'bookie-butter plan'?"

"I knew she wouldn't get it. Look at that hair!" Dad thought a bad hairstyle on a woman was a sure sign that there wasn't much under it.

"Hi there. It's just me." I made my best stab at sounding as though I was just in the neighborhood and thought I'd stop by, but my mother took one look at me and arched an eyebrow ever so slightly. That was all it took. "I don't want to talk about it" was all I could manage before breaking into hysterical sobs.

"I'll make cannoli," my mother said, heading for the kitchen. Making cannoli was her way of acknowledging that this was a "situation." She'd let my father deal with the worst of the storm and wait for me to join her in the kitchen when I could speak clearly enough to tell her what happened. The Conti women have always unloaded a lot of baggage around the stove.

"Come here, sweetie," my father said stretching out his arms. I sat down on the couch next to him and he wrapped me in a huge bear hug. He's six feet three inches tall, so when he puts his arms around me, I feel held. I get my height from him and, thank God, my ability to eat what I want and still be able to zip my jeans. Everyone says we look a lot alike even though our coloring is very different. We both have thick, wavy hair; his is a warm blend of light and dark grays and mine is very dark brown and shoulder length. His eyes are blue, whereas I have my mother's dark brown eyes, but Dad and I crinkle them in the same way when we smile. Our eyes weren't crinkling at that moment.

He kissed the top of my head. "You want to tell your da what's up?"

I told him my story and then added, "I mean it's not all bad. Most of the time we get along really well."

"Ah, Casey. Richard's a nice guy. But there's more to love than liking the same things. You have to want the same things and you and Richard are on different wavelengths there."

"Tell me about it. Sometimes I worry that maybe it's just me. Maybe I just want too much excitement. I'm afraid that I'll quiet down and be sorry I've thrown away a really solid relationship. How old were you when you quieted down?"

He gave me a devilish grin. "I'm working on it." Then he tightened his arm to pull me closer. "Honey, I want to see you madly in love. I want you to be deliriously happy, swept away, head over heels, lose-your-appetite in love. Do you know what I mean?"

"Well, I can't identify with 'lose my appetite,' but I get the rest. It just doesn't seem to be there."

"Then he's not the one for my girl."

I could smell the cannoli shells frying so I kissed him on the cheek and went to the kitchen to see how they were doing. Cannoli have been my favorite sweet since I was a toddler. When I was two years old, I stood up in my highchair to reach for one on the table and fell to the floor, breaking my collarbone. I moved so fast, no one saw me. I've always been enthusiastic about food.

My mother keeps round disks of dough in the freezer so she can make cannoli at a moment's notice. The disks are less than a quarter of an inch thick, so by the time she heats the oil, sifts the sugar, and drains the ricotta the dough is pliable enough to wrap around the molds.

When I walked in, she was pulling a stool up to the cupboards to reach the top shelf for a bag of miniature chocolate chips for the filling. My mother is petite. Everything about her seems to be in miniature. Her hands are small. Her feet are small; I outgrew her shoes when I was in the third grade. Her dark brown eyes are so expressive that we all know immediately what she's thinking and feeling. Dad calls them "espresso eyes." Right now, they were saying "worried" to me. I was grateful they weren't saying "I told you so." When I moved in with Richard she spent at least a week raving that I was damned forever. Many of my friends' mothers warned about "not buying the cow if the milk was free"; mine took it all the way to eternal hell flames.

"I'll get those, Mom. Want me to mix the filling?"

"That'd be great. I've already sifted the sugar."

Four fried cannoli shells, still on their metal tubes, were draining on paper towels and she was working on four more pieces of dough. While she worked her rolling pin—really an old broom handle—over the thin circles of dough, stretching them into even thinner ovals, I told her about Richard and Italy. She continued to roll. My mother makes cannoli by rote, so I knew she heard every word I said even though she never stopped working. Well, not until I told her about saying *vaffanculo* in the hallway. Then her hands stopped and she looked up at the ceiling. "Jesus, Mary, and Joseph, Casey. Tell me you didn't say that. It's not something you're supposed to say out loud. Did anyone hear you?" The problem with these dialect words and phrases is that I know under what circumstances I've heard them, so I know when to use them, but I don't always know exactly what I'm saying.

"Only the nuns getting off the elevator, but they just said, 'Same to you,' so I don't think they damned my soul."

She squinted at me to make sure I was kidding and then went back to her dough. While I chopped candied orange peel and ate handfuls of chocolate chips, she wrapped the dough around metal tubes and slipped them into the hot oil. "So what exactly does 'a break' mean? Is that just a little time apart?"

"I don't know. It was his idea," I mumbled through a mouthful of chocolate chips, then stirred the few left in the bag into the bowl with ricotta, sugar, vanilla, and orange peel.

"What do *you* want it to mean, Katherine?" she asked as she put the crisp shells down in front of me. She scooped some filling into a plastic bag, twisted one corner, and cut a large hole in the opposite corner. I pulled a pastry bag out of the kitchen drawer where my mother keeps the kitchen tools she never uses and the sexy aprons my father gave her that she wouldn't even think about showing to anyone, let alone wearing.

"I don't know that either. I mean, most of the time we're so comfortable together that it seems perfect. But then I get to wanting more than comfort. I want passionate, exciting, spontaneous."

"I would have thought you had enough of those things for the two of you. Whatever happened to 'opposites attract'?" She picked up a shell and smoothly squeezed the filling from the bag into the pastry. I was trying to pipe my filling into the shell, but I was having trouble finding the center because tears were clouding my vision.

"I think someone forgot to finish the thought. Opposites attract but they don't always make it for the long haul. It's just too hard. You and Dad are an exception."

My parents have been married for thirty years, and it's hard to imagine two people who could be more different and still adore each other as much as they do. My mother is from a traditional southern Italian family. Her mother, my Nonna, raised three boys and two girls the way she had been raised—in the *old country*. She kept a tight rein on her five little Contis, intimidating them by claiming she had "eyes in the back of her

head." Whatever admonitions Nonna overlooked, the good
nuns covered in fourteen years of parochial school and two
years of Catholic college. The result of all this rigid upbringing
is the outward appearance of a controlled, somewhat prissy
person. In fact, Mom can be downright prudish, but beneath
the surface, there's a wild woman looking to escape. No doubt,
it was that side of her that attracted my father.

Lots of people think that Costello is an Italian name, but it's
Irish, and Dad inherited more than his share of blarney, charm,
and "bit o' the devil." When he met my mother, she thought he
was too wild to bring home. But it wound up being a good
match. She gave his life structure; he gave her structure life. I
am their only child, and that has always been just fine with me.
In spite of what the third-grade nuns tried to drill into me, I
think sharing is highly overrated.

Mom put her arms around me. "I don't want it to be hard
for you, and if Richard is not the right one, better to find out
now."

I hugged her back and it made me feel a little better. We
talked about some of the places I'd be seeing in Italy while we
filled the rest of the cannoli and dusted them all with powdered
sugar. We brought Dad his share of the feel-better pastries and
watched a little television before I headed off to bed, dreading
the morning's commute and contemplating the various mean-
ings of "break."

A WEEK LATER, I was still contemplating, when, as I
was nibbling on the leftovers from a morning shoot, Richard's
receptionist called my cell to say that she had to reschedule my
next week's appointment.

"To when?" I asked.

"I don't have an opening right now."

I couldn't believe it. Richard and I hadn't even spoken to each other since the argument and now he was turning "break" into "breakup." With a canceled dental appointment! How low is that? *Well, no way,* I thought. I decided to go to his office and let him know that *I* was breaking up with *him* and getting a new dentist. It was quarter of one, and Richard always went to lunch from one until two. If the entire staff was out, the office would be locked. If someone stayed behind, I could sit in the waiting room and read the latest copies of six-month-old magazines until Richard came back. The door was open and the waiting room was empty, but I could hear faint giggling coming from one of the operatories. Realizing that one of his assistants or hygienists must be there, I went back to say hi.

The giggling was coming from Lexi, Richard's provocative, nineteen-year-old chairside assistant who wore gauzy, see-through white uniforms that looked as though they came from show-all.com. At the moment, she was sitting on my boyfriend-on-a-break's lap and showing all to him.

"Casey!" Richard jumped up, dropping the assistant on the floor. "What are you doing here?"

As if that was the predominant question. "What's going on here?" Okay, that was a dumber question, but my brain couldn't wrap itself around what I was seeing. And then I couldn't see at all, because my tears were blinding me. Lexi was still in a crouch position where she had been dumped, and she was clutching her barely-there uniform in a futile attempt to cover what I resentfully noticed was an ample bosom. I gave her a nasty, teary look and screamed, "You should be ashamed of yourself. *Puttana!*" before running out of the operatory. Richard followed me and grabbed my arm.

"Casey. Don't run off. We need to talk about this."

"Seems to me there's not much to talk about except why you couldn't have at least let me in on your definition of a break. I thought that meant time to think things over, not to work over your assistants."

"That's sick, Casey." He lowered his voice and spoke slowly, as if to show by example that it would be more adult and more civilized to remain calm. "You're not being reasonable. You're letting your anger take over." That's when I stomped down on his white shoe and left in a stream of Neapolitan expletives.

I walked and wept for ten blocks before taking the subway to my train. On blocks two, three, and five, I tried to call my cousin Mary, who is six months older than I am and happens to be my best friend. She wasn't picking up her cell, so on block seven, I called her work number.

"I'm sorry. Miss Alfano will be at a meeting all afternoon."

"*All* afternoon?"

"If this is an emergency I can reach her." I had tried not to sound hysterical when I called, but it obviously hadn't worked. I sounded like an emergency.

"No. Thank you. I'll call back."

Each one of my pounding steps beat out a rhythmic "I hate him. I hate him." What is it that makes us feel so miserable when a guy we're planning on deep-sixing anyway picks himself right up and goes out with someone else? I had pretty much come to the conclusion that I didn't want him, but I sure as hell didn't want him to want someone else. At least not right away. A little mourning period would have been in order. But then, what can you expect from someone who uses a canceled dental appointment as a breakup strategy?

As soon as my parents saw me, my mother headed for the kitchen and for once in his life my father was speechless.

"Don't bother," I said, shaking my head. "There aren't enough cannoli shells in all of Little Italy to make me feel better." I sobbed my way through the story, through dinner, through the first fifteen minutes of *Wheel of Fortune,* and then went up to my room exhausted.

Mary called just about the time I had torn up the last photograph and thrown out all my floss.

"Look, I know it hurts, but you have to keep reminding yourself that the relationship was a failure anyway."

"Yeah. Well, the breakup didn't work out so well either."

"Seeing Richard like that is the pits. But if you think honestly about it, you didn't really love him."

"I was trying to."

"Not good enough. The right guy is out there waiting for you, and you're not going to have to *try* to love him."

"Well, he's going to have to wait because I'm giving up dating and getting a gerbil."

"Do you want me to come over?"

"Thanks, no. I'm going to squeeze all the sample toothpastes down the toilet and go to bed. It's been a rough day."

Four and a half weeks later my father was still driving me into the city. He said he had business there, but I know he just didn't trust me near the train tracks.

Chapter 2

My future ain't what it used to be.
—*Lonnie Spiker*

I love a TV studio early in the morning. Just like me, it wakes up slowly. When I arrive, the lights are low and whatever noises the prop men are making get lost in the immensity of the room. This will all change in about an hour when the control room opens, the camera and sound crews arrive, and the line producers converge on the set. The show's hosts, Jim and Karen, don't join the chaos until about ten minutes before airtime, but sometimes Art, the weatherman, wanders into the kitchen early because he likes to cook and wants to get a few pointers.

There's always a breakfast buffet set up on a long table in the hallway right outside our studio, with plenty of good coffee, lots of cut-up fruit, every flavor of yogurt, and an Atkins-horrifying abundance of carbs—bagels, at least four kinds of muffins, croissants, three varieties of Danish, sticky buns, English muffins, scones. It's like a huge room-service bread basket but you get to pick more than two items. I took a corn muffin, a sticky bun, and a carrot-and-zucchini muffin for my vegetable, plus two large coffees, and headed back to the prep kitchen to start work.

The prep kitchen is a tiny, ten-by-sixteen-foot kitchenette that was never meant to be used to prepare anything like the amount of food we need for televising. It was there for any staff or crew member who needed a refrigerator to hold a lunch or a stove to heat soup or boil water. When Sonya, our executive producer, was able to sign Sally Woods on to the show for regular appearances, she pressed the too-small room into service because it was close to the set and already had appliances and running water. We've made the room even smaller by building a butcher-block work island in the center of the room, leaving just enough space between it and the counters for one of us to stand. Two people passing each other qualifies as an intimate relationship, so we call the table Romeo. Right before the show goes on the air at seven o'clock, a heavy soundproof door closes us in—"us" being my assistant, Mae, two stagehands who are assigned KP duty, and me. At some time during the morning, Sonya, the talent, and a set-designer-slash-food-stylist will also cram themselves into the space to check things out. We've learned to work around one another nicely, but we all keep an eye on the monitor that pipes the show into the kitchen so we'll know when there is a commercial break. Then we can open the door for a breather.

Mae was already there when I walked in. I hoped she had her own breakfast. I wasn't sharing.

"Hey," she said as she continued to unpack groceries, opening wrapped packages to check them against my shopping list. The first rule of television food production is to make sure the food is all there and it's what was ordered. On one of my early days with the show, I'd ordered salmon fillets. When I'd opened the wrapped package close to airtime, I'd discovered that the shopper had bought a slab of smoked salmon instead. Fortunately, the talent that day was dear, unflappable Sally, who has seen it all and dealt with it all in her twenty-five years of cooking on television. She told us to "oil the bejabbers" out of the salmon and ordered the cameras to stay back. It worked out fine, but it was a lesson. Check the supplies in time to replace them if necessary.

"Hey, yourself. How's it going?"

"Way cool." For twenty-three-year-old Mae March, life is always way cool. She comes from a bit of a zany family, Mr. and Mrs. March and their daughters, April, Mae, and June. Most people think she's joking when she tells them that. Mae has her own sense of style—or antistyle, depending on how you look at it. She wears a traditional white chef's coat to work, but she funks up everything else—from the long, gauzy vintage skirts that end midcalf, just above the high-heeled, black Doc Marten–type boots, to the small green star she applies with a Magic Marker under her left eye every morning. She wears her long chestnut hair pulled up and held with a variety of animal-shaped hair clips and a couple of chopsticks for good measure. Occasionally she colors a small tuft of hair in the front. Today it was a deep maroon, which matched the color of her fingernails. In spite of her attempts at bizarre, she's a knockout, with a flawless creamy complexion and high cheekbones that get a delicate shade of pink when the kitchen heat is on. Her soft gray eyes have a come-hither look even when she's inspecting groceries.

Her costuming makes it hard to take her seriously until she starts to work. Mae learned all she knows from high school home economics classes and her parents' restaurant. She avoided all the culinary school egotism of thinking she's a star chef and learned the importance of speed, accuracy, and getting along with people in small spaces. Our kitchen motto at *Morning in America* is EOT: Eye on Target. Mae has no problem with that. Neither do our cute young stagehands, whose target happens to be Mae. We have four stagehands available to us—all named Tony. At first, we tried to distinguish them by calling them Tony G. and Tony M. and so forth, but we could never keep that straight so we gave up. It actually works out okay, because when we need something done we just say, "Tony" and someone does it. Two stagehands stay in the kitchen with us to wash dishes, sweep floors, empty trash, and peel, trim, and chop. The other two are always nearby to run errands, carry trays, repair props, and so forth. Two Tonys arrived just as Mae was finishing unpacking and they tripped over each other to help her. It was like watching puberty on speed.

That morning we were doing a live spot with Tina Lovely, a tall, willowy movie star with a glorious mane of strawberry-blond hair. Working with celebrities is fun from a starstruck point of view, but can be frustrating from a culinary point of view. Unlike Sally or our guest chefs, stars are not food professionals, and we sometimes have to do some cookery sleight of hand to make the recipes work. Tina planned to demonstrate her method of growing herbs under special lights in her sauna. Not exactly a tip with universal appeal, but she happened to be dating a rock star who was all over the news because one of his band members had been caught in a indelicate situation with an underage girl who had turned out to be the daughter of a well-known British politician.

Tina was writing a cookbook. Actually, it seems as though every other person I meet lately is either writing a cookbook or planning to. Thanks to Sally's years of overwhelming culinary influence, food is fashionable and trendy, and lots of people who were raised on TV dinners and frozen fish sticks are now gourmet cooks. If you're a celebrity like Tina, publishers are eager to bring out your work. I have no problem with this because I love the food world and the more people in it, the merrier. And, of course, the more work there is for me.

After showing how to pot the herbs, Tina planned to offer some examples of how to use them once you get out of the sauna. She'd given us her recipes for herb-roasted chicken, baked potatoes with chive sour cream, and a sort of French bread with basil. We had to make her food look good, even though the recipes were not really workable.

Mae picked up her copies of the recipes and sat down next to me. I moved my muffins out of her reach. As usual, she got right to the point. "Her recipes suck. Do you think she actually makes this stuff? She cooks the chicken to death. She wraps the baked potatoes in foil, for God's sake. Even lousy restaurants don't do *that* anymore. She so can't cook. I'll bet she doesn't even eat. She's so skinny."

I looked at my remaining muffin and thought of Tina chewing gum for breakfast. "Probably not. I told Sonya the recipes needed tweaking and she tried to convince Tina to let us redo them. But Tina said her dinner guests always gobbled them up."

"She probably never looked under the parsley left on the plates."

"Since she's not actually giving recipes but only showing how to pot the herbs and offering some ideas of how to use them, Sonya said to go with them. We just have to make the food look good. Don't wrap the potatoes or they'll shrivel. I'll explain that to Tina. We'll make sure the chicken is fully cooked, but get it out of the oven before it takes on too much color." Food always looks darker on TV than it really is, so timing is especially tricky with chicken and turkey. Poultry has to be fully cooked in case the host tastes it, but if it cooks too long, it looks black and shriveled. In the "old days," magazines used to paint barely cooked birds with a combination of dish liquid and shoe polish so they would have a golden-brown glow. We don't ever do things like that.

"If I make the bread her way," Mae pleaded, "it won't even look good. Her recipe is a joke."

Tina's basil French bread called for mixing the traditional ingredients of yeast, flour, and water with sauna-raised basil, all of it to be whirred in a food processor and plopped (her word) on a baking sheet, then coaxed into a rounded shape and baked. Voilà, a French *boule*. She insisted that the dough didn't have to rise. *Stunad!* (My word.) Bread has to rise.

"All right, Mae. Make a few loaves the classic way. Let them rise and give them surface tension. We'll slice those so the pieces look like bread and hide Tina's blob behind Jonathan's props. I'll start with the trays."

Work on a cooking segment begins a few weeks before the day it is televised. Sonya picks the chef or celebrity, known as "the talent," who will appear on the show, and then together we choose from the recipes the talent suggests. Sonya decides if they fit into the overall programming; I decide if they are visually interesting and technically possible. Once we've agreed on the recipes, it is my job to break them down into what needs to be seen and how to show it in the time allotted, which is usually only three and a half minutes. After Sonya approves my recipe breakdown, I can make shopping and equipment lists for the crew and write the scripts. The scripts are not dialogue scripts with lines for the talent to memorize. They outline what steps and in what order the recipes will be shot. From the scripts, I determine what needs to be done ahead of time and then make prep lists for Mae and myself.

Since we can't leave any ingredients or equipment on the set before the cooking spot is ready to air, we set everything up on large cafeteria trays, which wind up scattered all over our tiny workplace. The trays are key. Each one of them represents a different part of the recipe that the talent will demonstrate. We put large pieces of masking tape on the trays and mark them with numbers according to their place on the set. In the three minutes of commercial break time just before the food segment begins, we have to get all that food to the set, and union rules allow only the stagehands to carry it. The numbers on the trays tell them in what order to set the trays down. Mae and I follow right behind, remove the items from the trays, and place them where the chef can easily reach them. We work all of this out before the show even begins so we are not guessing in this brief time where to place things and inadvertently put something down in a place that blocks the camera's view of the food. Jonathan, our set designer and food stylist, is right behind us making the setting attractive with napkins, plates, some flowers, and occasionally an objet d'art that he finds irresistible. He tweaks the food using tools from his stylist's basket—tweezers, toothpicks, a water spray, a jar of oil, and paintbrushes in various sizes.

There was a nice rhythm going in the kitchen when Jonathan stormed in, demonstrating that he was already having a supremely awful day. He was cradling a box of little clay pots in one arm and holding a large bag of potting soil in the other hand. He lifted the soil up above his head as though he were about to auction it off. "It's all brown. The pots are brown; the food's brown; the dirt's the color of shit. Brown bread, brown chicken, brown potatoes—all brown. How the hell can I make that pretty? Doesn't anyone consider color when they suggest these spots?"

I was accustomed to Jonathan's irritable disposition. It no longer gets a rise out of me, but he keeps trying. "Good morning, Jonathan. Had your coffee yet?" He is particularly unpleasant before he has had coffee, and never goes for it himself. A Tony dropped his dish towel and ran for the buffet as though he were afraid he'd be blamed for all the brownness. I made a halfhearted attempt at appeasement. "A lot of food is brown, Jonathan. We have nice red cherry tomatoes and lots of parsley that you can put around the chicken."

"I can't keep covering everything with parsley. Next you'll be asking me to drape it over a chocolate cake." He took out the only key in existence that opened his private cabinet. Inside was a wild assortment of scavenged dishes, napkins, vases, bowls, candles, and art objects. It looked like a garage sale waiting to happen. He made more noise than necessary as he moved platters around to find one that would make the chicken presentable for morning TV.

Before long, Mae had four batches of basil dough mixed and rising in bowls. There's no wiggle room in live television, and that accounts for our second motto, CYA: Cover Your Ass. In food television, that means "make more than you think you need."

While the bread dough was doing its thing, Mae was creaming a couple of pounds of unsalted butter against the side of a mixing bowl with a wooden spoon. She had already chopped the mounds of herbs we needed, which a Tony had washed, dried, and stripped from the stems, and they were lined up in front of her. One Tony was scrubbing baking potatoes and another Tony was oiling the racks that would hold the roasting chickens. There was happy chatter going on and I thought of what Sally always says when she is in such a kitchen: "Isn't cooking together fun?" It is indeed.

Mae and I each took a chicken and carefully slipped our hands under the skin to make a space for the herb butter. We picked up the softened butter, worked it under the skin, and began to massage it over the meat. If your head is in that place, it is a very sensual sight and the Tonys kept elbowing each other and whispering. I couldn't hear what they were saying, but I heard what they were thinking.

We rested the birds on their sides on Tony's well-oiled racks in roasting pans, massaged the outsides with more butter, and slid them into the oven. I went back to the trays to recheck the setup and make sure I hadn't forgotten anything. I always talk myself through the script so I can anticipate what might be needed: "Tina and Karen each open a potato and break up the pulp" *two knives, two forks* "and each spoon sour cream inside" *two spoons* "and taste" *extra forks because the first ones may look yucky from breaking up the potatoes.* Viewers truly write us letters about things like that. If there's a question about whether something is needed, I put it out anyway. It's a CYA lesson I learned the hard way. On an earlier show, I had to crawl on my hands and knees below the camera's eye to put a whisk in Karen's hand when the talent asked her to beat some eggs. It was an okay way to get it there, but I took a lot of razzing from the camera crew.

I gave an empty tray a number and wrote on the tape "Finished bird, beautifully garnished on pretty platter." The chicken hadn't finished baking, and Jonathan was still stewing about the platter, but everything happens so quickly right before airtime that we might forget what goes on it and where it goes. I marked another empty tray "1 uncut finished blob, 1 sliced bread" as well as "bread basket, napkins, butter dish, and butter knives" and told Jonathan we'd need these items. He ignored me. He was standing at his cabinet with four different platters lined up at his feet. He had one hand curled up so it made a lens-like circle and he was turning his hand camera from one dish to the other. It's not as though we had all morning, but I knew better than to rush him. "You have *way* too much free time, Jonathan," I said under my breath.

By seven-thirty, things were beginning to steam up in the kitchen, literally. The two fat little chickens were roasting away, and each time we opened the oven door to turn or baste them, thyme-scented steam filled the room. Mae, who was now shaping breads, had entered another zone. In one smooth motion, she ran her hands over the top of the puffy mound, stretched a thin layer of dough down the sides, and tucked it under the bottom as she lifted and turned the *boule*. She repeated the motion three or four times with each ball of dough, sending little poufs of flour into the space around her. Sally had taught her this French technique for creating surface tension and Mae had it down. It was sweet to watch. Unfortunately, Sonya chose that moment to arrive with Tina, who was not as impressed as I with Mae's technique. "What are you doing?" she exclaimed. "Is that my bread recipe? *Don't* do it that way. Just plop it onto a baking pan."

Tina picked up a perfectly formed mound of dough and looked around for a pan, all the while juggling the dough, and jabbing her long, perfectly manicured red fingernails into the lovely smooth surface. By the time she got it into the pan, it was the misshapen blob of her dreams. Mae kept looking from the dough to Tina as though the star had just snatched her first-born baby off her lap and given it to a mother gorilla. I was glad Mae practiced Zen meditation, because otherwise I think she would have hit Tina.

Tina seemed oblivious to Mae's wrath. "That's all you have

to do. It's so easy. That's why I love it. Oh, the chickens smell so good. Do you think they'll be done on time?"

"I'm sure of it," I reassured her, and I explained about the dark color the camera created. She understood.

"Believe me, I know what lighting can and can't do for an actor, even if it's a bird," Tina chirped. "Let's light that mother right and shoot it from its best side." With the exception of Mae, we all gave a little laugh at her movie humor, and I took that moment of discussing personal appearance to mention that we were going to leave the foil off the potatoes so they wouldn't wrinkle.

"But how will the audience know they're cooked if they aren't wrinkled?"

I started to explain that baked potatoes don't have to be wrinkled, but at that moment she reached up to push back a lock of hair and I noticed that two of her fingernails were completely gone and bits of polish were missing from a few others. "Oh gosh, Tina, look at your hands. You've lost a couple of press-on nails."

"Shit. That's why I always wear rubber gloves when I cook."

I fondled the dough a bit and found the fingernails. I wasn't worried about the polish in the bread because it looked like herbs, but the fingernails needed to be returned to their hand before showtime.

Sonya took Tina by the elbow. "We better go back upstairs to makeup for a repair. Everyone all set with Tina's instructions?"

Tina gave us one of those smiles that must have wowed the movie moguls and then walked out. Sonya turned back to me before joining her. "Do what you have to do," she whispered.

When all was said and done, the food looked pretty damn good on the monitor. Tina even came back to the kitchen to thank us. She was so gracious and sincere that I almost felt bad for trashing her recipes.

The Tonys cleaned up; Mae went outside for a smoke; and numerous members of the crew wandered into the kitchen for leftovers. Out of habit, I turned on my cell to see if Richard had called. We usually spoke as soon as the show was over to discuss cooks and patients. He'd get a hoot out of the fingernails in the bread and probably would have some funny patient story to tell me. Nope. I had accepted that it was over, and I didn't want him back, but my ego had been seriously wounded. I wanted him to call and tell me how sorry he was. I needed groveling.

I was opening and closing my cell when Mae walked back into the kitchen. She knew my old routine.

"Casey?" She raised her eyebrows.

"What?" I said, feigning no knowledge of her accurate assumption.

"Duh. You *know* what. The man is scum. I mean, I know you were totally zapped, but if you can't let go of it, you can't move on."

"I'm not moving anywhere, Mae. I've decided that I'm no good at relationships."

"That's another thing. Stop beating yourself up about it. You tried hard to make it work. It just wasn't the match for you. You have to let it go."

"Letting go is not part of my DNA. I just wish he'd call and beg me to come back so I could tell him to go fuck himself."

"Do you really think that's the best way to use one of life's three wishes?"

"Good point." I laughed. "Let's get to work." I pulled a thick packet of recipes and scripts out of my James Beard House tote.

Mae squeezed my hand and picked up her copies of the scripts. "So how are we for the rest of the week?"

"We have the live spot on Wednesday with Sara Paul, the vegan chef. Vegan chef—that's an oxymoron," I said to tease Mae. Although she follows no restricted diet, she is a definite fan of whole foods, organic foods, and vegetarianism—anything natural and good for you. I am less discriminating and tend more toward gluttony and cheddar cheese Combos.

"You should go to her restaurant," Mae gushed. "It's *really* popular. She does amazing things with grains. Like she shapes seitan into real-looking baby lamb chops. And around Thanksgiving she makes this turkey out of seven grains and serves it with a citrus, tamari, and cranberry coulis. It is *so* awesome. She's writing a cookbook, *The Gourmet Vegan.*"

"Those are two words I never expected to hear in the same sentence."

Mae rolled her eyes and punched my arm. "You wait. You'll be blown away by her food."

"Tempeh fajitas and chocolate tofu cheesecake. I don't think so."

"I've had the cheesecake. It's totally amazing."

I'll bet not as amazing as one made with Zabar's fresh cream cheese, but no point in pushing it. "You better tell Tony where to shop and exactly what to look for in tofu and tempeh. I'm betting any one of the Tonys is more a cheeseburger guy than a seitan lamb chop freak."

"I'll send them to my whole foods store." Mae looked at her scripts for Thursday. "Why's Sally not doing a live spot on Thursday?"

"She will be on live but she won't be cooking since she, Jim, and Karen are going to do a spot on the latest food trends. After the show, she'll tape the two segments. First we'll do the one with Sally showing Jim the proper way to eat a lobster and then we'll tape Sally making the tarte Tatin."

"Tarte Tatin. In three and a half minutes. I can't wait to see that."

"You know Sally. She loves to do the undoable. She's got it all worked out. That's why she needs the ten cast-iron skillets."

I pushed another packet of papers over to Mae. "These are for next week. Tuesday's a live spot with a pinch hitter for the New York Mets who's going to make his mother's calzone recipe. He uses packaged Pillsbury rolls. You know, the Doughboy ones."

"I thought he died from high cholesterol."

"The baseball player?"

"No, the Pillsbury Doughboy."

My turn to roll my eyes. "Very funny. Sally will be back on Wednesday for a live show and two tapes. The live show is going to be fun. She'll be with a kitchen brigade from a fire station north of Boston. They won this year's chili cook-off and they're going to show Sally their recipe. After the show, she'll tape a promo for Italy and then a piece on the hottest new cookbooks.

"The following week is the killer. I don't have any recipes yet, but on Tuesday we have a live spot with that crazy, neurotic Sal Vito." Mae groaned. Sal Vito was an Italian comedian who was volatile and unpredictable. Nobody liked working with him. "Wednesday we do a live spot with a new chef-owner and then tape two segments with him to air the week Sally and I are in Italy. He's never done TV but he's the new 'it' chef in town and Sonya wants to cash in. Danny O'Shea from Oran Mor. Thursday we leave for Italy."

Mae widened her lovely gray eyes and slapped both hands on the table as she lifted half out of her seat. "*Shut up!* Have you seen him? He's so hot. And he has that cool Irish accent."

"Now, lassie, would ye be talking about a lilting Gaelic tongue?" It was a poor attempt at an Irish brogue.

"Whatever. He definitely rocks."

"Where did you meet him? Have you been to his restaurant?"

"No way. It's much too expensive. I saw him at Dean & Deluca. He was doing a demo for Irish smoked salmon. Women were buying it by the armful just so he'd smile at them and say something in Irish."

"I think Sonya booked him for more than his cute accent. He's getting a lot of press. I'll get the scripts and lists to you next week."

"Okay, then. I'm off like a prom dress. See you tomorrow. I'll be at the family joint if you want to talk."

"Thanks, Mae. See ya."

I had to talk to Sonya about the Italian shows, and then my workday would be over. That's one of the perks of working morning TV: the studio becomes a soap opera set at one o'clock, so we always have to be out by noon. Since we're usually at the studio by five-thirty or six A.M., it's still a full workday; it just ends at a nice time.

Occasionally, I'll work on scripts with Sonya in the afternoon, but it's rare; I usually have the better part of the day to myself. The problem now that I no longer had city digs, though, was there wasn't much I could do. I didn't feel like going back to New Rochelle, but there aren't many places you can go in the city when you smell like the inside of a Dumpster. That's what cooking in small spaces does to you. If I were still living with Richard, I'd go to the apartment, shower, and change, then go shopping or to a museum or meet friends for lunch.

I left the studio and walked the four blocks to Sonya's office.

The executive offices are separate from the studio, probably so the suits won't pick up the Dumpster smell on *their* clothes. When I went into her small but windowed office, she was on the phone and rummaging through a pile of papers on the floor. Her desk was buried under more papers, stacks of video-tapes, and piles of books. It's always that way. Publicists continually send her their clients' material in hopes of getting a spot on the show. I don't know how she keeps it all straight, but she does.

Sonya Pierce-Jones is forty-five years old, British, and very good at what she does. She has worked, and worked hard, in American television for fifteen years. She became an executive producer when she brought Sally onto the *Morning in America* team, a decision that immediately and impressively raised the show's ratings. I love working for Sonya. She's tough and demanding but fair. Because of her accent, people often think she's stiff and formal, but I've gotten to know her warmer, laid-back side.

Sonya continued her phone conversation but stopped shuffling papers long enough to wave a videotape at me. That meant she wanted me to watch it to see if the talent had any talent. A Post-it stuck to the top said, "Ravenna?" We were planning to tape five segments, one in each of the five cities we'd visit. Sally would give a brief tour of the city, concentrating on culinary sites, relating some little-known fascinating food facts, and then invite an Italian cook from that city to demonstrate a traditional regional dish. We were still looking for someone from the Adriatic Sea area. I popped the tape into the VCR and watched a pretty, middle-aged Italian woman in a flowered housedress and frilly apron hold up various fish and shellfish as she spoke to the tape in rapid, enthusiastic Italian, espousing the virtues of the seafood. She was standing at a battered wooden table in what appeared to be her own kitchen. After she finished showing off the fish, she beheaded and eviscerated them, and then washed them in a chipped white enamel bowl full of water that sat on the table. She put the cleaned pieces on a brightly painted platter, chosen, I'm sure, with less deliberation than our Jonathan would have required. She poured olive oil into a large, slightly dented pot that sat on a small two-burner stove and then in a flash chopped a couple of onions and a good amount of garlic and put them in the oil. While the aromatics became, well, aromatic, she cut up a half dozen fresh tomatoes and a healthy amount of herbs and added them to the pot. She stirred everything around, and before long she had all the fish and shellfish in the pot. I understood the gesture when she pushed the point of a finger into her cheek and twisted it before she said the word *squisito*—delicious. There was a little break in the scene where the camera must have stopped to let the stew finish, but then our Italian mama was back ladling out the stew and insisting that the camera crew *mangia, mangia.* When Sonya got off the phone, she asked me what I thought.

"If she speaks English, it'll make a great spot. The varieties of fish are different from what we have here, but Sally can explain what to substitute. I even like the housedress. It's so homey. I think viewers will identify."

"That's what I thought. She does speak English. We also found a charming seaside restaurant where they cook eel in an outdoor fireplace. Might be fun to see. Do you like eel?"

"Sure. We eat it every Christmas Eve. It's a standard part of the Italian seven-fishes meal. It would be a great visual. Sally would like nothing better than to hold up a slithering eel for the camera. So we now have all five cities covered?"

"We do. I should have recipes for you by the end of next

week. Are you getting excited about the trip?" she asked somewhat optimistically. She knew I had hoped that Richard would be going as well.

"I am," I said in a totally unconvincing tone.

Sonya read it loud and clear and took off her glasses to look more intently at me. Richard is Sonya's dentist. That's how he got on the show in the first place. I knew she had seen him since the breakup but because she didn't say he had lost weight and looked like hell, I didn't press her for information. "It's going to be a great trip, Casey. I know you had other plans for it, but it's time to shake it off. Truthfully, I never thought you two were cut out for each other. I'm surprised that you were together as long as you were. You're very different people."

"Tell me about it. I'm politically opposed to fondling staff on my lap."

"But in favor of self-torture. You have to let go of it. You'll drive yourself crazy."

"Too late. I think I'm already marginally brain-dead."

"Well, you're not, but your teeth will definitely go bad." She smiled, showing her own beautiful white teeth. "You are going to be fine. He's the one who will regret this. Trust me."

"Thanks. You've made me feel much better, I think."

"Good. Because I'm about to make you feel a whole lot worse."

"Hmm?"

"George Davis is going to be in Italy when we're there."

"*What? What? Why?*" George Davis is a "celebrity agent." He appeared literally out of nowhere less than a year ago and somehow managed to glom on to Sally. "But he hates me," I whined.

"He hates me too. He hates everyone who was part of Sally's life before he arrived on the scene."

"But he hates me more."

"Probably because Sally likes you more." I had a momentary good feeling knowing this was true. I'd worked with Sally for six years, and in that time we'd become close friends and confidantes as well as a dynamite work team. We always had a great time together and I hated to think of George honing in on our Italian good times.

"Why is he coming?" I asked.

"Supposedly he has business in Italy, and his business involves Sally."

"When did she tell you he was coming?"

"She didn't. He did. He called to say he'd be there and suggested that I might want Carol Hanger to come along as executive chef. I told him we were all set, thank you."

Carol Hanger does what I do on a freelance basis. She appeared on the scene when George did, and the two of them seem to have a secret pact to make the rest of us miserable. She's unfriendly, haughty, and, although I hate to admit, really not bad at what she does. Not as good as I am, and that's not just my opinion. "That bitch! Over my dead body. What *is* his problem?"

"Sounds like a classic case of control. He's gradually been alienating anyone who has worked with Sally before. I've heard through the grapevine that he is talking to a different network about signing a contract with Sally for morning TV. He's meeting with our VPs on Wednesday to discuss her renewal."

"She'd never abandon you. She's been with you all these years. You're family!"

"That seems to be why he wants to remove me and you from her life."

"Can't you talk to Sally?"

"No. She isn't open to discussing George's choices for her."

"How bad will it be for you if she leaves *Morning in America*?"

"I doubt that I'll lose my job, but I definitely won't move upstairs."

I knew that Sonya was hoping for a promotion to the upstairs offices, which held the vice presidents. She had developed one of the most popular portions of the show and had earned the promotion, but the network would be fuming at the prospect of losing the major chunk of advertising revenue that Sally generated. I also knew that this revenue supported my job. Sonya wasn't saying it, but it might mean I'd soon be surfing Hotjobs.com. Things were beginning to look decidedly unrosy. "What can we do?"

"Hope that she'll see the real George Davis before her contract with us is up for renewal."

"Yeah. But, exactly *who* is the real George Davis?"

She raised her eyebrows and shrugged. "A good question."

Chapter 3

Some people walk in the rain, others just get wet.
—*Roger Miller*

Tuesday didn't start out to be the second-worst day of my life. I didn't have to be at the studio until after seven, since there was no live food spot that morning. After work, I was meeting my cousin Mary, who in addition to being my closest confidante and no-nonsense adviser is, to my good fortune, a buyer for Calvin Klein. Klein was starting a half-price sale tomorrow and if you added in Mary's discount, they were practically giving the clothes away. By going in a day early, I'd get first pick. Mary had convinced me that I needed a new wardrobe for my trip, and even though Insanity never complained about what I wore, I thought she might be right.

The extra few morning hours gave me time to blow-dry my hair and work the waves into something that resembled a "style." I put on makeup, concentrating on my eyes according to Mary's directions. Since we wouldn't be frying or roasting, I wouldn't leave the studio smelling like a greasy-spoon short-order cook. So I decided to go all out for my trip to Calvin

Klein. I put on a sheer silk Chloé shirt with a thin white jersey camisole underneath. The shirt was a pale, pale blue and I had just the right short Max Mara sateen skirt in a gray blue to go with it. There's nothing sweeter than a Bergdorf's designer sale. I slipped on a new pair of amazing Sergio Rossi suede mules with low heels and pointy toes. Mary would be impressed. I packed some of Mom's cannoli in a white pastry box to bring to the kitchen staff, and headed to the studio.

When I stepped out of the subway, four blocks from the studio, it was pouring rain. Did they say rain on the news? No one said rain on the news. You were supposed to say it was going to rain if it was going to rain. I tried to hug the buildings, but everyone on my side of the street was going the other way, and I kept getting pushed to the outside. By the time the truck splashed water all over me at the corner, I had given up trying to keep myself or my box of pastries dry.

I arrived at the studio with my hair and clothes soaking wet and watched the water as it dripped onto the floor just inside the studio door. My lovely white pastry box was now a dull, wet gray. Looking like hell is the same as feeling like shit. I went directly to the kitchen, hoping the Tonys had remembered to restack the drawer with clean dish towels. There was an unfamiliar stagehand sitting on the counter, drinking coffee and doing the *Times* crossword puzzle. Give me a break! They *are* given work sheets when they arrive in the morning. This was unacceptable—and a sitting duck for venting my annoyance.

"Good morning, uh, I'm going to guess Tony, but if it wasn't it is now because that's all we're used to. So, Tony, why don't you get that well-toned butt off the counter and at least *try* to look busy."

"Hmm. Me mam never said anything about Tony. She said she thought about Sean and Bryan before naming me Daniel, but I'll answer to Tony if that's what you like." The brogue was soft but undeniable. "As for the 'well-toned' observation, thank you. I'm on me feet a lot and I think that helps." He was obviously amused by my crankiness because his blue eyes were laughing at me as he slid off the counter. "And I'll be happy to look busy if you'll tell me what it is you think I should be doing."

I opened my mouth to explain but nothing came out. I was having trouble extracting my expensive new Sergio Rossi shoe from it. And even if I did, I couldn't think of an explanation other than "I'm the kitchen witch." So I said nothing and just stood there dripping with my mouth wide open.

He extended his hand. "Danny O'Shea. You'll catch flies if you keep your mouth open like that."

I closed my mouth. I was still holding the box, and when I turned to put it on the counter to free my hands, the wet bottom gave out, dispersing a shower of pastry, ricotta, and tiny chocolate chips in a cloud of powdered sugar at my feet. I ignored them.

"You must be Casey. A girl with a purple streak in her hair told me to look for a tall, pretty lass who'd be eating a dozen pastries in the kitchen. Seems to be you."

"I am not eating pastries."

"Some of them look to be in good form." He stooped down to retrieve the ones that had landed on the top of the pile. He was wearing faded jeans and a tight-fitting black polo shirt and I could see that his backside was not all that was toned. He looked to be about six feet two inches, and every inch was lean and hard.

I grabbed a tray and stooped down to help reassemble breakfast. "Chef O'Shea. I—"

"Danny."

"Chef Danny—"

"Just Danny, or Tony if you prefer." He was licking cream filling off his fingers and looking at me as though I was next.

"Cute." I picked up the tray and stood quickly and rigidly, hoping he would get the idea that I was immune to his bold flirtation. He slowly rose to his feet and I said, "Look, I *am* sorry about the mistake and the comments. I got caught in the rain, I'm soaked, and I've ruined a perfectly good pair of shoes. Trust me, I'm not always such a witch."

His eyes moved down but didn't make it as far as my shoes. They stopped briefly at my wet shirt and returned to my face. "I'm sure you're not. A bit flustered perhaps . . ." His eyes went south again and then returned, amused, to my face. "But perfectly lovely."

Was I blushing? I had no idea how transparent Chloé silk was when it was wet, so I lifted the tray breast-high to hide well, whatever.

"Would you like one?"

"Love one." He took a bite of a broken cannoli and looked into my eyes with lust written all over his face.

I was positively blushing, and it was flustering me. Caught off guard, I was behaving like an absolute dingus, and this man was outrageously bold with a libido that seemed to be in overdrive; he was also drop-dead gorgeous. His short black hair had a slight wave to it, and a few stands fell forward over a square face with well-defined features and a strong chin. His eyes were the killer. They were a deep blue outlined by dark eyelashes and they had a sensuous, suggestive glint that had probably gotten him kicked out of Ireland.

I was still wondering how much of me was actually showing when Mae walked in and answered my question by immediately handing me a chef's coat from her backpack. I needed to get control and take charge. I turned authoritatively to Danny and used my best executive chef's voice. "Do you know you're here two weeks early?"

"Not really. Sonya said I should come in this week to have a look around and discuss my recipes with you. I've never been on the telly before and I don't watch food shows, so I didn't know what kind of things you were looking for. I was on my way to the fish market anyway and thought this would be a good time."

"Well, we don't have a food spot this morning, so you can't see what actually happens. But since you're already here, we can discuss what you're going to make for yours."

"Brilliant."

I told him to sit down at Romeo, cautiously referring to it as "the island" while I gave Mae instructions for tomorrow's prep. The Tonys came in and I put them to work helping Mae but first asked them to clean up the residue of powdered sugar on the floor. I was giving orders a mile a minute and beginning to feel executive again. I took a legal pad and a pen from the drawer and sat down at Romeo, across from him. "Okay. What are your thoughts about what you'd like to demonstrate? You'll only have about three and a half minutes."

"Whoa! That's not a lot of time."

I explained about swaps and backups and asked if he had some signature recipes that he'd like to highlight. "You know, something you serve at the restaurant that is really outstanding."

"It's all outstanding."

Add nauseatingly arrogant to outrageously bold. "Did you by any chance bring a menu with you?" I was feeling totally executive again when Jonathan came in to complain about tomorrow's brown chocolate cheesecake and the brown tempeh fajitas. "Nice hair. What's with the eyes?"

I touched my head; my hair was still soaking wet, and I could guess where my carefully applied eye makeup was. "Is there mascara running down my face?"

Mae looked up from her work. "There is. It looks kind of funky cool." This from someone who paints her face with Magic Markers.

"I thought it was one of those new American looks. It's kind of sexy." Danny's wicked twinkle looked right into my mascara-streaked eyes as he said it, and I was back to feeling like a dingus. I stood up.

"You know what, Danny? This will be a lot easier if I have your menus first. Why don't you get them to Sonya or me as soon as possible and I'll look them over. I'm sorry that I'm not familiar with your food. I haven't had a chance to get to your restaurant."

"Oh, that reminds me." He reached into the pocket of a rain jacket he'd hung on a coat hook—he obviously listened to the right weather forecasts—and pulled out two envelopes. "I have an invitation for all of you and any of your friends for this Thursday night. Oran Mor will be a year old and we've decided kind of at the last minute to have a party to celebrate."

He handed me a generic envelope, and I could see that the other one had "Sally Woods" written on it. "I also have one for Sally Woods and wanted to deliver it to her in person. Is she around?"

I got it then. The outrageous come-on. He wasn't coming on to me; he wanted Sally. This wasn't the first chef to try to use me to get to her. Sally was the closest thing to a megastar the culinary world had to offer, and chefs wanted the celebrity status of having her in their restaurants. It guaranteed press at an event that might otherwise be just another night out. A lot of climbers in the field thought that if they befriended me, they'd get Sally in the bargain.

"Not today." Executive-chef tone.

Mae ignored my tone. "But she'll be here Thursday, and I'll bet she'd love to go. Sally craves a good party."

Danny turned his twinkle on Mae and handed her the invitation. "Brilliant. Would you mind seeing that she gets this, love? And I hope you'll be coming."

Way-cool Mae March simply melted in front of my eyes. Danny turned back to me and said, "If you come, I can give you the menus then, if that's soon enough."

"That'll be fine, if I can make it. Otherwise, can you fax them?"

"Not a problem." He smiled at me and left.

As soon as he was out the door, Mae let out her breath and said, "Isn't he gorgeous?"

"Actually, I found him arrogant, self-centered, and rude."

Mae looked horrified. "You have to be kidding. He was so charming."

"Charming? He's just another trendy chef, hoping to make the right connections that will make him a star."

"Wow." Mae raised her eyebrows, but said no more. I didn't mention that I did think he was one of the most gorgeous specimens of masculinity I had ever seen. Besides, I thought as I checked out my damp attire, I wasn't in my best connecting condition.

The rain had stopped by the time I left the studio, and I assessed the damage it had done before heading off to meet Mary. My hair was okay. At least it was dry. My skirt had lost the crisp sateen finish of its former life but it had dried evenly, so it looked okay. My shirt, however, had shrunk on my body, and my shoes were history. I didn't look quite as chic as I had planned, but I wasn't a total disaster. Mary, on the other hand, looked incredible and could easily be mistaken for one of Calvin's models.

We've always been just about the same height, but growing up she was many pounds lighter than I was. She was what you might call "gangling," if your definition included gawky and awkward. She had a Letterman gap between her front teeth, seriously mousy brown hair, and thick glasses secured to her head with an elasticized black strap. By her junior year in college, a large orthodontic bill, a talented Fifth Avenue hairdresser, and tinted contact lenses had re-created Mary as a knockout. Somehow, she'd managed to gain weight exactly where you'd want it, and had me beat by a cup size. She can apply liquid eyeliner evenly while riding in a taxi on the way to a date, of which she has many. She is my romantic adviser as well as fashion and makeup consultant. She has lots to say on all those subjects.

She led me directly to the sale rack and demonstrated the decision-making talent that had vaulted her to buyer in record time. She started at one end of the rack and began pushing hangers along it too fast for me to see what she was moving. "No. No. No. Yes. Maybe. No. No. Definitely not you. Yes. Yes. Yes." She went right to the end of the rack, pulling out the yeses and maybes and piling them in my arms. "All right. Try them on."

My arms were wrapped around a very heavy assortment of color-coordinated pants, skirts, tops, and dresses. Mary followed me into the dressing room so I wouldn't waste time wondering if something worked or not. She'd know immediately.

While I started to undress, Mary said, "Okay, let's *parle chiffon*." That's French for "have a girl talk." Her work involves numerous trips to France, and Gallic expressions creep into her conversation, making her sound feminine and sophisticated. I should think of that the next time I resort to Neapolitan profanity. "You know that lawyer, Bill, I met a few weeks ago? He has a friend who sounds terrific and Bill's looking to fix him up. I thought we could all go out together." She shook her head no to the skirt I had just tried on and handed me another one.

"You know I hate blind dates."

"But you're not doing anything on your own to get back in the game, Casey! It's been five weeks."

"Four and a half."

"Whatever. You have to get over it already! I'm begging you." Mary had exhausted her sympathy for my situation about week after I discovered Richard in his office with Lexi. That was so her. When Mary says she's leaving, Mary's gone. I'm more like a dog with a bone. I couldn't let go. She pretended she was strumming a guitar and sang a little George Strait: "If You Ain't Lovin' (You Ain't Livin')."

I picked up my imaginary guitar and sang her some Mark Chesnutt, "I'm Not Getting Any Better at Goodbyes." When we were growing up, we had a friend, Susie Jo Banks, whose father was from Nashville. If the stereo at her house wasn't playing country songs, he was singing them. Mary and I could probably carry on an entire conversation using country-and-western song titles and lyrics.

"I know, but I'm here to change that."

"I know you're right. I'd just like to have some—"

"*Please* don't say 'closure'!"

"I was going to say 'satisfaction.'"

"Well, in this case 'satisfaction' may well be in the form of some Italian dish, and I don't mean food. Try these." I zipped up a pair of cropped pants and she stood back and said, "I knew those would look great on you, and they travel well. I just bought the same pair for my trip."

"What trip?"

"I didn't tell you? Buying trip to Paris, in three weeks."

"So you'll be in Paris when I'm in Italy."

"*Oui.* Aren't we the sophisticated, continental family? Who would have thought?"

"I wish I felt as sophisticated as you do. You should have seen the ass I made of myself this morning." I told her about my encounter with Danny. She ignored the description of my bumbling behavior and zeroed in on his personality.

"Bold's not bad. Bold is where it's at. And why do you care if he just wants to meet Sally? Everyone wants to meet her."

"That's not the point. Going through me means he's a user. A user is not sincere. You can't trust them in business or in love."

"Is that the world according to Dr. Phil or according to cynic Casey Costello?"

"It's just a fact."

"So are you going to see this Danny again?"

"I'm *not* interested, Mary. He's an opportunist. But I will see him again and again. I have to work with him, and he's asked us all to a party at his restaurant this Thursday night."

"Are you going to go?"

"Yeah. I'm pretty sure Sally is going to want to go. She hasn't been to Oran Mor and she hates not being up on what's hot. That means I'll go. Why don't you come with us?"

"You don't have to ask me twice. I use all the connections I can to go everywhere. Wait right here."

Mary left and returned in a minute with a little black dress that was clearly not designed for warmth. "Here, try this on."

"Try what on? I don't see anything but a black handkerchief."

She pushed it toward me. "Try it!"

Had God been sitting in the dressing room, he would have listed the dress as the eighth deadly sin. It was a soft, smooth silk, and its only shape was my body. Thin spaghetti straps met a bodice cut so low you would see China if I bent over. It stopped about two inches above my knees and would stop my Nonna's heart if she saw me in it.

"You look incredible. You *have* to wear that to the party. Wear the black Jimmy Choo heels you bought in Nantucket last summer."

"Are you crazy? I'll get arrested, or at least propositioned on Second Avenue."

"You're not going to be on Second Avenue. You're going to be in the high-rent district, and this is what people are wearing."

"Not my people."

"No. You're right about that. Your people are wearing baggy pants with fruit all over them, white coats with little kerchiefs tied around their necks, and funny hats. Trust me, Casey. You look amazing. Chef Danny will see what's really cooking."

"I told you. I'm not interested."

"Well, that's the point. You want him to crave you for you, and then you can reject him for using you. Payback."

She had a point. Revenge goes with our heritage. I took another look in the mirror. The dress was skimpy, but it didn't reveal parts of me that I'd been taught to hide. After making sure the dress was shrinkproof in case of rain, I bought it, along with several stylish pieces for the trip. If you didn't count the sexy payback dress, the entire wardrobe barely set me back a week's pay.

Chapter 4

Cookin' good.

—*Nancy Apple*

Wednesday morning I ignored the pastries on the breakfast buffet and took a plain yogurt. No sense in risking a bulge in my little black dress. I ate half the yogurt and then started to unpack the organic groceries. Mae came in as I was trying to decide if tempeh really deserved a place in this world. I didn't have to guess where she would stand on the question. I hadn't seen her look that happy since, as my dad would say, "the pigs ate her little sister."

"Is she here yet?" she asked, dropping her backpack on a stool. "Sara, I mean."

"Mae, I have really bad news for you. They rushed Sara to the hospital with a severe case of additive deficiency. They're feeding her liquidized Chee-tos and pepperoni pizza through a tube, and she is responding well. She's begun to ask for take-out from Wendy's."

Mae lifted her arms into a cross as if to ward off evil spirits. "You shouldn't even contaminate the room with the name of that place. Trust me, you'll be eating your words as soon as you

meet Sara and taste her cheesecake." Cheesecake made me
think of the cheese Danish I had passed on earlier that morning. I figured one couldn't hurt and headed back to the buffet.

Our vegan chef, Sara Paul, turned out to be a delight, and
her tofu cheesecake was as delicious as Mae had promised. We
were even able to get all four Tonys to taste it. They declined
offers of the tempeh fajitas, however, and although I did taste
them, I didn't think the local beef-heavy, Tex-Mex restaurant
had to worry about being replaced. The morning's only dicey
moment was when I took Sara up to makeup and she asked if
the products had been tested on animals and no one knew.

"I just can't use them, then. I'm sorry, but the very thought
that they could have been is terribly upsetting to me. Can't I
just go on as I am?"

I took a good look at her. She was wheat. Her hair, her eyes,
her eyebrows, her complexion, her blouse, they were all one
shade of beige. The camera would have trouble finding her. "I
don't think so, Sara. Can you just get made up for the show
and we'll wash it off immediately afterward?"

She shook her head back and forth slowly. "I just can't. I'm
sorry. I think of those poor defenseless little creatures and it
makes me too sad."

The last thing I needed was a sobbing animal-rights activist
beating tofu, frying tempeh, and dedicating the segment to
helpless, chemically altered Spot. Not a good show. Then I had
an idea. "Wait here," I said and ran down to my socially con-
scious assistant. "Mae, do you have makeup with you?"

"Sure. What do you need?"

"Everything but your Magic Markers."

As I suspected, Meg's cosmetic bag held bottles and tubes all
clearly marked that they had not been manufactured at the ex-
pense of any critter two- or four-footed. Sara got a little color

and the audience got an exciting lesson in the uses of tofu and tempeh. Well, perhaps exciting is an exaggeration.

After the show, Mae went out for a smoke and I headed to the buffet for a muffin. I was fairly certain that I had burned off the calories of at least the Danish I'd already eaten by running up and down the stairs to makeup in search of politically correct cosmetics for Sara. I returned to the kitchen and sat down at Romeo to look over the scripts for Sally's two taped spots.

The prep for taped spots is different from that for live ones. If something goes wrong in a live spot, there's no way we can fix it; the talent just has to deal with it. So we only have to set it up once. With taped spots, there is always the possibility that we will have to do it more than once. If the talent makes a mistake or the camera misses something, the producer or director can ask for another take. So we have to have enough backup food prepped to repeat the shot as many times as necessary. It's not a problem if the food hasn't been disturbed, because then we can just wipe things clean and start again. But if the food has been cut or cooked or mashed about, we need backups. That means that for every food item on a tray that may be altered we need at least two identical items waiting in the wings. It's my job to know which ones and how many of them we need.

Mae returned to the kitchen with the Tonys. She was still going on about Sara to them. "You should *definitely* go to her restaurant. The food she serves will change your whole perspective on eating. You'll get into a whole new way of life." The Tonys were nodding their heads enthusiastically, but I knew the only thing they wanted to get into were Mae's pants.

I had made a huge number of notes on the tarte Tatin scripts and was trying to decipher what I'd written when Mae sat down. "Is Sally coming to the studio this morning?" she asked.

"She's going to try. She took an early shuttle from Washington and if it's on time and the traffic isn't bad, she told Sonya, she'll stop in."

"I want to give her the invitation for the Oran Mor party." It seemed to be all that was on Mae's mind.

"I told Sonya we were all invited and she said she'd tell Sally. I'm sure she's going to want to go."

"Well, duh! That's a def. Who wouldn't? You're going, aren't you?"

I tried to look bored. "I am."

"What are you going to wear?"

"Nothing."

"Huh?"

"Mary talked me into buying a dress that is so skimpy, I might as well wear nothing."

Mae leaned toward me and raised her eyebrows. "So, you bought a new dress? A skimpy new dress. Are you hoping to impress anyone in particular?"

I crossed my arms on Romeo and leaned into the distance she'd left between us. "Now, who could you have in mind? Mr. Love-'Em-and-Leave-'Em? Why don't *you* go after him? You're the one who thinks he's so charming."

"Because he's obviously into you."

"I'm going to assume that's a plural 'you,' referring to the majority of the female population in the midtown area."

"You're only guessing that he's a player, Casey."

"Trust me. It's a safe guess and I'm not interested. I bought the dress because I needed it." Even *I* didn't believe the sound of that. "What are you going to wear?"

"I'm putting together an Irish outfit." She leaned back and squinted in thought. "I haven't quite figured it all out yet, but I found the right color green spray paint." She didn't seem to have any idea how weird that sounded. "Speaking of clothes," she said and left the topic of spray paint, "did you find anything cool for Italy? You must be getting so psyched about going."

"Yes to the clothes. The jury's still out on the trip."

"Because Richard's not going?" She sounded ready to jump on me about it.

"Because George Davis is."

A look of disdain replaced her unsympathetic frown. "Hell-o! The Prince of Darkness. Who invited him?"

"He did. He says he has business with Sally there."

"Gross! I don't understand why she has anything to do with him. He's, like, so totally creepy. And, you know, he has her doing things that are so un-Sally. Did you see that commercial he arranged for her to do for laundry detergent? I mean, it's so embarrassing. His whole being around is a totally weird deal. He's like that Sven-something guy."

"Svengali."

"Yeah. Svengali. He's probably hypnotizing her into doing what he wants."

"I think that's a real stretch, Mae."

"Well, there *has* to be something. Maybe they're, like, getting it on. You know, a lot of lonely widows get trapped into doing crazy things by some young gigolo."

"Give me a break! Sally's suffering a lapse in judgment, not going blind. Have you taken a good look at George Davis?"

"You're right. He's pretty butt-ugly."

"Ugly's just the half of it. He's unkempt. Tina could start an herb garden under his fingernails. The dandruff, the dirty shoes. His clothes never fit. *Oh!*" I groaned. "And that smug look. There's no way he's Sally's type."

"Well, there must be something. It's too weird. If we were in a novel, we'd find out that he's secretly her son from a teenage marriage to a drug dealer who beat her and she had to give him up at birth because he was born a crack baby."

"*What* are you reading these days, Mae? Anyway, that wouldn't make sense even if this were a novel. Sally's life is an open book. Literally. With three different biographies written about her, someone would have found a skeleton if it exists."

"Hey, you never know."

"I guess. Whoa. Look at the time. We'd better get busy."

"Okay, tell me about the lobster spot."

"Sally is going to show Jim the right way to eat a lobster. Jim and Sally will each have a lobster, so I've ordered six, which should be plenty. It gives us two backups. It's just eating a lobster, not cooking it. What can go wrong?"

"Those are the four most frightening words in food TV."

"You're right. I take them back."

"Do we need any food prepped for that spot?"

"Just melted butter, and we can do that in the morning. We should also cut up some lemons in case Jim wants to squeeze some on his lobster. It's the tarte Tatin that's going to be a bitch." Mae and I each looked down at our recipes and scripts for the tarte Tatin. "With the tarte Tatin, Sally is not going to make the pastry crust but tell people to use their own perfectly made one. We can get those made today—three for three finished tarts, three for Sally, two of them backups. We can make the three finished tarts today and get all the apples we'll need peeled and cut. Sprinkle them with lemon and sugar so they won't turn brown. And be sure to leave some apples uncut, because Sally wants to show how to cut them up." After trying it a number of different ways, Sally had determined that the most efficient way to cut an apple into wedges was to cut it in quarters, core it, *then* peel it and cut the wedges. It eliminated the contest to see who could cut the longest unbroken piece of apple peel, but it was a lot faster.

I wasn't surprised that Sally had chosen to demonstrate a tarte Tatin. It was a classic French dessert, delicious, a challenge, and it had a good story. The famous tarte Tatin or, as it was originally called, *tarte des demoiselles Tatin,* was created by two spinster sisters of the Loire Valley who supposedly forgot to put the pastry in the bottom of the pie pan, put it on top instead, and then reversed it after cooking, creating the upside-down apple tart. Sally got a hoot out of calling these two talented hotel owners "spinster sisters," but what she really liked was the story, true or not, of how they just made the mistake work. More than once, she has told her audiences never to apologize to dinner guests. "If your cake is too moist and falls into pieces when you turn it out, scoop it up and call it a pudding."

"Okay. Let's start by giving assignments to the ten cast-iron pans and putting a Post-it in each one so we don't get confused." The Tonys each handed Mae a Post-it pad and a pen. She passed one of them over to me.

"When the segment opens, pan one will be on the stove with butter, already partially melted. Sally will add the sugar to that pan, then cook it until it caramelizes. Pans two and three are backups for pan one. Pan four will have already caramelized sugar and one partial circle of apple wedges. Sally will put on the second circle. Five and six are backups to pan four. She'll put pan four on the stove to cook the apples until the juices are thick and syrupy. Pan seven has the juices already thick, and Sally covers the apples in that pan with the pastry dough, which will be rolled out and on the counter. We won't need a backup for pan seven because it will be easy enough to pull the dough off without disturbing the apples. Pan eight is a finished, baked tart for Sally to turn out; nine and ten are backup finished tarts.

"In case she drops eight."

"Please, Mae. Not you too." When fans meet Sally, they feel compelled to tell her how much they loved the show when she accidentally dropped poached eggs on the floor. But people remember it differently, so sometimes they say chicken, sometimes leg of lamb, sometimes a great huge fish. Sally never corrects them; she just says, "Yes, wasn't that funny?" Some people remember incorrectly but with such detail that you can only wonder. One guy could hardly talk when he recounted to Sally how he and his wife almost wet their pants when she dropped the éclair on the floor and it landed frosting down. "Remember how you scraped the frosting off the floor and squiggled it back on the éclair? It was hilarious." "Wasn't it?" was all Sally said.

"I had to say it." Mae grinned sheepishly.

In no time at all, using Sally's apple-wedging technique, the Tonys and I had the bulk of the bushel peeled, cut in wedges, and sprinkled with sugar and lemon juice. Mae had made the pastry dough and divided it into six portions, and it was resting in the refrigerator. We were discussing the spot's degree of brownness in order to determine Jonathan's degree of annoyance when we heard an unmistakable "Woo-hoo" just outside the door. Our culinary superhero was here.

Chapter 5

God must have spent a little more time on you.

—*Alabama*

eventy-one-year-old Sally Woods galumphed into the kitchen with Sonya right behind her. Sally does galumph; it's part of her charm and, I suppose, hard to avoid with size eleven feet tucked into two-inch-high pumps. "Is *that Casey Costello?*" Sally said this as though she had just discovered the Queen of England cleaning the loo. It was her regular greeting, and it always makes me feel all warm and fuzzy.

"Can it be—*Sally Woods?*" I mimicked her tone and slight Georgian drawl as I stretched out my arms to join her in a big hug. Sally is my exact height, so hugging her is easy for me. Lots of people find their faces crushed into her ample bosom, a position that can be disconcerting when hugging someone as famous as Sally. "It's *so* great to see you."

Sally has been the biggest cheese in the food world for nearly thirty years. She has been declared a legend and a national treasure, been dined and feted by three presidents of the United States and one in France, and granted diplomas and awards more times than anyone of us can count, including Sally, who doesn't pay a whole lot of attention to such things. The man in the street knows her; children barely old enough to use the stove ask for her autograph; foodies swoon over her.

"It has been much too long, honey," she said and then turned to hug Mae, who did stand on her tiptoes to avoid the bosom crush. "And here's our Mae." There was never any question about who belonged to the Sally family. They were "ours."

As big a deal as Sally is, she never acts like one. The first thing she did after the hugging us was pull an apron out of her tote bag and ask what needed to be done.

"Well, we still have apples to peel and cut. All the dough's made and chilling and needs to be rolled out and we have to caramelize enough sugar to cover . . ." I looked down at my notes. "Six—no, seven pans."

Sally looked at the ten cast-iron skillets stacked up on the counter and let out one of her great hoots. "Huh! Just look at those pans. Isn't this something? I'd like to make the caramel."

Sonya reached for an apron and asked what she could do to help. Her question brought panic to Mae's eyes. Sonya is a genius at producing food shows but a real klutz when it comes to actually cooking. The last time she helped, she came close to chopping off two fingers. Between getting her to the hospital for stitches and washing blood out of the potato salad, we were lucky to get on the air in time. At some point one of us was going to have to level with her, but for now, I just had to find her a task. "Would you mind going over my notes for the tarte Tatin setup? There are so many pans to deal with; I want to make sure it's all there." It was a stopgap measure at best. It wouldn't take her all that long.

"Sure," she said without enthusiasm and sat down at one end of Romeo with my script. Mae dusted the other end of

Romeo with flour and lined up six plastic bags, each containing a perfectly smooth, flattened cake of *pâté brisée*. Sally gave the bags affectionate pats on her way to the stove. "Those are lovely, Mae." She slipped one out of its plastic cocoon, broke off a piece of the raw dough, and popped it into her mouth. It's not for nothing she's the best; she tastes *everything*. "Mmm. Buttery and delicious," she said before going over to the stove.

"I just followed *your* recipe. It's, like, foolproof." Mae was beaming even as she tried to make a perfect circle out of the cake with the missing mouthful. I measured out the sugar and butter for the caramel and put it on the counter next to Sally, who was trying to get the uncooperative electric stove to deliver a moderately high heat. Any serious cook uses gas, not electricity, and this particular stove always presents a challenge. She turned on all four imperfect burners and waved her hand a few inches above them to see which ones were responsive. "You can be sure no cook ever designed a stove like this. And who sells these? Someone who last week was working in men's socks? It's just a shame." Knowing what little control electricity provides the cook, I gave Sally a cut lemon. A few drops of acid added to the butter and sugar will prevent the caramel from crystallizing should the electric coils go mad.

"Oh yes, my friends. There is a God and he's painted my world red." An obviously jubilant Jonathan walked in carrying a small crate with six bright red steamed lobsters. He immediately spied Sally and set his bounty down on the counter. "Mrs. Woods! How wonderful to see you again!" He ignored the rest of us to get to Sally and took her hand in both of his. He was uncharacteristically all smiles. "How are you?"

"Just fine, honey." Calling him "honey" without using his name meant she knew she knew him and knew that he was one of us but just couldn't bring up his name quickly. It's a tactic she uses often and well. "How have *you* been?" When Sally asks that, she really wants to know. I know this because months after she has chatted with a fan she'll talk about how he or she lives in a trailer park, or was a pothead in the sixties, or has ten children. People fascinate her, and that has a lot to do with the kinship they feel with her. It's why they never hesitate to approach her—in restaurants, airports, on street corners and in the market. One woman actually slipped a piece of paper under the door in a ladies' room and asked for her autograph. Sally wrote "tinkle, tinkle" on it and slipped it back.

Sonya's cell phone rang and I said a little prayer that it was something that would need her attention elsewhere for a while so I wouldn't have to manufacture another task for her. It was and she mouthed, "I'll be right back" as she left the room with the phone still glued to her ear.

Meanwhile, Jonathan was relating in long, painful, drawn-out detail exactly how he had been. Sally listened and commented as she heated the butter and sugar, coaxing it into a caramel with a clean wooden spoon.

". . . so, after I spent my own money to paint the living room, and the bedroom, and put wallpaper up in the bathroom, just to mention a few things I've done, I may have to leave my lovely little apartment and look in a less desirable neighborhood—with my two cats and my dog, who really does *not* bark all day. It just doesn't seem right since I've . . . Mrs. Woods? *Mrs. Woods?* Are you all right? Can I get you something?"

"Wha eet err tuk."

I dropped my apples on the counter and turned. Oh my God, I thought, she's having a stroke. She had her hand to her mouth and seemed to be struggling. Her eyes were watering. Jonathan was visibly shaken but immobilized. I reached her just as she pulled a chunk of caramel out of her mouth. "It got stuck in my teeth and I couldn't get it off," she croaked.

"Jeez, Sally. You put hot caramel in your mouth? What were you thinking?"

"I didn't think. I just did." She gave me a Sally look that is seldom seen by the public. It is the sheepish grin of a schoolgirl who has just been caught executing a major prank. I'm sure she perfected the look in her younger days, because she is known to have created more than her share of mischief.

"Didn't it burn?"

"Well, *yes!*"

"I'll get some ice for you to chew. And for God's sake, keep the spoon out of your mouth." She gave me more of that impish grin.

I hadn't always talked to Sally like that. When I met her six years ago, I was so in awe of her stature that I addressed her with exaggerated reverence. At the time, I was teaching at a local cooking school that had been asked to organize a charity event at which Sally was the main attraction. It was held in a theater, so a makeshift kitchen had to be built on the stage. The "kitchen" consisted of a long skirted table with a cutting board, knives, a two-burner hot plate, a standing mixer, a food processor, and a large jar holding an assortment of cooking utensils. Sally stood behind this table facing the audience. Several feet behind her were two other skirted tables. One held three big buckets of water and served as our water source and cleanup area. The second table was our prep area and on top were another hot plate, cutting board, knives, utensils, and the food. Underneath were pots, pans, numerous small appliances, and several electrical outlets.

Sally was demonstrating trout mousse rolled inside salmon fillets and napped—such a nice word—with hollandaise sauce.

She made the hollandaise on her hot plate and handed it to me
to keep warm on our back-table hot plate. When I took the pan
from her, smiling for the audience, I could see that it had cur-
dled; little bits of hard yolk were visible up close. I wasn't exactly sure what to do about it. I certainly didn't want to point
it out to her, but I knew she wouldn't want to use it as it was.
So I made another one. I melted butter on my hot plate and
crouched under the skirted table with the butter, egg yolks,
lemon juice, and the blender. I waited for Sally to turn on the
food processor to puree the trout, and then, knowing the
processor would drown me out, I turned on the blender and
whirred yolks, butter, and lemon juice into a perfect hollandaise
and put it in a pan identical to the one Sally had handed me. I
saved hers just in case she was planning to discuss curdling, but
when I handed her the newly made one, she just gave me that
schoolgirl grin and said, "Nice work" and went back to the
demonstration.

That night, Sally asked me if I would be available to assist
her whenever she was working in New York. I guess being able
to cook on the floor is a valuable asset. My first official gig with
her turned out to be an eighteen-hour marathon of television,
demonstrations, and eating. We started our day at five in the
morning right here at *Morning in America*. Back then, they had
no prep chef, not much equipment, and no Romeo, so the re-
sources weren't much better than the makeshift theater kitchen.
But we managed to pull off one live show and three taped
shows without a hitch. We congratulated ourselves with a four-
course lunch and some very fine wine. Before going on to the
evening demonstration, we stopped off at a champagne-and-
chocolate-ice-cream tasting that the James Beard House was
sponsoring. At six o'clock, we were back in another theater
setup, where Sally made gumbo for three hundred people in

two electric woks. She was amazing. When the show ended at ten o'clock, the sponsors brought us champagne to toast the evening. Up until this point, I had been sensibly sipping the spirits, knowing that I wasn't called "Thimble Belly" for nothing, but now that the day was over I greedily held my glass out. As I was draining my second glass, Sally asked me where I'd like to go to dinner. Who was thinking about dinner? Mentally, my head was already on a pillow. We chose a homey little Italian restaurant, and after dinner, and more wine, I was showing Sally how to burn amoretti papers and coming close to burning down the restaurant. The next morning we met for breakfast, and I thought I should explain my behavior.

"Sally, I think I misjudged my dinner wine last night. I seem to remember dancing on tables."

She put her hand on my arm, got that impish look in her eyes, and said, "You were. But you were very good." From that moment on, I saw her not as a star but as a cool person, and before long, we saw each other as really good friends. When the position at *Morning in America* came up, she told Sonya she had to have me. That led to the happy place where I am today.

"Cooking together is such fun," Sally exclaimed between ice cubes.

"It sure is," Mae and I echoed each other.

Jonathan, however, did not look as if he were having fun. He might have been unsettled by the realization that the all-time greatest cooking personality could have keeled over in the middle of a conversation with him. He would become the medical case model for proof of dying from boredom. "I'm going to go to the fish market to see if I can get some seaweed for the lobsters," he said.

"Great idea. Did you remember the lobster tools?" I checked my notes to see what else was on my list. We'd spent so much time on the tarte Tatin that the lobster spot was getting short shrift.

He rolled his eyes and smirked as he held up claw crackers and lobster forks.

"It's my job to ask." I smirked back.

"How about lobster bibs?" Sally asked. She never confused cooking with heart surgery and was always ready to ham it up a bit. Not that lobster bibs were so weird, but many of our guest chefs wouldn't consider wearing a plastic bib with little cartoon lobsters running over it.

"What a fabulous idea!" Jonathan was clearly into this lobster thing. "I'll get some of those too. Do you think Jim will wear one? He's so conservative."

"If Sally does, he will." Mae was right. The show's hosts were well aware that Sally was a beloved figure, and they were happy to follow her lead in hopes of glomming on to some of her star power.

Sonya came back into the room just as Jonathan was leaving. She spent a little more time with the script before setting it aside. "I think this is just fine, Casey. What else can I do?"

I looked around to see where we were. I was working on the last apple, Mae had all the dough rolled out, and Sally's butter and sugar were now caramel. We were in safe territory. No more knives or heat. "I think we're ready to assemble the tarts. Let's line the pans up on Romeo."

We put seven pans in a row down the center of Romeo and I switched the Post-its from inside the pans to the surface next to them. We took our places, two on each side, and began our assembly.

Sally had stopped chewing ice and was now munching apple wedges. Between chews, she said, not so subtly, "I met the nicest young man in Washington, last week. He's a sous-chef at

Citronelle and very jolly. I think you might like him, Casey."
She was so sweet that way. Before I met Richard, she was
always suggesting men she thought would be good for me.
During one of my particularly long dating dry spells, she mentioned that she had a friend who was a "bit crumpled and
dusty" but a fine fellow. Would I be interested? I thought she
meant that he was a poor dresser, but it turned out that he was
a very old, weathered college professor who, fortunately, found
a mate before I had to tell Sally she must be crazy. Since I had
kept her up to date on the turmoils of my transition from break
to breakup with Richard, I imagine she was dusting off a lot of
old friends.

"Didn't I mention that I bought a gerbil? I've really grown
very fond of him."

"You did. But I thought that just might be a passing fancy."

"Nothing passing about it. Gerbils can live for two or three
years. That's a lot longer than my past relationship. 'It's not
love, but it ain't bad,'" I sang.

"Don't know that one. Roy Rogers?" Sally isn't much of a
fan of country music—she's more of a Gershwin devotee—but
she likes to hear me sing.

"Merle Haggard."

"Never heard of him. I think you should come to Washington and meet this chef." She raised her eyebrows in a question,
and I smiled at her.

"We'll see," I said.

She turned her attention to Mae. "What about you, Mae.
Are you still seeing that cute boy, Timmy?"

"Tommy. No. I ended it last week and I'm so over dating
twenty-year-olds with overdeveloped sex drives and underdeveloped communication skills. I'm looking for an older, sen-
sible man who doesn't consider beer guzzling and giving his

friends wedgies cultural events. But, it's so not happening."
Mae was in a tough position. For all that she looked like she's
playing dress-up from her nana's closet, she is very mature.
Older guys just don't give her a chance to prove it.

"What's 'older'?" Sally asked.

"At least in his thirties."

"Huh!" said our septuagenarian.

"I guess everything is relative," Sonya said. The truth is that
none of us ever thought of Sally as any age but ours. It wasn't
that she *tried* to act younger than she was; she *was* younger.

"Hey, most boys do outgrow beer guzzling and wedgies at
some point." I wasn't certain about the "most"; it was probably more like "a few."

"It's not just that. Whenever he calls to go out, he says things
like 'Hey, you wanna go out sometime this week?' I say, 'Sure,
that sounds great.' Then he says, 'Cool,' but he doesn't say
where or when. At first I'd suggest something and that's what
we'd do. But it really began to annoy me that he wouldn't at
least once have an idea of his own. You know, call and say,
'How about catching some sounds at the Knitting Factory Friday night' or 'Let's go for Thai food and a flick on Tuesday.' So
after a while, when he'd call and say, 'Wanna do something?'
I'd say, 'Fine' but make no suggestions. And he'd just hang
there waiting for me to decide what we'd do. That would go on
for days. He'd call and ask, 'When can I see you,' I'd say,
'Whenever you like,' and he still didn't come up with an idea.
I think it's a definite sign of a couch potato in training." She did
have a point.

"You can do better, Mae." Having been married to the same
handsome, adoring, man for over twenty years, Sonya was a
creditable adviser. "I think that Danny O'Shea is pretty cute.
And he's single."

"I think he's into Casey. He was, like, totally coming on to her but, you know, she was acting all chefy."

"Hey, I was nearly naked. I felt vulnerable. Besides, coming on to women seems to be his natural persona. He was much too obvious about it. I didn't take it personally."

"I liked that he was open and direct. I'll bet when he calls a girl he's got definite plans," Mae said.

"I'm sure he does. And I'd bet those plans aren't dinner and a movie."

Sally thought that was pretty funny. "What makes you think that?"

"He's flirtatious as hell and full of himself. He just acted like someone who spends all his free time seducing women."

"A real Casanova," Sally said.

"You got it."

"In my day, they would say that young men just need to sow their wild oats."

"Well then, my guess is that Danny O'Shea qualifies for a farm loan."

"So what about his party tomorrow night. Shall we all go together?" Just as we'd suspected, Sally was craving to go.

"Definitely," said Mae.

"Since you're staying out in New Rochelle, Casey, do you want to change at my hotel room tomorrow? As a matter of fact, it's a suite, so why don't you spend the night."

"That would be great. I was going to sleep on Mary's couch, but it's about two inches shorter than I am and it's hard to stay curled up all night."

"I'm going to lunch at *Gourmet* tomorrow, so I'll bring you your own key in the morning and you can just help yourself."

Finally, the apples were all in place. We covered three of the pans with Mae's perfect circles of dough and slid them into the oven. As soon as they were baked, we would be ready to call it a day. Sonya looked at her watch and said she'd better run. I remembered that she was meeting with George and the suits and I was grateful the offices were in another building. I really hated to be in the same room with him. Sally said, "I think we should go out for a good, big lunch today. How about that?"

"Count me in," I said.

"Oh, bummer." Mae frowned. "I have to work at the family place this afternoon. We're short-staffed since April and June are gone."

"The months or your sisters?" I asked.

Mae had to be sick of my inane jokes about her family's names. "That's so lame, Casey."

"I know. I am sorry you can't come, though."

"Thanks."

Sally suggested we try Jean-Georges Vongerichten's new place.

"Well, good luck, Sally. That's one of the most happening lunch places in the city. I *wonder* how we will get in," I teased. Never had a restaurant been too crowded to seat Sally.

Sally took out her cell phone and little black address book. "I'll make a call." After waiting a few minutes for an answer, she boomed into the phone, "Jeannie, this is Sally . . . Woods. Do you think your brother could get two of us into lunch at Jean-Georges's new place, today at one o'clock? Okay, call me on my cell phone." She gave Jeannie her number and folded the phone shut.

"Who's Jeannie?" I asked.

"She's my hairdresser here in New York. Her brother is a dishwasher at Jean-Georges's."

"Did it occur to you just to call the restaurant and tell them

who you are? Or, for that matter, just say, 'Hi, I need a table.'
Everyone knows your voice," I said.

"Oh. They wouldn't care that it was me. They see real star
types all the time." Sally was probably the only one who really
believed that restaurants weren't wild to have her eat there.
Even the haughtiest of places are willing to bend over back-
ward to accommodate her. When we were in San Francisco on
our way to Napa Valley, we decided at the last minute to eat
at a trendy new restaurant known for its crab claws and attitude. I got there before Sally, and when I asked the very bored
maître d' for a table for three he looked at me as though I had
warts covering my face and asked if I had a reservation.

"No. We just decided at the last minute because we heard
how remarkably good the food is."

My flattery did not impress him. He made snooty, snorting
sounds and said, "We are full months in advance. And we
never have empty seats." That's when Sally and Sonya arrived
and Sally asked me if we could get in.

"Not for a few months," I said.

There was a lot of undecipherable stammering on the
maître d's part, but we did make out the words "sudden can-
cellation." Next to the crab claws, the best part of lunch was
having him fawn all over us.

Just before noon, Sally's phone rang and she had a brief
conversation with Jeannie. "We're all set," she told me. I hope
we don't have to wait a long time at a crowded noisy bar. I'm
hungry."

WE ARRIVED AT THE restaurant, and Jean-Georges himself met us and led us to a table in the center of the room,
where a nervous-looking waiter was shifting flatware and
plumping napkins. Jean-Georges pulled out a chair for Sally

and with some effort shifted her back in to the table. "We are so happy to have you here, Mrs. Woods. We'd love to send some *amuse-gueules* to the table for you." Loosely translated, the term refers to small, one- or two-bite portions of food meant to tickle the appetite. I was tickled already.

Sally folded her hands together in prayer-like fashion and dipped her head demurely. "That would be lovely. Thank you."

"I guess he had time to Google you up and found out you were somebody," I said when he'd left the table. "That's great, because now we'll get all kinds of goodies."

The goodies began to arrive in short order. In addition to the appetizers we had chosen, the waiter delivered three complimentary ones from Jean-Georges. Sally finished the soup she had ordered, tasted my crab spring roll, and was plunging her fork into a complimentary mushroom tart when she reached her free hand over to touch my hand, the one that wasn't shoveling food into my mouth. "You're still very sad about Richard, aren't you?"

"More disappointed. And still angry, I guess. But, truthfully, the breakup was coming for a long time. Our relationship wasn't going anyplace. When we weren't arguing, we were more like good friends than lovers. I just hate how it happened."

"It was mean. In my day, you did such things directly, like a gentleman. Unless, of course, it was during the war and you were in a hurry to marry someone else. Then you sent a 'Dear John' letter, but it was on decent stationery and included a little chitchat."

"Well, there was definitely no chitchat. Not even 'Remember to floss.' "

"It's this high-tech generation." I knew she wasn't criticizing technology in general, because she herself was very much into the latest in hard- and software. "People are just not as courteous as they used to be. But Richard's in the past and you have to move on to something other than a gerbil." I gave her a sarcastic smile. "Do you know what you want?" she asked, taking another forkful of my spring roll.

I thought for a minute before saying, "I'd love to have what you and Peter had."

Before he died three years ago, Peter Woods was a brilliant government scientist whom Sally had met when she was a sophomore at Goucher in Maryland. He was eight years older than she was, but according to both of them, it was love at first sight and they married the day after Sally graduated from college. Peter was amazing—brilliant and charming. It was Peter who introduced Sally to good food and encouraged her to take cooking classes whenever she could. They went everywhere together. He was in his early seventies when he died of a heart attack. I know Sally misses him, but she loves to talk about him and their times together. At least, she usually does.

When I mentioned his name, she said nothing for a minute and then sighed and said, "Things aren't always what they seem."

I was stunned. "What do you mean? Weren't you happy together?"

"We were very happy; it's just that recently I've learned . . . " She paused, choosing her words carefully. "Things I didn't know when we were together."

A number of ugly thoughts raced into my head, and I said the only nonugly one that came to mind. "Oh, Sally. Peter loved—no, adored—you. It was so obvious."

"I know that, but it doesn't change everything."

I waited for her to tell me more, and when she didn't say anything I asked if she wanted to talk about it.

"I'd rather not, Casey. Forget I said anything. I'd rather talk about how you are handling this breakup with Richard."

Or not handling it, I thought, looking at the beautiful food Jean-Georges had sent to the table. It deserved better conversation. "Screw it, Sally. Let's not talk about either of them."

"Good idea. Pass that one over here."

Somewhere between devouring the entrées we had ordered and doing our best with the gratis ones, we began to talk about Italy. "I understand that George Davis is going with us?" I said.

"He's not going *with* us. He'll be there when we are. We have some business there." Sally's tone said that was all there was to discuss, but I couldn't stop myself.

"What are you going to be doing?" My tone was light and inquisitive, not pressing.

"It's personal. Not anything you need to know."

Whoa. This was as close as she had ever come to telling me to mind my own business, and I felt shamefully out of order.

"I didn't mean to sound short with you, honey, but George is, well, a temporary situation." That was sure good news. "I have some business with him and when it's over, I don't expect he'll be around anymore." That made sense to me. Maybe her new lawyer had arranged the deal with George and Sally was too honorable to back out of it.

"When does your contract with him expire?"

"We don't have a contract per se. It's an agreement."

I looked up from my forkful of braised duck. "Can you get out of it?"

She shook her head. "No. I can't now." She put her fork down and looked straight at me. "*I* know he's a sleazeball, Casey . . ." In spite of the unpleasant topic of conversation, I had to smile at her choice of words. Sally has such a charming way of blending words from all the eras she has lived in. She didn't try to imitate contemporary slang, but every now and then threw in a word or two that would seem out of place with her age, were she not who she was. "And I know you must wonder why I've let him handle my business. It's complicated. I've wanted to say something to you because I know he treats you rudely, and you and I have always been able to talk to each other." I put my own fork down and sat quietly, ready at last to hear what was going on. But the next words were not from her.

"I don't believe it! My two favorite people at the same table!"

We both looked up and saw Suzy MacDonald. "Suzette! What are you doing here?" Suzy is an American who teaches cooking classes in Paris, hence the "Suzette." She had worked with Sally and me on a number of projects, and her bubbly personality makes her one of our favorites as well.

She immediately had Sally wrapped in a big hug. "I've come over for my brother's wedding. I'm meeting Linda here for lunch." Linda is the food editor for *Cooks Today* and every bit as lovable as Suzette.

"You have to join us," Sally insisted.

Suzy pulled out a chair and sat. "But of course!" She said it with a French accent. "This is *très* fabulous!"

Linda came along soon and, exclaiming her joy at finding us all together, sat down. Our lunch, laughter, and guiltless gossip went on for over two hours, and by the time we'd finished the last of the eight complimentary desserts, I was no longer thinking about the unpleasant topics that had started our lunch.

Chapter 6

Famous last words of a fool.

— *George Strait*

At eight forty-five the next morning, Sally was sitting in a chair on the studio set, which was designed to resemble someone's cozy living room. She was chatting with Karen and Jim, who were sitting next to each other on the sofa. The cameras were rolling and Sally was telling the hosts what she thought the future was for fusion food, architectural food, and no-carb diets. She predicted that none of it would outlive just plain old good cooking.

"Rather than no-carb, don't you think no-fat makes more sense?" Karen asked.

"*No!* If you don't eat fat, you'll get dandruff. 'Everything in moderation' is my motto."

Sally really glowed on camera. Her sky-blue eyes were full of expression, and her short, soft curls in many shades of honey shone under the lights. In spite of the wrinkles and age spots that makeup could not completely camouflage, the camera, as they say in show business, loved her. She had "it," that indefinable, unforgettable magic that makes a star.

The show would be off the air at nine, so I took yet one more look at the setups for our taped spots. The lobster trays were ready to go. Jonathan had definitely outdone himself with the seaside theme, having managed to find some seaweed, as well as a weathered lobster trap complete with a faded buoy attached by a rope—and the bibs. The tarts were looking better than good.

When the show was off the air, Sally and Jim went upstairs to change their clothes. I don't know which of the staff keeps track of such things, but on the day the lobster spot airs, Jim will be wearing the same clothes he chooses for today's taping. He'll be on the living room set and will say something like "When we return, I will join Sally Woods, who's waiting in our *Morning in America* kitchen. She's going to show us the proper way to eat a lobster, so don't touch that dial." After a commercial break, he will reappear on the kitchen set with Sally, and his clothes will give no hint that it's not the same day or that Sally isn't really there.

As soon as we got the all-clear call from the studio, we brought the lobsters and ocean paraphernalia to the set. We positioned two lobsters in the center of the counter and surrounded each with plenty of seaweed, the claw crackers, lobster forks, and picks, bowls of melted butter, the lobster trap with attached buoy, and the plastic bibs. We added a bottle of wine and two stemmed wine glasses to the seascape. Jonathan fussed over his set, which did look incredible, spraying water over the seaweed and painting oil onto the lobsters to keep everything glistening. Sally and Jim took their places, the sound technician wired them, and we kitchen people stepped back so they could do a run-through. The run-through shows the director what is going to happen and where it will happen. That way he can direct the cameras where to be once they are rolling. Sally and Jim walked through all the steps, never, of course, actually disassembling the lobster. They finished by pretending to pour wine and then for real clinked their glasses in a toast. Perhaps because the glasses were empty and Sally was a little too enthusiastic, one of the glasses broke. Jonathan was on the set in a flash, cleaning broken glass out of the seaweed and off the counter while I went to the kitchen for replacement bowls of butter. I didn't know if any glass had landed in the butter, but CYA is what my job is all about. I gave the new bowls of butter to a Tony to bring to Jonathan and I checked once again on the tart setup. The lobster would be a piece of cake, but I still felt some angst about the tarts.

Returning to the studio just as the director asked for "quiet on the set," I took a place off to the side, next to Jonathan. The floor manager broke the silence when she began her countdown. "In five, four, three . . ." She stopped speaking aloud and held up two fingers, then one, and then made a small circling motion with that finger to indicate "now." Jim waited his usual three seconds before he began to talk, in order to give the editor some wiggle room, then said, "Sally, why do you think we need a lesson in eating a lobster?"

"I've watched so many people in restaurants struggling with them. Some people even throw away good parts that still have delicious meat in them."

"That's terrible."

"It is. But as we say in Georgia, 'Some people are as lost as a goose in a snowstorm.'"

Jim laughed. "Okay. So where do we begin?"

Sally handed him a bib. "You'll want to put this on to save that tie, which is quite handsome."

"Thank you. My wife picked it out."

"They always do." They each tied on their lobster bibs and Sally picked up her lobster and wiggled it at the camera.

"This is a fine fellow. Probably about a two-pounder." She turned it over and looked at the underside of the tail. "Well, it's a she, so we will have the delicious roe to eat." We had ordered only females according to Sally's directions.

"How do you know it's female?"

She pointed to the small joints under the tail near the chest. "In the female, these little swimmerets have tiny hairs. The male swimmerets are bald and pointy." Poor Jim didn't seem to know where to go with that. "I see."

Sally plowed right along. "Start with a claw and grip it firmly." She took a good hold of hers and waited for Jim to do the same. "Now snap it off. Wump!" They did it together.

"Is the claw meat tastier than the body meat?" Jim asked.

"It's a matter of preference. I'm a body person myself. Now break off the knuckle." Sally gave a good snap and the knuckle separated from the claw. Jim followed suit. "To get at the claw meat, you'll need a good set of lobster crackers." Sally searched on all sides of her lobster. The crackers weren't there. What the hell! I'd seen them there, but they were gone now. Sally kept going. She had begun her television career in what is known as "live to tape," so no matter what happened she was not about to stop until someone directed her to do so. She looked totally undaunted as she said, "Or you can just give it a good thump," and she picked the claw up over her head and gave it a good whack on the counter—or, actually, on the seaweed, since Jonathan had completely covered the counter's surface. The shell on a two-pound lobster is pretty thick, and the seaweed cushioned the blow, so even the second whack that Sally applied didn't so much as dent it. So, she picked up the Joyce Chen scis-

sors meant to cut through the thinner tail shell and tried to slice
into the obstinate claw. She needed a starting point and didn't
have a good one. Meanwhile, Jim was thwacking his shell on
the seaweed and having no more luck than Sally had, but he
kept at it. Finally, Sally grabbed the scissors so they were point
down and prepared to stab the point into the enemy claw. It was
beginning to look like a massacre scene from a bad B-movie. All
that was missing was the blood, and if Jim moved any closer to
Sally, we would have that too. Before Sally's scissors plunged
into the claw, the director called, "Cut. Hold it. Please."

When the director tells us to "hold it" or "please wait," he
means don't touch or move anything until he checks the tape
to see if he can fix the problem in editing. If he can, he tells us
where he'll pick the tape up and what he needs to see. If he
can't fix it, then we start from the beginning. In that pregnant
time, I turned to Jonathan and screamed in a furious whisper.
"What the hell happened to the lobster crackers? I touched
them twice. They were there." The minute I saw his face, I
knew he knew what the hell had happened. He reached into his
stylist's basket and pulled out the two sets of crackers.

"When I cleaned the broken glass off the counter, I picked
everything up. I guess I didn't put these back."

I tried not to sound too sarcastic. "Guess not."

"I—I—I—I can't believe I've messed up like this. Kill me.
Just take your chef's knife and run it through my heart."

What a tempting thought. The truth was, I couldn't believe
he'd messed up either. Jonathan is meticulous and doesn't make
mistakes. Anyway, killing him wouldn't exonerate me; ulti-
mately anything that goes wrong with setup is my fault.

"Hey, get a grip. It's okay. We've got backup, and anyway,
the director may be able to pick it up from where they broke
off the claws."

Or maybe not. "We'll start from the beginning. Setup please." Mae was ready with the backup trays, and as soon as we got the word, she and two Tonys appeared with fresh lobsters and clean bibs. Two other Tonys carried empty trays to remove the used lobsters and bibs.

"I can't find the crackers, Casey. They're not in the kitchen," Mae said in a panicked tone as she hurried by me.

"It's cool. We have them." Mae looked surprised but didn't ask. There wasn't time. The director was already asking, "How long?" Together, we cleared and reset the set. Jonathan put the crackers in place, and I made sure I was the last one to check the set.

"In five, four, three . . ."

"Sally, why do you think we need a lesson in eating a lobster?"

On went the bibs, off came the claws, and this time up came the crackers. Sally showed Jim how to crack the claw, and then she easily slipped the meat out of the shell in one piece. Jim did the same.

Sally dipped her lobster claw in the melted butter and took a good big bite. There was no acting involved; she was eating lobster and enjoying every minute of it. "Umm, ummm, that is just delicious. Try it."

Jim may have been waiting for Sally to finish chewing before he bit into his lobster, so that one of them would be able to speak without a mouthful of food. Forget it. Sally was already taking a second bite and umming some more, so he went ahead and dipped his claw into the butter and took a bite. I'd like to say he said, "Ummm, ummm" as Sally had, but he didn't. He opened his mouth, but nothing came out. He reached his hands up and clutched at his throat. Jim was choking—a frightening choke that made his eyes go wide and brought three of the crew rushing onto the set. Sally was already close to him, so she immediately grabbed him from behind in a ferocious bear hug and administered an insanely violent Heimlich upthrust that lifted the host several inches off the floor but did not dislodge the lobster. Sally did it again, and this time a large piece of partially chewed claw flew across the set with astonishing force and hit Jonathan in the face. I shouldn't have considered it revenge for the crackers, but I did. Jim held up a hand to indicate that he was okay and then began making small coughing sounds before finally managing to say, in a squeaky voice, "It went down"—*cough, cough*—"the wrong way." *Cough.* "I'm okay." And he sipped some of the water one of the stagehands had brought him.

Meanwhile, I was beginning to imagine the unimaginable. I was pretty sure there was no way to edit that take, so this next one would exhaust our supply of lobsters. If something went wrong with the next take, we'd be screwed.

Mae was standing next to me, waiting to see if we needed to clear and set up again. One of the reasons I like working with her is that she never says such dumb-ass things as "Do you realize there are only two lobsters left."

"Mae, I don't think they can fix this one, so if something goes wrong with the next take, we need a backup plan. I was thinking that they could start the spot with one claw already off. Sally can say something like 'I've already removed one claw and separated the knuckle.' Then she can say, 'I did it like this and blah, blah, blah' as she pulls off the claw that's attached. She won't like it, but we have no choice other than scratching the whole thing. Put the lobsters from the first take back on the trays with their detached claws and we'll see if it'll fly."

Mae went to the kitchen and was back in a flash. "We have a problem. The Tonys ate the claws."

"What! They know better. Shit! Which Tonys? They are so dead."

Mae looked confused. "I don't know. I mean, I know who but I don't know which ones they are. The taller, skinnier ones."

"Whatever, they are so very dead."

"They feel wicked bad. They didn't think we'd ever need a separated claw."

"We are so screwed. Let me think. These lobsters"—I nodded my head toward the set—"each still have one claw attached, and the two in the kitchen each have a whole claw. We can take the claws off the ones in the kitchen, put them with the ones on the set, and go with my backup plan of having lobsters with a claw already off. Did Jim and Sally both pull off the same claw?"

"I think so," Mae said.

"I do too. Do you think we can get away with lobsters with two left claws?" At that moment, ten more seventy-dollar-apiece, fully cooked lobsters sounded like a steal.

Jim vocalized something that sounded like "Ee dee ee do" and then announced that he was fine. The director called for us to start from the beginning, and we set up again.

"In five, four, three . . ."

"Sally, why do you think we need a lesson in eating a lobster?"

Put on bibs, shake the lobster for the camera, tickle its swimmerets, remove and crack the claw, dip and eat. Cut open the stomach, taste tomalley and roe, remove body meat, dip, and eat. Suck and nibble on legs and tail flaps.

As Jim poured Sally and then himself a glass of wine, I said, "Thank you God" under my breath repeatedly.

They picked up their glasses and held them ready for a toast. "Thank you, Sally, for a great lesson. It was delicious. *Bon appétit.*" And Jim ever so gently tapped Sally's glass.

"Or as we sometimes like to say, bon appe-titty."

They smiled for the camera and the director, who was probably replaying the tape to see if he'd heard correctly, asked us once again, "Hold it, please."

"Did she *really* say that?" I said to no one in particular and then answered myself. "Of course she did. She's Sally."

"What should I do, Casey? The lobster-with-two-left-claws bit?"

"You know what, Mae, they're going to be able to fix that with a voice-over or something. Let's get ready for the tart." I probably sounded surer than I felt, but I couldn't even consider the possibility of one more take. It was aging me.

"That's a wrap. Thank you everyone. Next setup please."

Sally left to change her blouse and I went back to the kitchen. Two tall, skinny Tonys tried to avoid eye contact as they scooted by me on their way to clear and wipe down the set, but I put a hand on each of their pathetically underdeveloped chests and stopped them. "Never, never, *nev-er* eat so much as a piece of parsley until you hear me say, 'We are completely finished, there is no more, I'm going home.' Even if everyone else in the studio drops dead and the studio is struck by lightning and burns to the ground, leaving only the food from the show remaining, do *not* touch it until *I* say it's okay. If I die before I say it, then the food rots here without ever being touched. Is that clear?" They nodded their fuzzy chins like bobblehead dolls.

Coming on the heels of the almost blown "piece-of-cake" lobster spot, the tart took on a new dimension. I began to look over the pans and consider all the things that could possibly go wrong. The caramel could burn. "Mae, ask a Tony to turn the large front burner on the set up to a medium-high temp and then stay there so no one burns themselves." I wanted to make sure the stovetop would cooperate. "And measure out two more butter-sugar backups and put a cut lemon on the tray." If we needed more apples, we could always scoop them out of one half-assembled tart and add them to another. I made a note of which tarts could be emptied if needed. If Sally missed the unmolding three times, chances were good we could slip one of them back in the pan to be re-unmolded. Unless she dropped it on the floor. Apple pudding. I couldn't go there.

I went out to check the set and brought a number of tools to put on the shelf below the counter in case Sally needed something that wasn't on the counter. I checked the burner to make sure it was heating, then stayed on the set until Sally came back in a pretty apple-green blouse. That was a good sign.

"Quiet on the set," said the director.

"In five, four, three . . ." said the floor manager.

In exactly three minutes and thirty seconds, on the first take, Sally pulled off the making and unmolding of a perfect tarte Tatin. From the control room, the director's voice was warm and genuine. "That's a go. Nice job, Sally. Thank you, everyone." Mae, Sonya, Jonathan, and I clapped. Sally made a little bow and then followed us to the kitchen, where the Tonys were hovering close to but not touching the tarts. "We are finished. You may eat now," I said.

"I think that went well." Sally never boasted about her work; that was about as close as she came to patting herself on the back. It was well deserved.

"Piece of cake," I said throwing my head back and rolling my eyes.

"Well, I'm off to my lunch at *Gourmet,* and then I'm going to do a little clothes shopping." She opened her purse and handed me a card key. "Here's your key to the hotel room, Casey. Just make yourself comfortable. Did you bring your suitcase?" She looked around the room, and I pointed to my overnight case in the corner.

"That's a very small bag."

"It's a very small dress."

"Huh!" She turned to Sonya and Mae. "Why don't you come to the hotel beforehand and we can have a little drinkie and then all go to the party together?"

"Lovely," said Sonya before turning to me. "What about Mary?"

"She's going to meet us at Oran Mor. She's getting ready for a Calvin Klein show and may be late."

Sally walked to the door, then turned as though she had forgotten something. "Oh. By the way, George said he wants to go also and will meet us there."

No one said "Great" or "Lovely" or even a noncommittal "Gotcha."

As usual, Sally's hotel accommodations were over the top. The management had covered the highly polished wood tabletops with bouquets of fresh flowers, bowls of fruit, and little silver dishes with chocolate candies that had the hotel's logo molded into them. There were two large bedrooms, a spacious sitting area with an office desk, and a small kitchen stocked with wine, liquor, mixers, and assorted edibles.

I telephoned Mary to remind her about the party—like she might forget—then drew a bath and soaked for a while before washing and drying my hair. Wrapping myself in the hotel's big fluffy white robe, I went to the little kitchen to check on ice, glasses, and nibbles for our little preparty party.

As I was setting out a tray of glasses, the phone rang and I went to the desk to answer it. I said hello a couple of times before realizing it was the fax machine, which stopped ringing and began spitting out a piece of paper. It was from George and, thinking maybe it was him saying he couldn't make it tonight or wanted to be picked up or wondered what time, I read it, in case I needed to call Sally on her cell. At least I tried to convince myself that was why I was reading it. His message had nothing to do with the party. It was to tell Sally that the appointment to discuss the new book contract was set for tomorrow morning at Farrow Publishing and they insisted that she be there. I read it again. What's that all about? Farrow's not Sally's publisher. Welling is. Welling has published all thirteen of her books and Jill Jennings has edited every one of them. Looks like *Morning in America* is not the only one on George's shit list. I wondered if Sally was aware of what permanent damage George's temporary status was causing. I knew that Sally wouldn't discuss George in front of the others, so I hoped that she would be back before they came. But she still wasn't there by the time I started dressing.

I put on the "little" black dress and slipped on my Jimmy Choo spiked heels, which made me an even six feet tall. I checked myself out in the mirror; the dress looked even skimpier than I had remembered. I was prepared for that and had packed a red antique French damask shawl that Mary had given me for Christmas. I draped it over my shoulders and across my chest, and as I teetered on my Jimmy Choo's, I had one thought: If I concentrated on my walking, I would make it through the night without tripping.

As it turned out, Sally came dashing in just before the others arrived. There wasn't time to talk. She looked at the fax from George and said, "Damn him."

"You didn't know he was speaking to Farrow?"

"Oh, I knew, but after he did, he went back to Welling and they reluctantly agreed to meet his price." I noticed that she referred to it as "his" price, not "my" or even "our" price. "He knew I wanted to stay with Jill, but he must have gone back to Farrow for more money and gotten it. If he wants me there, he must be ready to sign the contracts."

"Can't you just refuse?"

"No, I can't. I'd better get dressed." She threw the fax in the trash as she went into her bedroom.

Chapter 7

Whose bed have your boots been under?
— *Shania Twain*

I'm not sure what I expected the Oran Mor party to be like. The restaurant had been all the rage with the in crowd since it opened a year ago, but trendy spots come and go in New York like dot-com companies. What was hot last week may well wind up tepid and tired on a steam table tomorrow. But there was nothing tepid about the looks of Oran Mor. When we arrived, there was a crush of happy-looking, with-it people waiting to get in the door. A man dressed all in green was checking invitations and wishing everyone "top o' the morning" in spite of the fact that morning was long gone.

"Whoops. Who remembered the invitation?" I hadn't seen the generic invite since the day his nibs had handed it to me, and I wasn't sure Sally had actually gotten the one with her name on it.

"I have it. Good thing you brought me." Mae was heavy into this party. She had colored her hair tuft an emerald green, and her straight, ankle-length taffeta skirt was about the same color. Somewhere she'd found a gauzy white blouse with shamrocks on the collar. Her vintage strappy shoes were sequined and green; she said she'd spray-painted them. In the taxi on the way over, she'd applied a shamrock decal to the spot under her eye where her star usually shone. She had extra decals for the rest of us. We put them on our wrists.

We got in line with our invitation but needn't have bothered. Rent-a-Leprechaun spotted Sally and came hurrying over. "Mrs. Woods. It's such an honor to have you here. Please come right in. They've set aside a table for you in case you'd like to sit."

Mae offered the leprechaun her invitation, but he ignored it and her, in spite of her colleen appearance. Then he seemed to have second thoughts, snatched the invitation from her hand, and focused again on Sally. "Would you mind autographing this for my mother, Mrs. Woods? She is such a fan. She still laughs about the time you dropped the goose on the floor. It was so funny."

"Yes. Wasn't it?" said Sally as she pulled a pen out of her purse and signed the invitation. Signing an autograph in a crowded venue is always a mistake, and sure enough, a splinter group of the people crush broke away and, without apologies, pushed Sonya, Mae, and me aside to get to Sally. They held out invitations, grocery lists, bank deposit slips, and what looked like a used Kleenex for Sally to sign. After about five minutes of this, Sonya took charge and announced to the crowd in a no-nonsense tone, "That's all there's time for now. We have to go in." The crowd immediately backed off. That's why Sonya gets the big bucks.

Sally tucked her pen away and said quietly to Sonya, "Thank you. Why do you suppose they want old pieces of signed paper anyway? And what do you suppose they do with them?" The leprechaun led us inside the restaurant and left us in the care of a not very tall but very blond beauty.

"Hi." She twittered the word. "I'm Kim, your greeter." Was that a new front-of-the-house position? "We're so thrilled that you are here." I took that to mean all of us, even though she looked only at Sally. If possible, Kim the greeter's Kelly-green dress was cut even lower than mine was, and she filled the top out a hell of a lot more generously than I did. I hoped that "greeting" didn't involve bending over. She had a small nose-gay of shamrocks pinned to her hip, which was the only place there was room. I'm not sure she looked any better in her dress than I did in mine, but who could tell since I had taken the cowardly route of camouflaging mine with a shawl.

Kim the greeter led us to a round six-top table situated in a high-visibility area so we could watch the room and the room could watch us. A waiter immediately arrived with a tray of drinks. There were flutes of champagne, glasses of warm, dark Guinness stout, and stemmed martini glasses that held a pale green cocktail that the waiter told us was an Oran Mor specialty called a "Shamrock Mintini." I think we were supposed to choose from the tray, but Sally told him just to put the whole lot in the center of the table and he said, "Good choice" as he set the drinks down. I took one of the Mintinis; it was very good and probably lethal. I guessed vodka, an apple liqueur, and a touch of mint.

The room was comfortably crowded with clusters of smiling people scrunched around tables and sitting and standing at the bar. Many more were circulating through the dense crowd, in all likelihood searching for the most important person to be standing next to when the *W* photographer snapped a shot. Waiters in starched white shirts and cute green bow ties were weaving in and out of the throngs balancing trays with drinks and hors d'oeuvres. Small nosegays of raffia-tied shamrocks were everywhere.

I immediately saw that this was the culinary A-list. The media was out in full force, as were a number of entertainment personalities known for being foodie groupies. Three food editors from competing culinary magazines were in a tight circle, laughing and probably surreptitiously trying to find out what the others were planning for future issues. A columnist noted for his exhaustive, in-depth columns on such microscopic topics as the Croatian Dalmatian Coast juniper berry and Uruguayan Baerii caviar was rapidly jotting notes on a steno pad as he talked to a waiter who held a platter of smoked salmon. My guess was he was asking if that particular salmon swam to the right or the left of the rocks on its way to spawn. A popular radio-show host sat at a table with two of the doyennes of cookbook publishing, and whatever he was saying, he had them howling. Well-known chefs were scattered throughout the room; I wondered if people knew not to eat in their restaurants this night. It was amazing. Danny had been in this country for just a year and yet he had managed to gather everyone who was anyone to his party. If they all had been female, I would have had my own theory on how he did it.

A tall, pretty redheaded chef with a generous scattering of freckles approached our table. She wore an impeccably clean white chef's coat with a green shamrock and the name Erin stitched over her heart. Erin was carrying a sizable platter of food, and a busboy followed in her steps, carrying an equally large platter. "Chef fixed these special for ye and wanted me to thank ye for being here," she said as she and the busboy put the platters on the table. One platter held two fillets of salmon, each thinly sliced and surrounded by appropriate garnishes and small rounds of dark bread. The other platter had a lush assortment of appetizers.

"Why, that's perfectly lovely," said Sally, who immediately had a brioche round swathed with foie gras on the way to her mouth. I attacked the salmon. Between chews, Sally managed to say, "Please thank him for us. I'm sure it's a sweatshop in the kitchen, but when there's time, I'd love to meet him."

"I'll be sure to tell him. Right now he's a bit like a chicken without its noggin."

"This salmon is delicious. Do you smoke it yourself?" I always like to compliment freebies from the kitchen. It usually keeps them coming. This time I was being totally honest; the salmon was incredible.

"Aye, we do. And the other salmon fillet on the plate is cured in tequila and lime juice. We do that here as well. And we bake the brown bread that's with it. All of our salmon comes from Ireland, as well as the dark flour for the bread. A bit of the 'old sod' in the kitchen is what one of the American chefs calls it."

"Did you come from the 'old sod' with Chef O'Shea?" Sonya asked.

"Aye. I did. I was working with him for three years in Dublin when he moved here and asked if I'd like to come. It's a brilliant opportunity, I can tell ye. He's taught me so much." I didn't doubt that for a minute. "Well, if there's anything we can bring ye, please let us know and we'll be happy to do it."

As soon as she left, we began to concentrate in earnest on the platters in front of us. Chef Danny O'Shea had truly outdone himself. In addition to the two types of salmon, and the foie gras brioches, of which Sally had just taken a second, there were artichoke bottoms filled with chervil-laced lobster, potato gaufrettes slathered with crème fraîche and topped with caviar, and wedges of hot fingerling potatoes coated with melted cheese and sprinkled with crumbled bacon. Carefully trimmed vegetable crudités garnished the platter of appetizers.

"What beautiful presentations. We should show how to do some of this on one of our shows." Sonya was never far away from producing.

Mae, who was rapidly working her way around both platters, said, "The important thing is they *taste* good. Remember the cake."

"Remember the cake" was our inside reminder that food is supposed to taste as good as it looks. A few years ago, a local baker who had wanted to appear on our show had pitched herself by presenting us with an elaborately decorated cake complete with a painted marzipan sculpture of herself appearing before a chocolate camera. Sonya was blown away and said we definitely should get her for the show. When Mae and I tried the cake, we said, "You've got to be joking. It tastes awful! It's a packaged cake!" Foodies have their priorities.

Small groups of friends wandered over to our table to chat or, more likely, to see what we had to eat that they didn't. They talked, nibbled, and then continued to circulate. The talking, tasting, and sipping Mintinis was keeping us so busy that I didn't notice Mary until she was standing right next to me. "Wow," she said. "I practically had to make an obscene offer to that ridiculously cheery green man outside to let me in ahead of the crowd. What a party!" Mary, who had met Sonya, Mae, and Sally on a number of occasions, displayed her continental sophistication by kissing them all on both cheeks. When she kissed me, she whispered in my ear, "What's with the shawl?" Then she sat down, took a glass of champagne and an artichoke bottom, and asked, "Did you see the Chihuly up front? It is *so* incredible. It blew me away."

Mae tilted her head. "What's a chihuly? A type of salmon?" We food people can be so single-minded.

"Dale Chihuly. Probably the foremost glass artist in the world today. His works are in museums all over the world and then in places you don't expect to see them. Like the Rainbow Room, St. Peter's church, and right here. They cost a small fortune. That piece out there is a lot of smoked salmon, believe me. The restaurant must be doing really well."

Sonya said, "Well, if this crowd is any indication it sure is."

"You were smart to get the chef for the show, Sonya." Sally was never threatened by other people's success. In fact, she had helped more than one food star rise to the top.

"I think he'll be a hit with viewers," Sonya said. "He's good-looking, charming, and personable. Who knows? He may become the next star chef with his own show." If so, Danny wouldn't be the first chef she had introduced to the public who'd wound up with his own TV show.

"I wonder if there are any chefs today who don't want to be television stars. Seems like none of them want to stay in the kitchen and just cook," I said. "You know, today he's curing his own salmon. Tomorrow he's touring the country and ordering packages of cured and sliced salmon from a food distributor."

Mae said, "That's not true of all chefs. Lots of them can do both—be on television and run a great restaurant."

"Do you think this chef is more interested in stardom than his restaurant?" Sally asked me.

"Oh, I don't know. He certainly is egotistical and arrogant enough to want to be a real big deal. He *does* spend a lot of time all over the city doing demonstrations for Irish products. And just look at this crowd. He sure spent a lot of money to impress the press." I reached for another piece of salmon.

"Aren't you biting the hand that's feeding you home-cured salmon—*avec garni?*" Mary can be so annoyingly frank.

"Hey, I'm not criticizing. Large egos usually go hand in hand with success. I'm just stating a fact."

Someone came up behind me and spoke directly in my ear in a low, sexy voice. "Hello, darlin'. Having fun yet?"

"Sully! What are you doing here?"

"I've come to see you, my darlings." Sally Sullivan owned a highly successful public relations agency in Boston and possessed the three most coveted qualities in the PR business: connections, connections, connections. She knew just about everyone, and if she didn't know someone, she knew who knew them. On top of that, she had an outgoing personality and a droll wit that made her great company. If her approach to PR was hard sell, you'd never know it. We knew her because she pitched a number of her clients to *Morning in America* and usually came to the studio when they appeared on air. I introduced her to Sally and Mary.

Sully shook hands with Mary while telling her she'd obviously gotten the looks in the family, then shook hands with Sally. "Great name," she said to her.

"You too. Are you Sarah or Sally?"

"Sally. And Sally-May-Jane when I'm wooing a southern client, or good old gal Sal when I'm pitching anyone over sixty. Unfortunately, since a long childhood bout with tomboy behavior, born simply from wanting to play touch football with the boys next door, my friends have always called me Sully."

"Did you come to New York just for this party?" Sonya asked.

Before Sully could answer, I knew. The A-list of people, the Mintinis, the green man. "Is this your doing?" I asked.

"If you're having a great time, it is. If not, then blame it on that party crasher from the Johnson PR agency over by the bar."

"It's, like, the best," said Mae.

"I thought the leprechaun was a bit much," I said, raising my eyebrows.

"Careful, Casey. Those are my people."

"How do you know Danny?" Sonya asked.

"I didn't before I got involved in this event. One of Danny's chefs, Brian Reardon, came here from a Boston restaurant I represent. Danny wanted to have a party to celebrate still being around after a year, but he was going to invite a bunch of friends and spend all his money to drown them in Guinness. Brian convinced him to call me and see if I could make a press event out of it. Danny was a bit hesitant, at first. He's not much of a star fucker, pardon my English. Besides, he didn't know any of the movers and shakers in the business. With all due respect, Sally, he'd never even heard of *you*."

I got "So there" looks from everyone except Mae, who said, "So there!"

"Okay. Okay. Okay. So, he's not a user. I still think he's egotistical, arrogant, and, don't forget, a major womanizer."

"In my business, most people are egotistical and arrogant, but what makes you think Danny's a womanizer?" Sully asked.

"Just the way he looked at me when I met him."

"You were naked," Mae reminded me. "So he copped a look. Who wouldn't?"

"Half naked! It's not the same thing," I said, but I wasn't sure of the distinction.

"Which half?" asked Sally.

"Does it matter?" asked Sonya.

"Someone tell me what's going on or did go on," Sully said.

Mae filled her in, adding, "Just for the record, I thought he was perfectly charming."

"He *is* charming. And gorgeous. I certainly wouldn't mind him looking me over," Sully said.

"I'm dying to meet him," Mary said.

"So am I," said Sally, "but I think he's still very busy in the kitchen."

Sully cringed. "Ouch. A PR nightmare. A chef who'd rather cook than circulate. I can't get him to stay out here. I'm going to go fetch him. Meanwhile, be sure and taste the potato wedges. They have Irish cheese and Irish bacon on them and are out of this world." Sully headed for the kitchen.

"See if he has any crow on a cracker for Casey to eat," Mae called after her.

A waiter came by to check on drinks, friends and fans continued to stop by to socialize, and we kept on drinking and eating. My seat was facing the entrance, so I was the first to notice Kim speaking to the gruesome twosome: George Davis and Carol Hanger. In spite of what appeared to be an attempt at dressing the part of party animals, they looked woefully out of place. George was wearing his usual ill-fitting pants but, for some God-only-knows reason, had on a red smoking jacket and an ascot. Noël Coward in a smoking jacket and ascot was classy and elegant. George Davis looked like an ass. Maybe he knew it and had put on the large sunglasses to disguise himself. When Mr. Hollywood stepped aside, Carol came into full view. She had squeezed her thick, round figure in some sort of pink jersey pantsuit, and its stretch ability was being tested to the limit. She should have brought a change of shoes, because the psychedelic green sneakers she wore for walking did not go with the suit. Then again, I'm not sure anything would go with that suit. Her short, straight haircut (which always reminded me of what Mary's had looked like when she was eight and I had put a bowl on her head to cut her hair) was dyed a new color. The label on the box of the do-it-yourself dye kit had probably said something involving the word "red," but it had turned her mop into an unreal rose color that came close to matching her suit. I wondered if they thought this was a costume party. Kim started them on a path to our table, and I caught Sonya's eye and nodded in their direction.

"Anyone have to go to the ladies' room?" she asked without missing a beat. Mae saw what was coming and left with Sonya. I had to hang around to see Mary's reaction when she got a load of these fashion statements. She didn't disappoint me. When George and Carol got to the table, she choked on her champagne, sending a thin spray of bubbles into her napkin, which she brought to her mouth just in time.

"Excuse me. The champagne went down the wrong way," she said.

"That can happen when you drink too many glasses of it. How many of those have you had?" That was Carol. All tact.

"Carol, George. This is my cousin Mary Alfano. Mary, George Davis and Carol Hanger."

George and Carol nodded at Mary without smiling and turned away so quickly that they left Mary with her hand outstretched. They said hello to Sally and sat down in the seats vacated by Sonya and Mae. Sally said hello to both of them; no kisses, no "honey."

"Is this what they're serving?" George asked, looking over the drinks on the table. He had a very high-pitched, effeminate voice and an affected accent, the origin of which was difficult to trace other than, perhaps to a constant hair across his ass. Before anyone could answer him, he raised his arm above his head and snapped his fingers at a waiter, who came right over. In an exaggerated gesture, he removed his sunglasses and said, "I'll have a Seven and Seven in a tall glass without too much ice. Carol?"

"I want a Diet Coke in a large glass with a glass of ice on the side."

I was so hoping the waiter would say, "Give me a break," but he said, "Right away, sir," and departed for the bar.

George turned to Sally. "Did you get my fax?"

"I did."

"Good. I'll meet you there then." He turned to me and gave me a look that I could read only as "Up yours." I turned away to talk to Mary. She was trying to make conversation with Carol, who was piling food on a napkin, but it was obvious that Carol had dismissed Mary as a lush. I turned back to talk to Sally, but now George was leaning close to her ear and talking in a one-on-one tone that implied, "Don't interrupt." She looked so uncomfortable that I had the urge to put my hand on hers and ask her if she wanted to leave.

Mercifully, Sully returned to the table with Danny by her side. He had on a clean white chef's coat with the shamrock logo and just his name stitched on it—no "Executive Chef" or "Head Honcho." His hair was neatly combed, but there were a few stray strands on his forehead just above those startlingly blue eyes, which were smiling and twinkling right at me. "Hi, Casey," he said, putting his hand on my shoulder. My stomach did a complete flip-flop. It must have been too much salmon and the raw onion I ate with it. Then again, I seem to have a thing about men in white professional coats. I was crazy about seeing Richard in his dentist's jacket, and when I was nine, I'd had a major crush on the vet who treated my cat, Meatball.

"Hey, Danny. This is a terrific party," I said, looking around at the happy party people. "And the food is *incredible*."

"Thanks. I'm really glad you came."

Sully put her hand on Danny's arm and said, "Danny, this is Sally Woods and Casey's cousin Mary." She waited for them to shake hands and then added, "And George and Carol." I was hoping Danny would not think that they were friends. Danny shook hands all around; although George actually shook his hand, he didn't stand, and his wrist looked like a limp rag in Danny's firm grasp.

"Can you sit with us for a while?" Sally asked.

"It's a bit mad in the kitchen, and—" Danny began.

"Sit," said Sully as she pushed him into the chair next to me. She pulled an empty chair from the next table and squeezed it in between Danny and Carol. Danny scooted closer to me to make room; Carol didn't budge.

"Your food is just delicious, Chef," Sally said with obvious enthusiasm.

"Thank you. I have a great group of chefs to rely on."

"What part of Ireland are you from?" Mary asked.

"Cashel, in county Tipperary."

"That's a long, long way," I said.

"She has her father to blame for comments like that," Mary said.

Danny smiled and laughed. A good, honest laugh. "I've heard it before. Often."

"Where did you train, Danny?" Sally asked, reaching for a potato gaufrette.

"I studied hotel management at Shannon College. By the time I graduated, I'd realized that I didn't want to run a hotel, I wanted to be in the kitchen. So I went to culinary school at Ballymaloe, in county Cork."

"Oh, yes. I know it well. They do such a fine job. And the facilities are remarkable."

"I was very lucky to go there. I couldn't afford it, but the Irish government gave me a scholarship, no strings attached. It's why I do so many demonstrations for Irish products. To pay back, you know." Oh, Lord. The man's a saint.

Carol took a business card out of her purse and stretched her arm across Sully to hand it to him. "I do prep for the more experienced chefs who give demos. I freelance, so I can be available any time of the day. Of course, I need some notice since I am very much in demand." She then gave me a smug look.

Oh please! Professional competition from Carol doesn't concern me in the least, but fashion competition was approaching our table. "It's good to see you out of the kitchen, Danny," chirped Kim the greeter.

"Thanks, love." He slipped his arm around her waist. "Have you met everyone?"

She looked at Sally. "Yes, I have, thank you."

"How's it been going out here?" Danny asked.

"Totally amazing. Everyone seems to be having a blast. Is there anything I can do for you?" she asked, and I swear to God she bent over. And there it was: China.

"Thanks, no, love."

The minute Kim left, Mary put her arm on the back of my chair and tugged on my shawl so that it slipped off my shoulders. I tried to kick her under the table, but she had anticipated it and moved her legs well out of my way. Danny, however, moved his toward mine. "Great dress. I think I'll pray for rain."

"I brought an umbrella," I said. He laughed and gave my now bare shoulder a little squeeze. I did not take it personally, because in the course of the next fifteen or so minutes a number of scantily clad women approached the table to say hello to him, and they all got squeezes on one part of their anatomy or another. I would have bet anyone that a lot more happened in the kitchen walk-in than food storage.

Sally asked Danny about the Irish products, and he really lit up as he talked about the small farmhouse cheeses and the special feed for the pigs that gave up their lives for the bacon. He talked about the salmon fishing, a passion of Sally's, and they compared fishing stories. When there was a moment's break in the animated conversation, Mary said, "Danny, the Chihuly glass up front is totally amazing. Did you find it in New York?"

"For truth, it was a gift from the artist."

"Wow! Do you know him?" Mary was noticeably impressed.

"A bit. I met him in Ireland. He and my uncle used to hang out there together. The glass was a gift for the restaurant opening. He's a real generous guy." Danny turned his head to both sides, looking for someone. "He's here someplace."

"Are you serious? Where?" Mary sat up tall and looked around the room.

"I'm not sure, but he'll be easy to spot with that curly hair. Would you like me to introduce you?"

"Absolutely!"

"Okay. We'll find him." Danny stood up and walked around the table to Sally and shook her hand. "It's great to meet you, Sally. The kitchen is beside themselves that you're here. If it's not a bother, before you go, could you pop out and say hello to them?"

"I'd love to."

He said good-bye to Carol and George and then walked over to Mary. "You ready to look for Chihuly?"

"I'm right behind you," Mary said as she stood.

Danny put his hand on my back. "You coming, Casey?"

"No thanks." I might have gone, but I knew it would make George happy, so I stayed. Fortunately, Sully stayed as well and did her best to engage George and Carol in conversation. Carol was still making food piles. I was pretty sure she was slipping some of them into her purse.

"What do you do, George?" Sully asked.

"I'm an agent," he answered without looking at her.

"Literary or otherwise?"

George put his arm on the back of Sally's chair and gave Sully that smug look that just grates on me. "I represent Sally."

It was probably imperceptible unless you knew her well, but Sully began to throw her head back to laugh and then must have realized it was not a joke; she coughed instead. She looked at me as if to say, "He can't be serious," then turned to George and said, "Great gig. Do you handle other clients as well?"

"Not now."

"Oh. But you did before? Who were some of your clients?"

"I prefer to keep my client list confidential." Even I knew that was bullshit. Agents build their businesses by dropping names.

Sully kept plugging. I didn't know if she was really interested or just trying to make conversation, but I was dying to hear the details of George Davis. "A friend of mine has an agency here in New York. I'm sure you know of him—Marc Friedman?"

"I have only been working out of New York for a while, so I haven't had time to socialize."

"Where were you before?"

George's smug demeanor was gradually slipping, and a look of discomfort was replacing it. I thought I saw sweat running down the side of his face. Without responding to Sully's question, he looked across the room and said, "Oh there's . . ." I forget the name he used, because I'd never heard it. Sully had to turn around, but I was facing the direction he was looking so I saw his hand deliberately swipe a Mintini, sending it flying toward Sully. She jumped up quickly, but the green drink was already running down the front of her dress. George said, "Sorry," but that damnable smug look said otherwise.

"Let's get that washed off right away, Sully," I said. "I'll get some club soda and meet you in the ladies' room." I gave George a nasty stare as I stood, but he wasn't looking at me.

In the ladies' room, as I was less than successfully trying to remove the green from her dress, Sully said, "Who is that George character besides the guy on the far end of the evolutionary chart? He's all bullshit, Casey."

I was kneeling, so I looked under the two stall doors to make sure we were alone before responding. "I know. Nothing about him makes any sense. I'm pretty sure he knocked that drink over on purpose."

"Of course he did. He was obviously uncomfortable with my questions. It's not my business, but it's hard to believe that someone like Sally would let a sleaze like him represent her."

"I know. He's definitely not of her class."

"Class? He's not even her species. Is Carol his sister?"

I looked up at her, surprised by her question. No one had ever mentioned their being related. "Why do you ask?"

"Didn't you notice how much they look alike? Same shaped face. Same Slavic features. The same unfriendly, beady eyes that never look directly at you."

"Come to think of it, they do look alike."

"Mary to the rescue!" my cousin announced, marching in holding up a small vial of extra-strength spot remover. "When I got back to the table, Sally said you might need this. Let me do that, Casey. You should never travel without spot remover. How'd this happen? Did Carol throw a drink at you?"

"Close." Sully told her what had happened and then suggested she sit as far away from him as possible if she planned to ask him any questions.

"He left. Carol did too. Sonya and Mae came back as soon as they did." She stood up and admired her work on the dress. "There. Good as new." Sully thanked her and said she'd better get back to the party. As she was walking out the door, she said, "Watch out for that guy. Seriously."

"What's Sally doing with him, anyway?" Mary asked, handing me her lipstick and telling me I needed to put some on.

"Good question."

"Maybe he makes her a lot more money than she was making before."

Even though I always told Mary everything, I also always kept Sally's confidences. I was careful not to reveal the little Sally had told me about George. "Be real. Sally already has a lot of money. She gives tons of it away to charity. Besides, she doesn't care about expensive jewelry or yachts, that kind of stuff, so I don't see why the money would matter. I can tell you one thing though: there's not enough money in the world to get me to work with him." I shuddered just thinking about it. "By the way, did you meet Chihuly?"

"Yes indeed. Talk about charming, and he is *so* talented! He took my name to put on the invite list for a private party before his next New York show."

"You are amazing, Mary. You want something, you make it happen."

"Speaking of making things happen. That Danny's pretty hot." She widened her eyes.

"*And* he takes full advantage of it," I noted. "Did you see the women hanging all over him? And he seemed pretty cozy with greeter Kim. Tell me he's not a meadow vole?" Mary and I had read an article in the Sunday *Times* about the sexual habits of voles. Prairie voles were monogamous; meadow vole males mated with many females and then wandered off to be alone. My guess was that Danny O'Shea was a meadow vole.

"Yeah, well remember: one little gene injection in the head was all it took to turn meadow voles into faithful prairie critters."

BEFORE WE LEFT ORAN MOR, Sally, Sonya, Mae, and I went out to the kitchen. It was always such a good feeling to watch Sally as she walked among the young chefs, asking them about themselves and telling them to keep up the good work. Most likely, many were chefs because of her, and you could see how thrilled they were to meet her.

While Sally was signing the chefs' battered cookbooks, splattered aprons, and sweaty hats, Sonya, Mae, and I were having a look at some of Danny's menus.

"We change the menu every day. Some items we keep because people keep asking for them." He was standing behind me looking over my shoulder with his hand on my bare back. I wished I had brought my shawl, because his touch was making me uncomfortably tingly. Well, nicely tingly and uncomfortable that I felt so. I would have been perfectly comfortable with it if I hadn't seen him fondling bare female backs all over the restaurant all night.

"Which ones in particular?" Sonya asked.

"There's this great lamb dish we serve that people love."

"Do you have a recipe for it?" I asked, turning so that my back was away from his hand. Chefs don't always have exact recipes as they appear in cookbooks. Their versions are often just sketchy guides.

"Not for the lamb. We've all done it so often, we don't need to write it down. But you could come and watch me do it, if you like. We don't do lunch on Saturdays, so you could come in the morning and I'd have time to work with you."

"Can you do that, Casey?" Sonya never asked me to work on Saturdays, but we did need to get Danny's shows finalized. And I knew she knew that I wouldn't be hanging out with Richard.

"Sure, that's fine," I told her, then turned to Danny. "How's ten o'clock?"

"Anytime you want, love." He grinned at me, and I had the most insane feeling of wanting to stick my tongue out at him.

He walked us to the kitchen door, put his hands on my arms from behind, and said, "See you Saturday. If you need *anything* beforehand just call." He emphasized the "anything," and if I could have balanced on one Jimmy Choo, I would have kicked him in the shin.

Mary and Mae decided to stay at the party, but the rest of us left. Sonya shared a taxi with Sally and me back to the hotel, and we talked a bit about Italy.

"You know, I really am getting excited," I said, meaning it. "Are we flying over together? You two are going to put me in a center seat, aren't you?" I was already sitting between them in the back seat of the taxi.

"You and I are going together," Sonya answered.

"I'm going to go over a few days earlier to stop in London," Sally said. Peter had given Sally a London flat near Harrods for her fiftieth birthday. She thought it was the best gift ever, and she went as often as she could.

"Lucky you. Just for fun or do you have work there?"

"I'm going over to speak to a real estate agent about selling the flat."

Sally loved that flat, loved London. I wondered if she was selling because it *had* been a gift from Peter and she wanted to erase whatever the unhappy memory was. I thought I should see if she wanted to talk more about that unhappy memory. I was pretty sure she didn't want to discuss the "why" in front of Sonya, so I waited until we were alone at the hotel to bring it up again.

"I need the money, Casey."

I tried not to look as stunned as I was. Selling London wasn't about Peter; it was about money. How could she have financial problems? Maybe Mary was right about Sally needing George to help her make more money. "Is that why you've hired George? So he'll bring in more money?"

"Huh!" she said, throwing her head back. "He's why I need the money."

"Sally, what the hell is going on?"

"He has something I want, and I'm willing to pay for it."

"My God, Sally! What are you saying?" Of course, I knew what she was saying, but it was so unbelievable that I wanted it spelled out.

"Just that. So now you know why such a repulsive person is in our lives."

"Wait a minute, Sally. I don't really know. What does he have?"

"I don't want to tell you that now."

"You don't by any chance have a crack baby, do you?"

Sally laughed so hard it made me laugh, and neither of us could talk for a while. Then she said, "Let's go to bed. We both have an early morning."

"But I need to know more about this George stuff. I'm worried about you."

She gave me a hug and said, "I know you are, but you don't have to be. I know what I'm doing, and I know you'll keep this just between the two of us. *Sogni d'oro.*"

I wondered if she did know what she was doing. Right now it seemed as though the only gold in her wish of "golden dreams" was going to George.

Chapter 8

Wavin' my heart goodbye.
—*The Flatlanders*

Friday morning, Sally and I sent for a room-service breakfast of eggs, bacon, sausage, assorted breakfast breads, one side of blueberry pancakes to share, and the *New York Times*. She gave me the crossword puzzle and took the first section of the paper for herself. Even though we had eaten an embarrassingly large number of delicious appetizers the night before, we had never really had dinner, so we were both hungry. I guess the kitchen couldn't imagine two people eating all that food, because the waiter wheeled in the table and set out three place settings. I had a million George questions that had kept me awake most of the night, but as soon as I brought George up, Sally made it clear that she wouldn't discuss it further. Then she looked at me over the top of her reading glasses and brought up a topic of her own.

"I thought that Danny was awfully cute?" It wasn't a statement; it was a question requiring a comment from me.

"I think Danny is *very* cute, Sally. But I still think, as you so accurately put it, that he just needs to sow his wild oats and the last thing I need right now is an itinerant farmer."

That brought a glint to her eyes. "Who knows? Might be fun."

"Sally Woods! Shame on you!"

By the time we got down to sharing the last pancake, our conversation had moved from men to the cookbooks she was going to feature on next week's show. Sally does a cookbook spot on the show once a year. She and Sonya both receive just about every one that is published—over three hundred a year. Sonya gives hers to me to look over, Sally goes over the ones sent to her, and then she and I compare notes and select ten to feature. "I look at the recipes for chicken first. If you can't cook a chicken so it's not dried out, you have no business writing a cookery book," she had told me, using the quaint British term for cookbooks. "As soon as I see directions to cook a boneless chicken breast for one hour, the book is out the window. A good index is necessary as well."

"I think you have a great group of books this year," I told her now.

"I do too. It's amazing how many come out every year, and people still buy them. Thank God!" she said. "Maybe next year we should consider including some cooking CDs. I've been receiving a lot of them lately."

"Sonya has also. I honestly haven't had a chance to look at any of them. Are they any good?"

"Some are. I don't think they'll ever replace real books, but the ones that show actual techniques, like boning chicken breasts, can be quite helpful to the beginning cook." She looked at her watch. "Gosh, I'd better go."

"I'll walk out with you."

A car was waiting for her at the curb. We hugged each other, holding it a little longer than usual.

"Now, you put that Richard situation behind you, Casey. He didn't deserve you." She got into the car.

"Thanks, Sally. I'll give you a call over the weekend." I was hoping she might share more about her situation over the phone.

"I'll be away for the weekend, but I'll see you next Wednesday. We'll have a nice lunch after the show. You pick the place. Why don't you ask Mary to come along? She's such fun."

"Great. I'm on it." I wondered if she wanted someone else there to avoid talking about troubling issues, but I let it pass. "Love you. Mean it," I said as I closed the car door.

"Love you back." And she was gone, along with any immediate answers to the George dilemma.

I HAD A HALF hour to spare, so I walked to Sonya's office. She was on the phone when I walked in, and she did not look happy. She had her forehead resting in her hand, and her voice was a monotone of mutterings: "I know. I will. I did." She glanced up when she saw me and shook her head back and forth in a woeful manner. When she hung up, she let out a long, discouraged sigh.

"Well, that did not go well."

"What's up?"

"The meeting with George and the VPs on Wednesday was a disaster. He asked for triple the amount we pay Sally now or, he said, she'll walk. The VPs didn't come right out and say it, but they sounded a lot like they're wondering what I'd done to make her ready to leave the show or at least why I couldn't keep her here."

"Wow. Will Sally tell them it's not your doing?

"Sally won't have anything to do with any of the negotiations. She has authorized George to do all the talking for her, and quite honestly, it's pissing me off."

I wished I could tell her that George was a temporary problem, but I figured if Sally wanted her to know she would have said something already. "Will they pay the raise in salary?" I asked.

"I don't know. Right now, they're really steaming at being pushed like that. They feel like they're being threatened. You know, these guys have pretty big egos. They don't take well to being pushed around."

"But wouldn't the revenues from sponsors more than cover the salary increase?"

"That's another issue." She picked up a small Post-it pad and tossed it across the desk. It was just a gesture; I'm sure she wanted to throw something bigger and harder at our friend George. "God, it's been a hell of a morning, and it's not even nine-thirty. It seems that some of the commercials that Sally has been doing present a conflict of interest to our sponsors. Some sponsors are threatening to sue if she doesn't stop. They're going over the fine print of her contract to see if she isn't in violation."

"I can't believe Sally's lawyer didn't check that out."

"Sally's *lawyer* didn't deal with it. *George* did. Things like this were never an issue before he started directing her career. All these years, she's avoided doing anything that makes her look unprofessional or like a charlatan, and now it's as though she's going to allow that imbecile to plunge her career into ruin and not even say a word to stop him."

I had never seen Sonya so worked up. I knew she really cared about what happened to Sally; but just as scarily, she was fighting for her own career. And then the scariest part of the conversation came up.

"Casey, I wanted you to know how things look, because you should be prepared if, if, well, if things don't turn out the way we hope. Why don't you start to check around to see if other stations are looking for help? You're very good at TV work. There's also the strong possibility that if Sally does jump ship, she'll take you with her. She loves working with you."

"Oh, Sonya, I . . . " I knew I looked as though I was going to cry. I loved working with Sally, but I hated the thought of not doing it with Sonya.

"I'm not letting you go. I just want you to have some fall-back plans, should it come to that. I'm fairly sure that if Sally walks, a lot of heads will roll."

"I understand. It's not your fault. I know that. " I wondered exactly how soon George would be out of Sally's life. I was afraid that it wasn't going to be soon enough to save my job. We went over Sal Vito's recipe and worked on the cookbook scripts, and then I walked out into what had become a very gray day. Richard might have been responsible for my heart-ache, but George was causing me a major headache.

When I got home later, my parents were already asleep so I went into the den and booted up the computer. I decided to Google George up and see what I could find out about him. There were hundreds of George Davises listed, all variations and combinations of agents, representatives, celebrities, and the like, but after a long exhaustive search, none fit the de-scription of the migraine in my life. He certainly kept a low profile for someone professing to be a "celebrity agent." There *were* two other possible matches, but neither was identified as an agent. One promised a good time and a photo for a mere two dollars; the other listed his address as San Quentin State Prison, and was looking for a potential wife: "must own heavy digging equipment." I finally went to bed and fell asleep crying to the radio playing Emmylou Harris's pathetically sad "My Baby's Gone." My baby was gone, and my job wasn't looking so good either.

Chapter 9

Down to my last teardrop.
— *Tanya Tucker*

Saturday morning, I forced myself out of bed early. I was emotionally exhausted and wanted nothing more than to pull the covers over my head and rescript yesterday, but I knew I'd need a lot of time to camouflage my swollen red eyes before going to Oran Mor. I dug my beach bag out of the closet and rummaged through until I found the waterproof mascara I use for swimming. I prayed it would withstand the deluge it might have to face. Ten-foot ocean waves were nothing compared to what it would have to hold back if I got going again.

I threw on a scoop-neck white T-shirt, faded jeans, and grabbed a baseball cap. I didn't know how strictly Danny held to the health regulations about covering your hair in the kitchen, but I wasn't about to compound my already challenged looks with a hideous hairnet.

The front door of the restaurant was locked, so I knocked and a tall gangly boy of about seventeen opened the door. He had a short, unruly mop of red hair and his face held its own deluge — of freckles. Or perhaps it was the other way around; space between the freckles revealed a sweet face.

"Mornin' to you," he said with an unmistakable Irish lilt. "You'd be Casey. Chef's expecting you. I'm Cian." He gave me a big smile and held out his hand.

"Casey Costello. Nice to meet you, Cian. You look like—"

"Erin. I know. She's my big sister. She's helping me to learn the restaurant business. I'm just a busboy now, but I'm workin' my way up. Some day I'll have my own place, just like Danny." He looked so proud and was so cute that he made me smile for the first time that morning.

"Come on. I'll take you to the kitchen."

Danny was already at the stove, dressed almost exactly as I was. He looked a lot better in his outfit. When he turned around I could see his hat had THE CHIEFTAINS written across the front; mine said TEXAS ROADHOUSE and was signed by Willie Nelson. Oran Mor means "big song," and I thought it was appropriate that we were thematically outfitted.

"Hey, Casey," he said coming over and putting his arm around my shoulders. "I think you met the staff the other night?" I said hi to his sous-chef, Brian, then to Erin, then to two line chefs, recruited from excellent New York restaurants, and to Sweetie, the pastry chef, a cute, skinny girl from Ireland.

Danny clapped his hands together. "Okay. Where do we begin?" He seemed so enthusiastic about our project that I was sorry I wasn't in a more upbeat frame of mind. Usually, I find a restaurant kitchen more stimulating than a Broadway musical, but since I had spent yesterday in the middle of a Shakespearean tragedy, facing madness and eventual execution, I was having trouble finding my tap shoes. I tried not to show it.

"Well, let me look at tonight's menu, and watch you all work for a while. Then I should see copies of any recipes you do have for the dishes that I think will work."

"If you don't find something from today's menu, I can show you others."

"Great." With lively Irish music blasting into the kitchen, Danny and his staff moved through their preparations like seasoned dancers. It was pure art. Sweetie was rhythmically kneading brown bread to the Irish beat and Erin was cutting perfect sheer slices of cured salmon with a long, flexible-bladed knife. With his foot tapping, Bryan was dicing exquisite pieces of ahi tuna. I was impressed that they were all working by hand, not relying on machines. To me, that's a sign of a chef in love with his product.

Danny had several racks of lamb in front of him that needed to be trimmed so that all the fat and bits of meat were cleaned from the ends of the bones—or "Frenched," in culinary terms. His hands were strong and skilled, and he trimmed the bones quickly, with obvious expertise. When all the racks were trimmed, he browned some of the meat trimmings in a large sauté pan, then deglazed it with Madeira. He added whole shallots that he had cooked gently in butter in a separate pan, then poured in three different types of stock and let them reduce to a deep, rich sauce before stirring in duxelles and setting the pan aside. Watching him work and direct his staff in an easy, sure manner, I could see why his restaurant was so successful. I could also see that his staff loved him. It was a very touchy-feely place.

After about an hour, he asked me if I saw anything I liked. I had already jotted down numerous notes and dipped a spoon into everything that was finished. "Oh gosh, yes. Saw, smelled, tasted. The lamb sauce is delicious, and I tasted the cured salmon and tuna tartare. They are incredible."

"The tuna is strictly sushi grade, and we serve the tartare in baked sesame wonton cups. It's a good presentation. The salmon is from Ireland. Irish salmon is the best in the world, and we cure it ourselves. We also smoke our own salmon." He turned to Erin. "Love, bring out some of the smoked salmon for Casey to taste." I didn't mention that I had tasted more than my share at the party.

I decided on the tuna tartare, the cured salmon, and the lamb. Danny got me what he had in the way of recipes and we sat down in the dining room to go over them. As I spread the recipes out in front of us, he moved his chair so he was close enough to me for our arms to touch. Remembering his overactive libido from our first meeting, I shifted on my chair to put more distance between us. "The food is delicious," I began, "but its preparation, naturally, is designed for the restaurant, so it doesn't exactly work for the home cook. Sometimes you call for *too* many ingredients, and then there are ingredients that aren't readily available. We need substitutes, if possible. And we need to work out the measurements so they serve six to eight people rather than eighty.

"Also, the rack of lamb is great and I think you should show a little of how to trim the bones, but let people know they can buy racks that are already trimmed. We'll have one partially trimmed so you only have to clean one rib. How do you cook the racks?"

"I brown them quickly on both sides on top of the stove and finish them off in a hot oven."

"Great. That will work on the show, and it's a good thing for people to know about cooking red meat. The sauce presents a few problems. You use veal, beef, and chicken stock. Most people don't have all three on hand and wouldn't make them just to use a small amount for a sauce. Can you make the sauce with just one?"

"Sure. Not a problem."

"Good. The duxelles is another problem. It's delicious in the sauce, but most people don't know what it is."

"It's a combination of minced shallots, finely chopped mushrooms, Madeira—"

"*I* know what it is. I meant our audience might not know."

"I didn't know if you actually cooked or worked for the telly and got assigned to the kitchen."

Because I was feeling particularly sensitive that morning, I sat straight up and looked directly at him with all the superiority I could muster. "I graduated from the Culinary Institute of America. Second in my class."

The corners of his mouth turned up in a taunting grin. He saluted me. "Sorry, Chef. I didn't know."

I had wanted him to know that I knew my way around a stove, but I was sorry I had mentioned my class standing. It made me sound pretentious. Ignoring it, I went on. "The duxelles. You can mention that if someone has it on hand, they should use it, but for the show it would be better if you could make the dish with fresh mushrooms, shallots, and Madeira— build a duxelles in the pan. Do you think you can handle that?"

He put his arm on the back of my chair so that it brushed my shoulder and grinned at me. "I can handle anything." I knew he meant more than mushrooms in a pan and he probably could, but his bold conceit still got *my* Irish up. I gave him a sarcastic look and continued going over what we'd do with the cured salmon and tuna tartare. Then I asked him how he made the sesame wonton cups.

"It's simple, but we have to make some anyway so you can watch. Or, if you'd rather, you can help make them."

"I'd love to."

We went back into the kitchen and he handed me an apron and told Erin that I would be helping her make the wonton cups. He told her I was a chef; I was grateful that he didn't add "second in her class." Erin laid out several mini-muffin pans and handed me a pastry brush. "Brush the insides of the pans with that peanut oil. I'll get the wontons." We worked together, pressing wontons into the tins and then brushing them with a mixture of oil and cornstarch.

"Why the cornstarch?" I asked.

"It gives them a nice sheen and helps the seeds stay where they're supposed to."

Erin gave me sesame seeds and sea salt and told me to sprinkle them on the cups. Meanwhile, she cut a stack of wontons diagonally and arranged them on several baking trays before brushing them with the cornstarch oil and coating them with sesame seeds and salt.

"What do you do with the triangles?" I asked, sprinkling my wonton cups as directed.

"We bake them, just like the cups, and put four of them on the plate to eat with the tuna. They're really good just as they are, and at home I use them for all manner of dips."

We were working to the lively beat of the Chieftains' music, and I could understand why Danny chose the lively tunes. It was hard not to work at the fast pace of its rhythm or not feel happy while doing so. In no time at all, we had filled all the muffin tins, covered all the trays with wontons, and had them in the oven. Erin removed the triangles after six minutes, let them cool a bit on racks, and then handed me one to taste.

"Pretty good. Don't you think?" she said. I was already nibbling on a second one and wishing I had some hummus.

"Delicious!" I said between chews. "Well, I definitely think we should go with the lamb, the cured salmon, and the tuna tartare in sesame cups."

"So, what happens now?" Danny asked.

"I'll turn my notes into recipes and then into scripts."

"I'm going to have to memorize lines?"

"No. The scripts are not dialogue. They tell you what you will do and in what order. I'll get them to you beforehand so you can look them over."

"When will that be?"

"I'll have them ready Monday afternoon and either fax or e-mail them to you." I picked up my pad and pencil. "Do you have an e-mail address?"

He rolled his eyes and said, "ODannyboy@oranmor.com. Don't groan. My staff set it up for me."

I wrote the address on my pad and started to hum. " 'Oh Danny boy, the pipes, the pipes are calling . . .' "

"I'm begging you. Please don't."

I sang the next words quietly: " 'From glen to glen, and down the mountainside . . .' "

"I'm not listening." He turned to the stove and began sautéing more mushrooms.

I leaned right up to his ear. " 'The summer's gone and all the roses falling . . .' "

"I can't hear you."

" ' 'Tis you, 'tis you must go, and I must bide.' " At that point, the rest of the staff joined in and we sang loud enough to drown out the Chieftains.

" 'But come ye back . . .' " Brian and the two line chefs had their arms around each other's shoulders and were rocking side to side as they sang. One of them was a pretty decent tenor. Erin and Sweetie were harmonizing and pretending to dry their eyes with chefs' towels.

"You're all fired!" Danny yelled above our singing.

" ' 'Tis I'll be here in sunshine or in shadow. Oh, Danny boy, oh Danny boy, I love you so.' "

"I hope you're happy to bring all this chaos to my kitchen," he said when we'd finished and the guys were taking a bow.

"You should change your e-mail address. Should I fax the scripts instead?"

"Maybe I could pick them up and watch a show from behind the scenes to get an idea of how it works, now that I know what I'm going to be making."

"Sure. Tuesday's a good day. We have a live spot and we'll also be prepping for a Wednesday spot with Sally. So you'll get to see what both involve. I'll be there at five-thirty. You can come anytime. Bring your tools. I'll put *you* to work"

"Brilliant. Will Sally be there Tuesday morning? I really enjoyed meeting her. She's a trip."

"No. She doesn't get in until Wednesday," I said and then remembered that I was in charge of lunch reservations for Wednesday. I thought it would be a nice gesture all around to come here, so I asked Danny if he could seat three of us.

"Brilliant. I'll put you down." He made a note on an order pad and then asked, "Do you have to go now or do you want to work some more?"

Working with his friendly staff to the happy beat of the Irish fiddles was making me feel a lot better than I would have expected, so I stayed and peeled, chopped, blanched, and whisked my way to feeling pretty good. As Sally always said, cooking together was fun. When it was time for me to go, I removed my apron and went to the dishwasher's sink to wash my hands. Dishwasher's sinks have a low faucet and a high shower-style faucet for rinsing the dishes. I realized too late that I'd turned on the high faucet, and a shower of cold water streamed down from the faucet suspended above me. It was directed right at me, and before I could move, I was drenched right through my T-shirt, right through my half-price Calvin Klein bra, and all the way to me. I didn't have to turn around to know that Danny had seen what I'd done. I could hear him laughing.

"You seem to favor that wet look."

"Not on purpose," I said, crossing my arms over my chest.

He looked down at my crossed arms and said, "No need to be shy. I've seen them before."

I was going to punch one of his arms, but I didn't want to uncross mine. "Very funny. I can't go out like this. Have you got something I can borrow?"

"Sure. Come on." He led me back to his private office, which was a small, windowless room with just about enough space for his desk, which was against the wall. The walls were lined with bookshelves and cookbooks, lots of cookbooks. It was orderly but undecorated. Danny took a jeans jacket off the hook of an old wooden hat rack.

"Will this work?"

I rolled up the sleeves. "It's perfect. Thanks. Is it okay if I give it back to you on Tuesday?"

"Fine." He leaned back against his desk and smiled at me— a killer smile. "I'm sorry you have to leave. It was nice having you here."

"I really enjoyed it. You run a great kitchen."

"Thanks. You're very efficient yourself. Ever think about restaurant work?"

"No. I don't like the late hours."

"But if you don't work lunch, you get to stay in bed all morning."

"Staying in bed all morning has never been my bag."

His smile became a wicked grin. "Maybe you just haven't had the right company."

He had that right. I put my hands on my hips and squinted at him. "Are you hitting on me, Danny O'Shea?"

His grin widened. "Second in your class and you have to ask."

"Well, you have to stop."

"Why? Are you attached?"

"That's my business." Please don't cry. Please don't cry. "Besides, that's not the point."

"Well, what is the point? I like you. I'm attracted to you."

Me and the entire attractive female population of the five boroughs. "The point is, you're a meadow vole."

He laughed. "A what?"

I crossed my arms over my chest and looked square at him. "A meadow vole. A Don Juan, a Casanova, a womanizer, a player."

"I think you have the wrong idea about me." He took a step toward me and straightened my collar. "But I think you like me anyway."

Oh, the arrogance!

I grinned back at him. "Okay. I'm done having this conversation. Thanks for the jacket."

"Don't mention it. But you looked better without it."

He was laughing as I left.

Chapter 10

Let the morning in, but keep it under cover.
—*The Slip*

I woke up Sunday morning to the smell of gravy cooking. It was the same heartache therapy that working in the kitchen had been yesterday. Gravy is what Italian-Americans call tomato sauce, the three-hour kind with enough meat to feed a small country. My mother makes a huge pot of it every Sunday. It isn't so much about cooking as it is about connecting with her heritage. She likes knowing that generations of her maternal ancestors spent their Sunday mornings stirring what they called *ragù* in their own kitchens. Even when we ate Sunday dinners at Nonna's, my mother made her own gravy before we went. She'd give half the pot to me to bring to the city, and before the end of the week we had each used up our share for lasagne, sausage-and-pepper sandwiches, baked stuffed peppers, and veal parmigiana.

I looked at the clock and saw that it was only eight, so I closed my eyes and enjoyed a morning when I didn't have to get out of bed at an insane hour. Seduced by the familiar aroma, I drifted into an alpha-wave sleep where images of my mother making gravy played out like a TV food show. She moved gracefully about the kitchen cradling a large gold can of olive oil, dangling a long string of Italian sausage links in front of the camera, straining tomatoes, and finally putting her hands on her hips, smiling at her audience, and saying, *"Buon appetito."* Sally couldn't have done it better.

I heard the car pull into the driveway and knew that would be Dad returning from Piri's Bakery with loaves of bread for dinner and pastries for breakfast. Time to get up. I found some old jeans and a faded Johnny Cash T-shirt in the closet and threw them on before snuggling my feet into my slippers and padding downstairs to meet the day.

My mother had just finished kneading a large mass of pasta dough and was patting it into a nice round ball before putting it aside to rest. That meant ravioli. We always began Sunday dinner with either ravioli or lasagne. The homemade pasta meant ravioli, because we buy the large sheets of dough for lasagne from Costantino's. Sitting on the stove, waiting for the oven to get up to temperature, was a roasting pan holding a large pork roast studded with garlic, glistening with olive oil, and surrounded by rosemary sprigs. My parents looked at me without saying anything, and I could see that they were assessing my emotional state before speaking. Over a month had passed since the Richard fiasco, but they were still cautious.

"Good morning," I said in a cheery tone. I could see them relax.

"Ah, she lives and breathes," my father said as he cut the string wrapped around the white pastry box from Piri's.

"Mmmm, *sfogliatelle, zeppole,*" I cooed while lifting the cover. I kissed him first.

"Good morning, Mary Sunshine. What makes you wake so

soon? You used to wake at twelve o'clock and now you wake at noon." My mother had greeted me with that nursery rhyme as far back as I could remember, and I never grew weary of it. When I was little, I did wonder why she didn't know my name, but I liked the rhyme so I let it pass. This morning, I was grateful because I knew I looked nothing like sunshine.

"I'm here to help," I said with a mouthful of *zeppole*. "Are you ready to make the *braciole* and meatballs?"

"In a minute. Finish your breakfast first."

One *sfogliatella*, two *zeppole*, and couple of new Dad jokes from the bakery later, I was ready to go into culinary action. Dad took his newspapers into the living room and Mom and I did what we love to do together—cook and talk.

"How are you doing, sweetie?" She was using a meat pounder, a *batticarne*, to even out thin slices of beef top round before stuffing and rolling them into *braciole*.

"I'm okay." I took out the box grater, found dried pieces of Italian bread, and began to grate bread crumbs for the meatballs. "You need bread crumbs for the *braciole*?"

"About a cup. You're going to be just fine."

"I know. Any Parmesan?"

"Grate me a good cup. I feel sorry for Richard."

"For *him*! Why's that?" I put the few pounds of ground meat into a large bowl and added some beaten eggs, the bread crumbs, grated Parmesan, and salt and pepper.

"Because he missed out on the best."

"Thanks. You want me to put raisins in any of the meatballs?" Italians are territorial about their gravy and meatballs. My mother's heritage is Neapolitan; her people do not put garlic or tomato paste in their gravy and or raisins in their meatballs. My Aunt Maria's mother-in-law, Louisa Alfano, who always comes for Sunday dinner, is Sicilian. She uses garlic, tomato paste, and raisins and likes to point out that they are missing in my mother's gravy and meatballs.

"Madonn'." She pinched her fingers together and wagged them in the typical Italian sign language for exasperation. "That woman! Make a few with raisins."

I began to mix the meat and eggs and bread crumbs and cheese into a homogeneous mass. "Who'll be here today?"

Mom began to count with her left hand, never missing a beat with the *batticarne* in her right hand; she is an expert at multitasking. "Nonna, Mrs. Alfano, Aunt Maria, Uncle Tony . . ."

Mom's older sister, my aunt Maria, is married to Tony Alfano, a pediatrician. Uncle Tony grew up three houses away from the Contis' and started hanging around Aunt Maria when they were twelve. Mom says the whole street could hear Mrs. Alfano yelling from her second-story window, "Anthony! Anthony Alfano, you get away from that girl. Anthony!" They have five children: Matthew, Mark, Luke, John, and Mary. Yup.

". . . Mark will be here. The other boys are away and Mary has to work."

The boys might well be away, but I knew that Mary was actually going out with her new lawyer friend, Bill; only that is not considered an acceptable excuse for being absent. My cousin Mark is twenty-five, and the bassist for a rock band that actually earns money, at least enough for him to rent a one-room apartment in the city. He still has to go home to do laundry and get groceries. Mark worries about his music, feeding the hungry, and saving the environment. My aunt Maria worries about feeding him and saving his environment from being condemned by the health department.

"Remember five." Mom stopped counting long enough to season the meat with salt and pepper, cover each piece with a slice of prosciutto, and mix the bread crumbs and Parmesan with some olive oil and chopped parsley. She used her right hand to sprinkle the crumb mixture over the prosciutto and resumed counting with her left.

"Okay, Russell and Sharon will be here with Ben, but Uncle Bob and Aunt Ellen are away . . ."

My Uncle Bob, named Roberto after his father, is the oldest Conti. Since he'd retired a few years ago, he and Aunt Ellen spend most of their time golfing in hot, sunny places. Their skin is so weathered from the sun that their son, Russell, says they would make a great handbag and pair of shoes. Russell is twenty-seven and bright, with an offbeat, irreverent sense of humor. He is married to Sharon, who is pretty, sweet, and seems totally overwhelmed by the number of people she now calls family. Ben is their adorable but discipline-challenged two-year-old.

". . . Uncle Mike will be here, but Aunt Connie is out of town. I'm not sure about the boys . . ."

Aunt Connie is not out of town. She and Uncle Mike are separated, but the older Contis don't discuss it. Uncle Mike has what Russell calls a "side order" and what Aunt Connie calls a "slutty bitch whore homewrecker." They have three grown boys who will come to dinner unless Aunt Connie threatens to throw herself out a window. Uncle Mike is a big man who smokes big cigars, wears big, flashy gold jewelry, and looks as though the slutty bitch whore homewrecker is not all he has on the side.

". . . I won't count them. Little Joey and Aunt Gina . . ."

Uncle Little Joey is the youngest Conti, and is still called "Little Joey" even though he is six foot two and built like a Jets linebacker. Little Joey is married to Aunt Gina, who is even more petite than my mother. You just have to wonder.

". . . Raymond."

Uncle Little Joey and Aunt Gina's son, Raymond, is seventeen and his specialty is being sullen. He doesn't even have to work at it. It's odd, because as a little boy he was adorable. He'd run around the neighborhood in yellow tights and a red cape, pretending to be Mighty Mouse. Sometime around puberty, he started running around with a crowd into personality-altering substances that are not so adorable. Uncle Tony referred him to a youth therapist, but the work doesn't seem to have penetrated. I've learned to ignore the ridiculous fuzzy, sparse goatee and the pierced tongue and eyebrow, but I still get queasy looking at the screaming mouth oozing droplets of blood tattooed on his cheek.

"How many is that?" Now that her counting was over, Mom was using both hands to roll the meat up and secure each roll with a toothpick.

"Fourteen with you, me, and Dad and not counting Ben." I didn't have to think about the number because I had rolled a meatball each time Mom had raised or lowered a finger. I'd rolled the ones with raisins into meat ovals.

She turned toward the living room and raised her voice so my father could hear her. "Mike, we'll need to put two leaves in the table." She slid the pork roast into the oven, browned the *braciole* in a cast-iron skillet, and added them to the sauce, along with my meatballs. We don't brown our meatballs; they are more tender if they are just added to the sauce.

My father came in for a chair count and was sidetracked by the loaf of Piri's bread. He broke off a piece, dipped it in the sauce, and declared it the best ever. The sauce tastes the same every Sunday, but my father's that kind of guy. He sat down at the table. I needed to keep my hands busy and away from the bread and the pastry, so I offered to go on to the next task. "Want me to start the ravioli?"

"Not yet. Sharon wants to learn to make them, so she and Russell are coming over early. I thought you might like to show her."

"You've got to be kidding! Sharon doesn't cook. She calls the kitchen the room with the big white things. Her oven is a storage bin for Ben's toys." If there is a hand equivalent to foot ineptitude, then Sharon had two left hands. She tries, but there is a gene missing there.

"Oh boy, Paula. I hope you have a backup first course." My father had been to more than one meal at Sharon and Russell's house, and he knew the pitfalls.

"Anyone can learn to cook." God bless her. My mother refuses to think badly of anyone in the family. Outside the family was another story.

"There are exceptions. You don't know Tina." Truth be known, Tina Lovely was a step ahead of Sharon, but I needed support for my argument.

"Who's Tina?"

"One of the exceptions. Why does Sharon want to learn to make ravioli? Microwavable fish sticks are more her speed."

"Because Ben loves them."

"Doesn't she know she can buy them frozen in any grocery store?" I'd never tried them, but I'd seen them.

"Watch your mouth, Casey." My father, who grew up on canned Franco-American spaghetti, was now a pasta snob.

"Nonna already showed her how to make the pasta dough, so you only have to teach her how to make the filling, roll the dough, and shape the ravioli."

"Why me? Maybe Nonna would like to show her the rest, since she started."

"She won't get here until late. Mrs. Alfano wanted to go to High Mass at St. Michael's."

"Ah, smells and bells," said my father, nodding his head. "I wonder whose pain and demise Mrs. Alfano is praying for." On Sundays, Aunt Maria and Uncle Tony take Nonna and Mrs. Alfano to church before bringing them here. Aunt Maria and Uncle Tony try to find the shortest service possible, one where you could slip in the back door, catch Communion, and leave. Mrs. Alfano insists that salvation can be had only in Gregorian music and burning incense and demands that they go to High Mass at St. Michael's. My parents go on Saturday night so my mother can start cooking at the crack of Sunday dawn. She's stopped asking me when I go.

"Well, I better shower and change now, because there will be no time later if I have to wait for Sharon to get the hang of making ravioli."

WHEN I CAME BACK downstairs in clean jeans, a shirt with a collar—my mother's only criteria for dinner—and shoes, Sharon was waiting for me at the kitchen table with a pad and pencil. She used to be a court stenographer, and she takes copious notes on everything. Ben was sitting on the floor covered in powdered sugar and *zeppole* cream, and I could hear Russell laughing with my father in the other room. "Hi, Sharon," I said. "You ready for the ravioli lesson?"

She wrote "Ravioli Lesson" on her pad. "Hi, Casey. I'm sorry about Richard. What a terrible thing to do." Sharon and Russell had been on vacation when it happened, and when they got back, Ben came down with chicken pox. This was the first time I'd seen her since the "incident." "You okay?" she asked.

"Thanks, Sharon. I'm fine." Then, in an upbeat tone I had practiced while changing, "Okay, ravioli. We'll start with the filling." She wrote "Filling" on her pad. "We're going to make spinach-and-cheese ravioli today . . ." I was going to mention that they can be filled with a variety of ingredients, but realized as she was writing "spinach-and-cheese" that this would take forever if she was going to record all the possibilities.

I had her scoop the ricotta cheese into the strainer and explained that it was necessary to drain it and remove the excess water so the filling wouldn't be runny. As she was writing that down, I washed the spinach and described the process of wilting. So far, so good. I let her grate the Parmesan and felt bad when she scraped away two fingernails and let out a squeak. Ben began to cry and Sharon picked him up and called Russell to come and get him.

"Hey, Case. My favorite cousin." He calls all of us that. He had me in a bear hug as he said, "I heard about the tooth jockey? What a shit! Excuse me, Aunt Paula."

"She doesn't want to talk about it." Sharon gave him a pointed look. I made a mental note to show her how to make lasagne someday.

"I'm sorry." He held me at arm's length. "You okay?"

"Fine." I could see my mother raise her eyebrows.

Russell dipped a piece of bread into the sauce and then took Ben from Sharon and left the kitchen. I swept away the grated cheese that was speckled with bits of Sharon's pink fingernails and showed her how to keep her fingers tucked in to avoid losing them. I then showed her how to use the same finger-tucking technique for chopping the spinach. I stood right there as she chopped.

"Okay, Sharon. Mix the spinach and cheeses together. I'll get the pasta machine." I went around the corner to the pantry—really an old broom closet—and when I turned back into the kitchen, Sharon was opening and closing cupboard doors.

"What do you need?"

"The mixer."

Knowing her limitations, I probably should have said "stir" rather than "mix." I've known brilliant people who, when it comes to cooking, are two chips short of a cookie. They seem to put their brains on hold, and do all kinds of weird things. This is why Sally writes such detailed recipes in her books. She's fond of saying that a cookbook is only as good as its weakest recipe, and she doesn't want the success of her books to depend on an inept cook with no common culinary sense.

"You don't beat a filling for ravioli, Sharon. You want texture. Just use a wooden spoon or a fork to stir the ingredients together." She wrote that down, then began to stir them together while I added salt and pepper and grated in some nutmeg.

"How much salt, pepper, and nutmeg did you add?" She had her pencil poised. I could have told her what Nonna told me—"Enough"—but I knew that would not compute, so I gave her my best guess.

As I was clamping the pasta machine to the counter, the absolutely best thing happened. Nonna arrived. Church had let out early. It couldn't have been on account of good behavior, since Mrs. Alfano was there and "good behavior" is not part of her belief system. Didn't matter why. I knew Nonna would happily take over the ravioli lesson and do a much better job.

Aunt Maria, Nonna, and Mrs. Alfano came into kitchen together. Aunt Maria had a tray of delicate *wandis* that she had made. She rolls the dough in a pasta machine before shaping and frying the pastries, so hers are always very thin and crispy. Nonna had red peppers that she had roasted, cut into even strips, and laid out in rows on a pretty dish. Mrs. Alfano had a scowl. It was the one she had spent years perfecting and saved for Sunday dinners. Mrs. Alfano and Nonna are about the same age and both came to America from Italy as young girls, but the likeness stops there. My grandmother is as short as my mother but very round and cuddly. She has white hair that Rita's Hair House sets in rollers once a week and sprays so generously that it doesn't move until her next visit. She wears flowered dresses and colorful knit suits. Now that her children are grown, she has relaxed her parenting skills and enjoys being a grandmother.

Mrs. Alfano enjoys nothing. She's a big, stout woman, and regardless of what *Vogue* says, her standard black dresses and thick black stockings do nothing to minimize her size. She has dull gray hair that she pulls back in a bun, no doubt to show as much of the scowl as possible.

Mrs. Alfano grunted, "Hello," although it may have just been just a grunt and no hello, and then she sat down at the kitchen table to wait for something to happen that she could criticize.

Nonna hugged me and then did what she has always done with me: she put both her hands on my face and tilted my head down so she could look intently into my eyes. We grandchildren knew about the eyes in the back of her head and believed even the eyes in the front had some special gift of vision.

"You will be fine, *cara mia*. Richard was not the right one for you." She'd been saying the same thing every Sunday for five weeks. "I see a very different man in your life. You will not settle for a gerbil."

"You can see the gerbil?" I said, truly amazed.

"Your father told me. But I do see the man, and he's more special than that Richard."

Mrs. Alfano saw her chance and pounced. "I never liked him. He's a bum." She'd been saying that for five Sundays in a row. Even though she probably had it right, it was annoying. Nonna and Aunt Maria each broke off a piece of the bread, dipped it into the sauce, and told my mother how good it was.

Aunt Maria generously put a little sauce and a piece of bread in a saucer and brought it to Mrs. Alfano, who tasted but said nothing.

WITH THE EXCEPTION OF Mrs. Alfano, who continued to sit, stare, and scowl, we spent the next two hours fixing dinner and catching up. As I expected, Nonna was happy to finish the ravioli lesson with Sharon. She told Sharon to watch carefully and then she broke off an egg-sized piece of dough and rolled it through the machine several times to knead it. Even with her fingers badly bent with arthritis, she kneaded and stretched the dough more smoothly than anyone in the family could. She laid the long, wide sheets of pasta out on the floured counter and began to place little piles of filling evenly along the sheet. Sharon picked up her pencil and asked, "How much filling in each?" Nonna picked up some filling and held it up for Sharon to get a good look. "This much," she said. She had Sharon dip her finger in water and then paint lines around each pile of filling before folding the dough over and pressing where the lines were so the dough would stick. When she handed Sharon the ravioli wheel, I was going to mention the grated fingernails, but to my surprise, Sharon rolled perfectly straight lines without injury.

Meanwhile, Aunt Maria made a large salad and I peeled and cut up potatoes to roast in the pan with the pork. Mrs. Alfano ate the last *sfogliatella*. The rest of the family arrived just as we were ready to sit down, and the noise level went up considerably.

Until Nonna turned eighty last year, she had family meals at her house. And unless you were dead, you were there. On her eightieth birthday, her children finally convinced her to move into an assisted-living facility and Mom continued the tradition at our house. It's not compulsory anymore, but everyone still comes if they can. My parents had the wall between the dining room and sunporch removed and converted the entire area into a room with a table large enough to accommodate the entire family. Fourteen of us now sat comfortably, with our heads bowed, waiting for Dad to finish grace. Ben sat in a high chair smashing the olives. Dad asked God to bless the food and finished, as usual, with a request to bless all the people here with us. Fourteen pairs of eyes looked at the enormous spread and quickly shouted, "Amen."

Eating dinner together is not as simple as it used to be. Aunt Gina is lactose intolerant and can't digest the ricotta filling, so she cut her ravioli open, ate the pasta, and gave the filling to Uncle Little Joey, who is on the Atkins diet and can't eat the pasta. He ate the ravioli filling and licked the cream cheese out of the celery stalks on the antipasto plate. Mark is a vegetarian, so he ate the ravioli but asked for it without the meat sauce. Raymond is fasting for Rastafarian rights and only drank Coca-Cola. Uncle Mike is on a low-fat diet, so he ate Uncle Little Joey's empty celery stalks. Mrs. Alfano complained that the gravy was too thin and the pasta too thick and ate seconds anyway. Every Sunday, Mom pretends not to notice the food juggling, but poor Nonna always looks genuinely saddened by it.

"Michael, why can't you eat just a few ravioli? What's that going to hurt?" For someone of Nonna's background of lean times, not eating on purpose was just wrong.

"I can't, Ma. They're not on my diet. Besides, I drank a Slim-Fast before I came, so I'm not really hungry."

"I knew a man who drank that stuff for three days and then just dropped dead. He was perfectly okay before that." Mrs. Alfano always knows someone who did the same thing as someone else and did not survive, or at the very least was confined to a wheelchair and would forever be a terrible burden to the family.

"I doubt that it was Slim-Fast, Mom." Uncle Tony should have known better.

"You think they are going to teach you that kind of thing in medical school? If people don't get sick, what is there for doctors to do?"

"I heard a good one about doctors the other day." God bless my father. He had one for every occasion.

"This doctor is late for a meeting, so he rushes in and quickly sits down. The doctor sitting next to him looks at him strangely and then asks him why he has a rectal thermometer behind his ear. The doctor pulls it off and looks at it. 'Damn. Some asshole has my pen!'"

"Mike!" Mom sounded outraged, but I could see the twinkle in her eyes. The rest of us were laughing except for Mrs. Alfano, who was blessing herself.

"What?" Dad's innocent look was as funny as his joke. He loved to stir up a little trouble and then act as if he had no idea what he'd done.

"I know a woman who had her temperature taken that way in the hospital and they put a hole in something and now the family has to do everything for her. She can't get out of bed. They're all praying she'll die." Mrs. Alfano was on a roll now.

Russell was sitting next to me, and I don't think anyone but me heard him say, "Is that all it'll take? A little prayer and Mrs. A's gone?"

"Sharon made the ravioli. They came out really well. Brava, Sharon!" I wanted to give Sharon some encouragement. Besides, this seemed like a safe topic.

"I heard on television that ravioli were created to use up leftovers. So ravioli are really garbage." Just like Mrs. Alfano,

Raymond held to the if-you-can't-say-something-nasty-just-scowl school of behavior.

It was Aunt Gina's turn to be outraged. All five feet of her snapped into action. "Raymond! Leftovers are not garbage. That's an awful thing to say. Apologize."

"Hey, Ma. Chill. You've all said that Sharon's cooking is garbage." He laughed at what he thought was a good joke. The therapy is definitely not working.

"*Hey, Raymond.* Put a sock in it." Russell rarely showed anger, but he wasn't about to take any criticism about his wife's cooking when she'd finally shown some interest. I wondered if Dad was ready with a sock joke. We don't think that our table conversations should necessarily be polite, and they usually do grow loud and edgy. We're okay with that until we hear someone say something like "And just what is that supposed to mean?" or "I'm coming over there to knock your effing head off." Then it's time to clear the table and go on to another course. I got up and asked for help clearing the ravioli plates.

The second course went much like the first. Mark ate the potatoes, Nonna's peppers, and salad. Sharon is Jewish, so she passed on the roast pork and the sausage. Uncle Little Joey made up for no ravioli pasta with generous helpings of all the meat, and Uncle Mike pushed salad around his plate. Most of us followed our ravioli course with roast pork, roasted potatoes, peppers with sauce, *braciole*, sausages, meatballs, and heartburn. Nonna's remedy for poor digestion is salad, which she calls "the stomach's toothbrush." It does lighten the load, so that those who really wish to punish themselves can stay at the table and eat dessert.

Chapter 11

What am I gonna do about you?
—*Reba McEntire*

On Tuesday morning, my train was late and I arrived at the studio a little after five-thirty. I went straight to the buffet, grabbed a large coffee and a cheese Danish and told myself I'd go back for muffins later. There were too many to choose from and I wanted to get to the kitchen before anyone else so I could get organized before having to give directions.

Danny was already there. He was leaning against the far counter, legs crossed at the ankles, sipping a cup of coffee.

"Good morning, Chef," he said. "You're late."

"Well, good morning to you. You're very early."

He looked at his watch. "You said five-thirty?"

"I know. It's just unusual for chefs to get here so early in the morning after a restaurant night." I put my coffee and Danish on Romeo and then slipped my purse and tote off my shoulder and dropped them on the floor. "Don't you ever go to bed?"

The corners of his mouth turned up in a slow, wicked smile. "Whenever I get the chance."

"I meant, do you sleep?"

"Like a baby."

"Glad to hear it. I see you have coffee. Would you like a Danish?" I reluctantly moved my Danish to the center of the table. "There's also a huge buffet spread out in the hallway."

"No thanks. I never eat on an empty stomach."

"Well, mine never is." I broke a Danish in half to expose more of the cheese and took a bite.

"Okay. So what do I do?" Danny asked, walking over to Romeo and putting both his hands on the surface.

I reached into my tote and took out his scripts, as well as the recipes and scripts for today and tomorrow's shows. I was spreading them out in front of him when Mae walked in, followed by two of the Tonys.

"Well, top o' the morning to you," Mae said with a huge smile. "Hey, Casey. That was an awesome party, Danny!"

Danny gave a little bow. "Top o' the morning to you, love. I'm glad you had a good time. It's the truth I had nothing to do with it, except for the food."

"Well, that was the best part."

"I thought the best part was seeing you lasses all decked out for the party. You were a force, I can tell you. I'm glad you all came." He smiled, and I'm pretty sure I heard Mae sigh before getting to work on several cans of Pillsbury dough. We didn't need backups, but we did need a number of finished calzones for a beauty shot.

I sat down at Romeo with Danny, explained to him the difference between setups for live and taped spots, and showed him how that pertained to his scripts. He was fascinated and said he'd had no idea that cooking on television involved so much. "I would have thought you just cooked and the cameras rolled."

"Most people don't know how much preparation and product go into one brief cooking spot," I said.

When we'd gone over all the scripts, he reached for the chef's coat and tool kit he'd brought and asked, "So, what can I do?"

"Do you really want to work?"

"If you promise you won't sing."

"I'll try to control myself."

"Well now, don't go that far."

I rolled my eyes at him and gave him a pile of onions to chop for the chili.

Sonya popped in briefly to see how things were going. I had told her that Danny would be here to observe, so she wasn't surprised to see him.

"Good morning, all. That was a wonderful party, Danny."

"I'm glad you enjoyed it."

"Do you feel prepared for next week now that you have the scripts and a sense of how we do things?"

"No problem. Casey's been a huge help."

Jonathan came in as Sonya was leaving. "I am not happy!" he said, and in case we hadn't heard him or couldn't read the pout on his face, he repeated himself. "I am *not* happy!"

"Somehow, I'd picked up on that, Jonathan," I said. "But for your information, calzones are not brown. They're beige."

"Beige is just a variation of brown. And what about the salami? Caca brown. Couldn't you have thrown in some roasted red peppers?"

"It's his mother's recipe. He just didn't want to change it. Believe me, we asked." I knew Jonathan was very close to his own mother and thought this might temper his annoyance. It did as far as the calzones were concerned, but he had other issues.

"And tomorrow, what do we have? Brown chili. Don't even get me started on that." That's the last thing I wanted to do. "I can't wait to see next week's scripts. Let me guess: it's brown-meat week?"

"As a matter of fact," I said, handing him the scripts for Danny's show with the lamb dish on top, "it is." To ward off another hissy fit, I immediately introduced him to Danny and he politely shook his hand before going to his cupboard—still pouting but, thankfully, saying no more about the lamb. Danny shot me a questioning look and I mouthed the words "I'll tell you later."

At six o' clock, our cohost Jim came into the kitchen to see if our baseball player had arrived yet. He hadn't, but Jim hung around like a little kid outside a pro sports locker room. He shuffled around outside the door for a while, then came in and engaged Danny in conversation. He'd been to Oran Mor, and although he'd come hoping to talk batting averages, he seemed pleased to chat with Danny about Ireland. Our baseball player showed up around six-thirty, and it was hard to keep him on track since Jim was more interested in next year's starting lineup than provolone, salami, and the Pillsbury Doughboy. Luckily, they called Jim to the set just about the time he was suggesting "a little catch" outside behind the studio. He'd brought his own baseball.

The calzone spot wound up being a charming segment that looked very natural—just a couple of guys standing around, rolling up calzones, talking sports, and trying not to spit or scratch on national television. I told Danny that he would do his live spot with Karen instead of Jim and that she would keep things moving as far as timing and conversation were concerned.

"Lack of conversation is not an Irish affliction," he pointed out. I thought about my father and said, "I know. You'll do just fine." When the show was over, we took a break before going into high gear for tomorrow's prep.

"I'm going out for a smoke," Mae said.

"I'm going back to the buffet for some muffins. Are you ready for something to eat, Danny?"

"I don't know, but I'll go with you and see what they've got."

"Anyone else want anything?"

Mae asked for a raspberry yogurt and the Tonys both asked if they could go outside with Mae.

"Go for it."

To get to the buffet, we had to pass behind the set through a dimly lit passageway. I was all too acutely aware that I was alone with a bold flirt who oozed testosterone. I picked up my pace, but he took hold of my arm and stopped me. "Are you walking that fast to get away from me?"

"Why would you think that?"

"Because you keep ignoring my attempts to seduce you." He still had his hand on my arm and he ran it up to my shoulder. The touch sent an uninvited tingle through my body. "But I know you're crazy about me."

Oh! The arrogance! I thought he might get the point if I shrugged his hand away, but it felt pretty good where it was, so I let him leave it there. "We've had this conversation before and I told you, I'm not interested."

"And that's because you think I'm some kind of mole?"

"Vole. Meadow vole."

"Whatever. Is that the only reason?"

"That's pretty much it."

"I think it's pretty heartless to stomp on small critters before finding out if they mean you any harm."

"I didn't stomp."

He threw his hand over his heart. "You have no idea."

He looked so wounded that I laughed. "If you feel stomped upon by me, then I am sorry."

He put his hands on the wall on either side of me, locking me in front of him. "Well, you *could* make it up to me."

I ducked under one arm and continued to the buffet. "Not that sorry," I said.

"Look at all this!" he exclaimed when he saw the long buffet table. "It's brilliant."

"Well, the pastries didn't come from Jacques Torres, but they're not bad." I handed him a plate and he selected a plain bagel. He put a small container of cream cheese on the plate next to the bagel. I decided to take just one muffin, even though I had planned to take at least two. I grabbed a yogurt for Mae.

The kitchen was empty when we returned. We sat down at Romeo, across from each other. Danny cut his bagel in half and started to spread cream cheese on it. I offered to toast it under the broiler, but he said he liked it that way.

"You know, I don't know much about American baseball, but it occurs to me that I should have talked to that baseball player about the game."

"Why's that?"

"He might have had a few tips about what to do when you keep striking out."

I cocked my head and smirked at him. "You get benched."

"For how long?"

"That's up to the coach."

He took the last bite of bagel and grinned. "Well, that's good, because I think the coach is really hot to put me in the game but just won't admit it."

I might have told him he was wrong, but I think my body's sexual receptors would have reached out and slapped me. They wouldn't understand that at the moment, I was brokenhearted and vulnerable and no matter how charming this man was, he was not the answer to my problems. I was grateful that Mae and the Tonys returned before I had to say anything.

It was super having the extra pair of hands in the kitchen; we moved along at record speed. As Danny worked, he chatted and charmed the others, even Jonathan, who told him his lamb dish was going to be fine. "You won't believe what I can do with parsley," he told Danny, without looking at me. He probably knew I was squinting daggers at him. As for any more suggestive advances, Danny kept them in check except for the times when I passed him on my way to the sink. He had figured out that unless he scooted way in I was either going to skim my breasts against his back or face the other way and risk a summit of our backsides. He made it harder by backing up every time I had to go by him.

By about ten-thirty, we had finished just about all we had to do.

"Well, I'd better get back to the restaurant," Danny said, taking off his chef's coat and laying it on a stool. "They'll be well into lunch prep by now." He patted the Tonys on the back and thanked them, shook hands with Jonathan, and gave Mae a big hug and told her she was the best. I was next, and I figured I came under the hug category, so I was trying to determine if I should just hug him back or kiss him on the cheek, as I often do with the guest chefs I know and like. Before he came to where I was standing by the door, he picked up his coat and tool kit, which meant that there wasn't much arm left for hugging. What's that all about? One minute he's all over me and the next he's planning on squeezing me in between his dirty laundry and used chef's tools. I felt as though I'd just been voted off the island. He can forget the kiss on the cheek.

"I'll be seeing you, Casey," he said and bent down and kissed me. Just like that. On the lips. Not a long kiss, but one that felt so passionate and intimate that my toes curled and I was speechless. He walked out the door without saying another word.

I didn't say anything either until I noticed Mae grinning at me with raised eyebrows.

"What?" I said.

"It sure looks like you two have got it going on."

"No way, Mae. Flirting is just an extracurricular activity for him. It has no effect on me." Liar. Liar. Pants on fire.

I MET MARY FOR lunch at a small burger joint on a side street near where she works. The smell of burgers, bacon, and onions on the grill was so strong that I was sure people wouldn't notice that I smelled of hamburger, onions, and chilies. Mary was already sitting in a booth when I walked in.

"I could smell you the minute you walked in," she said. Hey, what are best friends for if not to tell you when you smell! The waiter came over and we both ordered cheeseburgers and Diet Cokes.

"What were you cooking?"

"Calzones and five-alarm chili. Danny was in this morning to help."

"So?" Mary raised her eyebrows at me. "How did that go?"

The waiter delivered our burgers and we greedily took big bites, letting the grease drip over our hands and ooze toward our elbows.

I told her about the trip through the passageway and then the kiss before he left. I finished by saying that I was *not* interested. She put her burger down, wiped the grease off her hands with several flimsy paper napkins, and put her elbows on the table.

"Casey, ever since the fifth grade when Bobby Morgan dumped you for Carla D'Angelo—"

"Carla D'Angelo was a skank."

"Whatever. Since then, you only go out with guys that *you* go after. Anytime anyone the least bit aggressive shows an interest in you, you write him off as insincere. The problem is, eventually you aren't happy with the predictable guys you pick. You want spontaneity, excitement, a little bit crazy. That's the forward, aggressive type, Casey. That's a Danny."

"That's a dangerous thought, Mary."

"*That's* what's so appealing about it. What are you afraid of?"

"Well, for one, my guess is he's just interested in a quick fling. Probably has them in the walk-in all the time."

"So you have a quick fling with him. He's pretty damn hot."

"You know, Mary, sometimes I think you're as bad as your mother thinks you are."

"Probably worse." She started to sing, " 'I want to get to heaven before I die.' "

"Nathan Moore," I said, identifying the singer.

"With the Slip at the Iron Horse. You were in the front row, screaming 'me too.' Remember?"

"I remember, but I have a feeling a fling with Danny would put me in the opposite afterworld."

"So, Dark Cloud, is there a number two on your list of reasons for turning your back on that gorgeous hunk? And if you mention anything about being in mourning over Richard, I'll throw up."

"It's not about Richard. I don't want to be in a contest with women like the hotties at the restaurant who were throwing themselves at Danny."

"Why not?" she said, finishing her last bite of burger. "You'd win."

Chapter 12

Hot mama.
—*Trace Adkins*

Sally breezed into the studio at six the next morning. After greeting me as though she couldn't believe her eyes that I was here, she said she'd arrived in New York late last night after spending a delightful weekend with friends north of Baltimore. She was in a very upbeat mood.

"I'd like to sit down and look over the cookery books first," she said. "There's nothing much for me to remember for the chili spot." Since the firefighter would be making the recipe, all Sally had to do was be entertaining and charming and act interested. She could do that in her sleep.

I piled the cookbooks on Romeo. "Do you have the scripts with you or do you want mine to ignore?" She gave me her sheepish grin. Scripts were merely guidelines for Sally; she'd do and say whatever came into her head and it would be better than anything we could have spent weeks writing.

Since we had gotten so much done on Tuesday, our work for the chili segment was pretty much a snap. Because it was a live show, we didn't need backups, and although there were a few swaps, we'd gotten them done the day before. Mae pulled a number of containers out of the refrigerator and transferred the contents to pans so she could reheat them. Jonathan came in and when he saw Sally, he quickly removed his pout and replaced it with a smile. He said nothing about the color of the chili but proudly showed her the flowers he had brought to decorate the cookbook set. "I'm going to put them in one of my special copper pans. A vase would be just too common. What do you think of that, Mrs. Woods?"

"I think it's a fine idea, Jonathan." I knew that Sally didn't care about decoration at all. As long as the food looked good, she was happy with a setup.

"Make sure the copper finish is dull, Jonathan," I said. "We don't want the lights to create a glare on the metal."

"I didn't start here yesterday, Casey."

I gave him a sarcastic smirk. "CYA" was all I said.

Before long, Sonya arrived flanked by a brigade of six strapping firefighters looking sharp and snappy in dark blue dress uniforms with double rows of shiny brass buttons. Only one of the men would be cooking with Sally—they chose him by picking his name out of a firefighter's boot—but they had developed the winning recipe together and they all wanted to meet her. Each had his hat tucked under one arm and something in the other hand for her to sign. If I were ever to be famous, I'd want to be just like Sally. She has such a genuine warm appreciation for her fans. They left the kitchen beaming and I knew she had made them feel that they were the special ones, not her. John McGuire, the firefighter who'd won the boot lottery, stayed behind so we could go over the script with him and give him tips on what to do and not do. John was a big burly man with a red complexion that I knew makeup would be hard-pressed to cover. He was chatty and full of the devil and would be great on the show.

In the segment before the commercial break that preceded the chili cooking, Karen and Jim introduced the six firefighters and showed footage taken of them cooking in their firehouse. We broke, John changed into a dark blue T-shirt and an apron, and when we were back on air, he was standing with Sally in the kitchen set.

"So, John, you have developed your own secret recipe for the best chili ever," Sally said with the camera shooting a close-up of her and John. Makeup had toned down his complexion considerably.

"I guess it won't be a secret after today," he said.

"Why, honey, I won't tell a soul. Where do we begin?"

The cameras moved in close to pick up several strips of crisp bacon inside a large pot on the stovetop. John said that the recipe began with bacon fat, so first you cooked bacon, then set it aside to be crumbled for the topping. He used long tongs to transfer the bacon to paper towels and Sally picked up a piece and took a bite. "What's next?" she asked.

John picked up a bowl that held small cubes of beef and, remembering our instructions, tilted it toward the camera and held it there for a few seconds. "Now we add the beef."

"And you've cut it up yourself. You don't use ground beef."

"No. The cubed beef is much hardier."

"Always good to have something you can really sink your teeth into," Sally said, taking another bite of bacon.

John put some of the meat on a paper towel and said, "You have to make sure the meat is dry or it won't brown. And you have to work in batches." Sally let him tell her that as though it were the first time she'd heard it. "And don't crowd the pan," he went on. The meat sizzled in the pan, John stirred it around for a second, and then he and the cameras switched to a twin pot that held chopped onions and jalapeños. "After all the meat is browned and out of the pan, you cook a couple of large chopped onions, six cloves of garlic, and some chopped jalapeños." The camera went in close to show that the onions and garlic were translucent.

"Now it gets a combination of these spices," Sally said, sweeping her hand by several jars. "This is your secret that won you the prize."

"That's right," John said.

"What was the prize?"

"A year's supply of chili powder."

"Very practical."

John poured dried oregano into his hand and crushed it between his palms before adding it to the pot. Sally added cumin and cayenne pepper according to his directions, and then he poured in a heaping half cup of chili powder.

"Goodness," said Sally. "That's a very large amount of chili powder."

John grinned at her and said, "We like our chili just like our women—hot and spicy."

Sally gave him her own twinkling grin and dumped in another quarter cup of chili powder. I'm pretty sure that much heat would make an inedible bowl of chili, but it was very funny.

John stirred the spices around and then poured in beef broth, water, crushed tomatoes, and a cup of coffee.

"I guess you always have coffee brewing at the station."

"Sure do," said John, "and most of it is only good for the chili pot. You let that cook for a couple of hours . . ."

"While you polish the truck and the fire pole," Sally said.

"Right," said John as he moved the unfinished chili aside and slid a finished pot to the burner in front of him. He stirred in about four cups of red beans and said, "Now stir in the beans and heat it up. We serve it with the crumbled bacon and these other toppings." The camera moved to a Jonathan still life of diced avocado, sour cream, lime wedges, cilantro sprigs, tortilla chips, and a small bowl of crumbled bacon. We had fried and crumbled more in the kitchen because we'd figured Sally might eat the whole slices and, indeed, she had somehow managed to consume two of them during the spot.

John ladled chili into two bowls and both he and Sally adding toppings and tasted. Sally declared it worthy of the prize and thanked John.

When the show was over, Sally went up to change her blouse and have her makeup tweaked while the Tonys cleared the set to ready it for the cookbook spot. We have a shallow wooden box that fits over the stove so that the whole peninsula becomes a counter. A Tony put it in place and then Jonathan did his thing, making a handsome arrangement of cookbooks and a dulled copper pot filled with flowers. We positioned a stool at the counter so Sally could sit high.

Jim and Karen had a few promo spots to shoot, so they changed and returned to the set and the crew began taping spots of one or the other of them telling the audience what was coming up this week and next and encouraging them to tune in. Sally returned to the studio, and we sat on the side and watched. We spoke only during the shooting breaks.

"So where are we going for lunch?" Sally asked.

"Oran Mor. Mary's going to meet us there."

"Perfect. I was hoping to get back there soon." She was quiet while Karen told the camera audience, "On Friday, the problem of bed-wetting will be solved." Karen made it sound so tantalizing that I made a mental note to tune in even though I didn't know anyone with the problem.

When the cameras stopped, Sally asked, "How are you getting on with Danny?"

"We're getting on fine." She gave me a devious, questioning look. "Sally Woods! If you're asking if I'm getting *it* on with him, the answer is *no*. And that's the way I want it."

"Huh!" she said.

We obeyed the quiet-on-the-set call, and listened to Jim tell us that tomorrow they would have an exclusive interview with a woman who had witnessed the mystical appearance of a weeping Madonna on a windowpane in New Jersey. I could miss that one; Nonna witnessed such things all the time.

It was Sally's turn, and after sending Jim and Karen off with big hugs, she did a promo to air the week before the Italian series would be shown and told the audience all they would miss if they didn't tune in to watch. "We'll be in Parma, Bologna, Florence, Ravenna, and the hills of Chianti with our own *Morning in America* chef, Casey Costello, who will cook right in the kitchens with real Italians. We'll show you how true parmigiano-reggiano is made and see the fat pigs that give us Parma ham. You'll learn how to cook a Tuscan steak the size of a cow, make a real Bolognese sauce, pasta the Italian way"—she leaned forward and gave the camera a coquettish twinkle —"and what to do with a squiggling eel." Who could resist?

We cleared out the kitchen so she could change her blouse without having to go upstairs and she took her place on the stool behind the cookbook display. She described what each one was about and why she had chosen it. Whenever she said, "You just have to have this one," I could imagine the stampede of feet as people rushed to their bookstores or the clogged phone and cable lines as they logged on to Amazon.com. A good word from Sally was all it took.

WE ARRIVED AT ORAN Mor just after noon; the restaurant was already crowded. Kim the greeter saw us come in and strode right up to us. "It's so good to have you here again," she said. She was looking at Sally, of course. "The rest of your party is already here." She led us to a table where Mary was nibbling on *amuse-gueules* and reading a menu. As soon as we had greeted each other, a waiter arrived, handed us menus, and announced, "Danny would like to send you a selection of appetizers but he said to order any that you like. The kitchen is very busy right now, but he said he'd be out to see you before you leave."

"Good," said Sally. "We'd love to talk to him. Just so you'll know, I have to leave by two-fifteen." I knew Sally was meeting George, and I was grateful that she hadn't let him worm his way into lunch.

"I'll let him know," the waiter answered and then offered us complimentary cocktails or wine of our choice.

Danny sent out four appetizers in addition to the ones we ordered. We managed to finish them all. In addition to our entrées, the waiter delivered the lamb dish that Danny was going to make on the show. "It's not on the lunch menu," he said, "but the chef thought you would like to taste it." I had tasted the sauce on Saturday but not the lamb itself. The tiny ribs were easily the best lamb I'd ever tasted. The flavor was meaty yet delicate, with none of the mutton taste of an older animal. He obviously had a special source. Sweetie herself delivered a large assortment of her desserts, proudly describing each of her own creations. We were passing them left to right when I saw Danny walking through the dining room. He had on a clean chef's coat, but it was obvious that he had been working hard. He had the glisten of someone who had just stepped off the StairMaster after a grueling workout. Mary nudged me under the table and raised her eyebrows. I ignored her. He stopped at several tables, shaking hands and saying a few words, before approaching our table. I hoped he wasn't going to kiss me again. That is, I hoped I wasn't going to want him to kiss me again.

Sally took hold of his hand and said, "That lunch was one of the best I have ever eaten, Danny."

"I'm glad you enjoyed it."

"Can you sit for a while?" Sally asked.

"Love to. The kitchen has finally quieted down."

"Where do you get your lamb?" I asked after he sat. "It's amazing! I've never had any with that much flavor."

"Neither had I. It's from a small farm in Pennsylvania. The lambs are raised on a special diet that includes herbs that flavor the meat."

"How'd you find the farm?" Mary asked.

"Before I opened Oran Mor, I spent a lot of time going to small farms and tasting the products. Product's what it's all about, and I'm always searching for good ones. I really enjoy that part of the business." He leaned his arms on the table. "I just heard about a wild guy in Long Island, only about forty-five minutes away, who raises chickens on a special feed."

"Michael McLaughlin," I said.

"Exactly," he said, seemingly surprised that I knew his name.

"I've heard he's a real character," I said.

"He sure sounded like it on the phone. He told me he'd have to meet me before he'd agree to sell me his chickens, so I'm going out this afternoon to try to convince him. He said his babies couldn't go to just any old eatery to be overcooked and oversauced."

Sally laughed and lightly pounded her fist on the table. "That's just as it should be. And good for you for searching for the best. Using only high-quality ingredients and careful cooking is why your food is so good and your restaurant so popular." The dining room was less crowded now, but for the past two hours it had been hopping. "Is it this busy for lunch *and* dinner?"

"Thank the Holy Trinity it has been."

"You probably have no time to yourself," Sally went on.

"Not much."

"Do you get back home to Ireland at all?" Mary asked.

"I haven't been home since four months before we opened. None of the staff has had more than a few days off at a time, so we're going to close for a week starting next Sunday and I'll go home. The last time I called, me mam said I sounded familiar, but she couldn't quite place the voice. I think it's time."

We could see Sally's car pull up to the curb. She stood up, telling us to stay put, but I walked out with her anyway. The driver held the door open for Sally and I saw that George was sitting in the back seat. Our eyes met, and I grudgingly said, "Hello, George." He said hello without using my name and then told Sally they had a schedule to keep and had to get going. When I leaned into the car to kiss Sally's cheek, he said, "We are going to be late. Please close the door." Sally squeezed my hand just before the driver shut her in and I gave George the evil eye, which he probably missed with his nose in the air like that.

When I returned to the table, Danny asked what else I knew about Michael McLaughlin.

"I heard that he named all his chickens Ella so he wouldn't get too attached to any one of them in particular. Then he named his rooster Sam and planned to call his farm Sam-and-Ella. His wife convinced him that it was a very bad idea. He said he wanted to discourage casual business."

"Well, that would discourage mine, I can tell you," Mary remarked, standing up. "Look, I have to run. It's been real, Danny. Thanks." She kissed him on both cheeks, threw me one, and was off.

"Back to McLaughlin," Danny went on. "I really want to persuade him to sell me his chickens. Do you know anything in particular about him that can help me do that?"

"Not really. Sonya had wanted to use him as a talent on the show. Crotchety is always entertaining, but he wasn't interested. 'Too much exposure,' he said."

"Why don't you come with me to see him this afternoon. Maybe we can both convince him?"

"How are you getting there?"

"Driving."

"You keep a car in New York?"

"Not exactly." He stood up. "Follow me." He led me to his office, where he handed me a motorcycle helmet and a leather jacket. "You game?"

"Sure," I said, noticing that the jacket was a woman's size and wondering how many had worn it.

"Brilliant." He took off his chef's coat and said he was going to wash up a bit and would be right back. He returned in clean jeans and a red plaid flannel shirt. "What do you think? Does it say 'trustworthy farm boy' to you?"

I was actually thinking "hunk," but I said, "Absolutely."

He changed from his kitchen clogs to short black leather motorcycle boots and grabbed his own leather jacket and gloves. "Okay. Let's do it."

We walked around the corner to a garage, where the attendant obviously knew him well.

"How's it going, Chef?"

"Great, Bob. How about with you?"

"Can't complain. You taking the bike out?"

"Yeah. It's a great day for it."

"Sure is," Bob said. "I just polished her this morning, so she'll look prettier than anything out there."

"He polishes your motorcycle for you?" I said as we walked down the ramp into the garage. Most people were lucky to find a garage in New York where the attendants didn't pass the time playing dent-the-fender with your car.

"Yeah. A few months ago I began to bring him food from the restaurant, and then he started polishing the bike. He knew it was special to me."

"What's so special about it?"

"Sentiment." He walked to an area that held a number of motorcycles. "It's over here." He removed a soft flannel cover from the motorcycle and said, "This is it."

I had no clue what was special about it. "It's really good looking," I said. "What a pretty color!" I didn't know enough about motorcycles to say more than that.

He patted the handlebars and smiled. "This, my friend, is a vintage 1962 Triumph Bonneville." He turned to me. "Triumphs are made in Britain. This honey was my da's. He gave it to me before I went to culinary school and we restored it together. The *pretty* color is British racing green. It's not the original color, but it's my favorite for a bike, so Da and I painted it."

"I can see why it's so special." Somehow, my mother had managed to pipe her voice into my head and I asked on her behalf, "Is it safe?"

"Of course. Put your helmet on."

I slipped the helmet over my head and began to struggle with the chin strap. Danny lifted my visor so he could see my face. "Here," he said, securing the strap. "You look awfully cute in that, Casey."

"I bet you say that to all your passengers."

"Only the cute ones," he answered, snapping down my visor. He climbed on the bike, and after warning me to keep my legs away from the pipes whenever we stopped because they would be hot, he took my arm and hoisted me behind him. I wrapped my arms around his waist and he took them in his hands to tighten my hold. "You don't want to fall off," he said and started the engine. It was a beautiful day, and the ride was incredibly therapeutic. I loved feeling the breeze around me and the sure, swift way we moved together with the road. In no time at all we were out of the city and moving along a back road that led to Michael McLaughlin's chicken hatchery. "Isn't this great?" he asked when we stopped at a light. "Who'd believe this was so close to the city? Are you okay back there?"

"Fine." My voice sounded as though it were coming from an echo chamber.

We found the tiny farm, where Mrs. McLaughlin answered the door. "He's out with his chickens," she said, pointing to the back of the house. "Around that way."

Michael McLaughlin was a big man, tall and rugged, with a mass of white hair, big bushy eyebrows, and a huge mustache. He was cooing to his chickens as he scattered feed to them. "Here, Ella, Ella, Ella. You too, Ella, Ella, Ella."

"Mr. McLaughlin, I'm Danny O'Shea." He shook Mr. McLaughlin's hand. "And this is my friend Casey Costello." I shook hands and then brushed the residual feed away on the back of my jeans.

"Look at these fine birds," Mr. McLaughlin cooed. "What makes you think your cooking is good enough for them?"

For the next twenty minutes, Danny charmed his way into Mr. McLaughlin's suspicious heart. He told him how he wanted to cook with only ingredients that were grown and raised with care and feeling. He said that no amount of culinary training could compare with the skill needed to produce those ingredients. The derivation of McLaughlin's name had not escaped him, and his brogue had become so thick I could hardly understand him. When he told Mr. McLaughlin about spending summers on his grandparents' farm and how they never ate anything that they didn't raise themselves, the older man put his arm around Danny's shoulder. I wondered if my summers at Girl Scout camp would have had the same effect. By the time we were ready to leave, Danny had locked up a place in Mr. McLaughlin's limited customer base and, seemingly, his heart; but Sam and Ella's dad still refused to appear on *Morning in America.*

"You're going to have to work on your blarney, Casey," Danny said as we were getting back into our helmet gear.

"Well, if anyone could teach me, it would be you. That was very impressive. Did you really spend summers on a farm?"

"Would I lie?" he asked with a grin.

"To get what you want? My guess would be yes."

He laughed and then asked if I was in a hurry to get back to the city.

"Not really. Why?"

"I know this great little place on the way back that serves the best *café liegeoise* this side of Belgium."

"What's a *café liegeoise?*"

"Hop on. You're in for a treat."

We drove for about twenty minutes and then Danny pulled off the highway, turned down a side road, and stopped in front of a small, charming bakery with blue-and-white-checked curtains and blooming flower boxes. Inside there were six small round metal tables. Danny told me to grab one while he ordered. "Do you want a pastry or two or a dozen to go with the *café*? It has ice cream, but you may want something else as well."

"I'll start with the *café* and see after."

He returned to the table with two tall, thick-handled glasses with soft whipped cream oozing over the top. He handed me a long spoon and a straw. "Which one do I use?" I asked.

"Both," he said, plunging his spoon into the bottom of his glass, taking a bite, and then sipping through his straw. I did the same, and since I'd never been to Belgium, I found it the most incredible *café liegeoise* this side of anywhere. The bottom of the glass held hot, strong espresso coffee, topped with vanilla ice cream—homemade, with visible flecks of vanilla beans. The ice cream was drizzled with a dark chocolate sauce, and the whole was topped with real whipped cream. The combination of flavors and hot and cold temperatures was totally seductive.

Danny was halfway through his when he looked at my empty glass and asked, "How many more do you want?"

"One should do it."

I forced myself to eat and drink the second one more slowly so as not to look like a complete pig and was halfway through when Danny finished his. When he took a spoonful of mine, I was sorry that I hadn't finished it before having to share.

"Aren't they good?" he said, digging in for another bite.

"Positively orgasmic," I answered, immediately regretting my choice of words.

"I wish I'd known sooner that a little ice cream and whipped cream was all it took."

"Let's not go there."

"Struck out again. I'm getting a complex."

"Look, Danny. I like you. I mean, you *are* arrogant—"

He put both hands on his chest, raised his eyebrows, and asked, "Me?"

I nodded at him. "Yes, you. But you are also very nice."

"Uh-oh." He looked wounded. "That's the kiss of death."

"What."

"Nice. 'Nice' is always followed by 'but' and some made-up excuse, like that your star sign is wrong for me."

"Is that a fact?"

He raised his right hand as if in oath. "Undeniable fact. Only you were probably going to say, 'You're nice *but* we can't ignore the fact that you are, after all, still a vole.'"

I raised my right hand. "Undeniable fact."

He fiddled with the spoon in his empty glass, then said, "You know, you didn't tell me the other day. *Are* you attached to someone?"

I was pretty sure I could talk about it without crying, so I told him that I'd just ended a long relationship.

"I see," he said. "What happened?"

"It's a very long story, but it came to blows over this trip to Italy. I wanted him to come along and play Gregory Peck to my Audrey Hepburn in *Roman Holiday*, and he wouldn't."

"You wanted him to do what?"

"It's an old movie, from the sixties. It was always my mother's favorite, and my father gave her the tape when I was a little girl. So Mom and I used to watch it together all the time. I liked the idea of two people riding a scooter through a foreign city better than an alien riding a bicycle across the moon." I told him the story, about how Gregory Peck is a journalist who meets Audrey Hepburn, a princess who has escaped her demanding duties for one day of freedom in Rome. At first Peck thinks he's going to get the story of his life, but in the end they just spend twenty-four hours exploring Rome on a Vespa scooter and falling in love. "It's very romantic."

"Why didn't your guy want to do it?"

"That's part of the very long and not very interesting story. I'd really rather not go into it."

"So, it's this long, uninteresting story that's preventing me, a lonely stranger in your country, from the benefit of your company?"

"You have my company. I'm here now. I'm happy to be your friend."

He grinned. "I should have said 'orgasmic' company."

"I'm sure you can find lots of that."

He leaned across the table toward me. "Not from someone like you. You're not only beautiful and smart, you have a very special spark about you."

Vole or no vole, he *was* incredibly charming and I couldn't ignore the fact that he was proving to be a pretty decent guy— full of himself, but decent. And if I wanted to be honest with myself, I'd have to admit that he did turn me on. But I didn't want to be honest about that, so I lied to myself. "Thanks, Danny. That's very sweet of you. But the answer is still no."

"Ah. 'Sweet' is a step up from 'nice.' I'm making good progress here. Slow, but good."

We rode back to Manhattan and he dropped me off at the train station. As he was strapping my helmet and jacket on the back of the bike, he asked if there was anything he still needed to know about next Wednesday's shoot.

"Yeah. Don't get in before me. You're making me look bad."

"Not a chance," he said, revving up the engine.

SONYA HAD NOT SCHEDULED any cooking shows for Thursday, Friday, or Monday so that I would have time to finalize the scripts for Italy. Since I was now single and had the weekend to myself, I finished them on Saturday morning. Sally was leaving for London that night, so I called her to let her know I would be e-mailing the recipes and scripts to her.

"Would you rather I faxed them to London?"

"No, e-mail," she said. "If I don't get a chance to open them now, I'll have my PortaPrinter with me and can open them anywhere."

"How are you doing, Sally?"

"Fine. I'm all packed up and ready to go."

"I meant *you*, Sally. How are you feeling about putting London on the market?"

"I told you, Casey. I have to, so I don't think about it. I just bull it through." That was so much like Sally. She was proud of the fact that she was descended from colonial Virginia settlers who had had to fight the elements, the Indians, and a shortage of taffeta. I wanted to believe that she would do what she had to do and be fine, that she'd just bull it through. But I was also afraid that, this time, the toreador might be tougher than the bull.

Chapter 13

You can't make a heel toe the mark.
— *Wanda Jackson*

The funny thing about a lot of comedians is that offstage they're not so funny. Sal Vito cracked people up when he was in front of an audience. Backstage, he seemed ready to crack someone in the head. Sal is an Italian comic—been around for years. He does a lot of nightclub work, mostly Vegas. Audiences roar at his routines, which typically poke fun at his Italian mother, who is constantly feeding everyone. What's so funny about that? Every few years he turns out another cheaply produced paperback cookbook: *The Mama Mia Cookbook, The More Mama Mia Cookbook, The Even More . . .* and so on. He comes on the show a few times a year, and we try hard to stay out of his way.

On Tuesday morning, Sal was the talent for a live spot. The recipe, his mother's pasta with cauliflower, was from his latest book. It's a good, simple Italian home dish and a pretty easy setup: finely chopped cauliflower, minced garlic, and a little hot pepper sautéed and tossed with spaghetti. The problem is, it's all white. Sonya had tried to talk Sal into doing something more colorful, but he'd blown her off—rudely. It would have been okay if the viewers were going to see the dish only when Sal put it together, because they would clearly understand what was going into it. But the director called down first thing in the morning for a beauty shot.

Usually, during variety shows, the monitor will display part of a segment that is coming up as a tease to the audience, so that they will stay tuned. The director asked us for a finished dish of pasta; that was the tease we call a "beauty shot." White pasta with white cauliflower would need a lot of makeup to be considered beautiful, and Jonathan was doing all he could to make it look appealing.

"It's better than brown, Jonathan," I pointed out, trying to encourage him as he got out a blue pasta bowl, some red-checked napkins, and a bottle of red wine.

"No. It's not. At least you can see the brown. This is going to look like a dish of Wite-Out."

The director agreed with Jonathan. When the camera lined up the shot, the dish didn't look like much.

"Can't we throw something red or green in there?" The director asked over the loudspeaker from the control room.

Sonya spoke into the microphone on her headset. "Well, there's nothing red or green in the recipe. I'll see if I can get Sal on the phone to check if it's okay with him if we add something just for the tease." She took out her cell, looked at her clipboard for the number, and started dialing. I went to the kitchen to see what we had in red and green.

When I returned to the set with a plate of cherry tomato halves, Sonya was again speaking into her headset. "He's nowhere to be found. He's not answering at the hotel or on his cell."

"Well, we have to take the picture now if we're going to use it during the show," the director said.

"Let's shoot it two ways, and as soon as I get hold of Sal I'll see if he minds if we add"—she paused long enough to look at what I was holding—"some tomatoes. If he does, we're just going to have to go with the white version."

I handed the tomatoes to Jonathan. "Okay, Jonathan, knock yourself out."

AT THE START OF the show's eight o'clock hour, the monitor began to run the teases, using the shot with the tomatoes. I figured Sonya had reached Sal and he was okay with it. We were ready for his live spot, so we were prepping for Danny's three shows tomorrow. At eight-fifteen, half an hour before he was to go on the air, Sal stormed into the kitchen. I was on the far side of Romeo, facing the door, when he came in, so I could see his face, which was not registering pleasure. Mae and Jonathan were on the other side of Romeo, with Jonathan closest to the door. "Who the hell fucked with my pasta?" Sal screamed.

Jonathan and Mae both started like jackrabbits, and Jonathan began to stammer at the same time that I tried to explain what had happened. Jonathan was closer to Sal, and either the big oaf heard only him or was deliberately ignoring me and picking his closest victim. In any case, from that point on, everything happened with such lightning speed, it was like a DVD on fast-forward. Sal, who was over a foot taller and about eighty pounds heavier than Jonathan, grabbed the startled stylist by his shoulders and lifted him off his feet. "Don't ever fucking mess with my food. Do you fucking *capisce*?" Even if Jonathan did *capisce*, he probably couldn't have said so because his teeth were chattering.

Again I tried to explain, but this time I was drowned out by our own sweet, nonviolent peace activist Mae, who picked up the bunch of scallions she was trimming and swung them so that the green ends hit Sal across the face. "Put him down, you animal," she ordered.

Sal immediately let go of Jonathan, who fell to the floor still clutching the napkins he had been folding into lotus blossoms. That left Sal and Mae face-to-face. He yelled at her, spraying spit all over the place. "Why, you little bitch. You can pack your bags now. You will be finished here when I get through with you." He took a small step toward her, and in a heartbeat two Tonys leaped over Jonathan and onto Sal's back, screaming, "Run, Mae, run."

The fact that Mae was wedged behind Romeo and had nowhere to run was beside the point; it was a sweet gesture. Sweet, but foolish. I was sure Sal was going to shake our boys off and make mincemeat of both of them. Now, absolutely nothing in four years of culinary school had covered anything like this particular kitchen disaster. Overbeaten egg whites, broken mayonnaise, fallen soufflés, yes, but not fallen set designers, broken necks, or beaten stagehands. On the other hand, twenty-nine years of Conti Sunday dinners had covered it all.

I lowered my shoulders and raised my hands up to either side of my chest, palms up and fingers pinched together. I vibrated my hands back and forth and raised my voice to a decibel level above Sal's. "*Stattazeet che cosa fa? Tu sei patzo.*"

Sal stopped moving, and the Tonys slid off his back.

He turned toward me and raised his right arm, bending it at the elbow and making a fist. He reached his left hand over and placed it firmly on his upper right arm, a gesture known as the Italian salute, which is equivalent to dropping the F-bomb.

I brushed four fingers of my right hand from my neck to my chin and thrust them forward, which I think means "Go to Naples, or hell, or anyplace but here—I couldn't care less." For good measure, I added a *vaffanculo*. The yelling and gesturing in Italian seemed to contain Sal's anger. He didn't try to hit me or lift me; he just kept giving me indecent hand gestures and foul words, which I matched pretty good for a Catholic girl raised in a middle-class neighborhood.

As I said, all of this happened very quickly. So when Sonya walked in the door, Jonathan was still in a heap on the floor, Sal had bits of scallions on his clothes, the Tonys were hovering behind Sal, ready to pounce if necessary, and I was giving Uncle Mike's version of the Italian salute, which is a bit more complicated but a lot more graphic.

"What the hell—" said Sonya.

"My neck is broken," Jonathan moaned. "Call an ambulance."

"Casey?" Sonya's face clearly asked, "What the hell is going on here?"

"Sonya, please, get Sal out of the kitchen."

Fifteen minutes later, I had Jonathan up to medical, the kitchen back up to speed, and the sound on the monitor as low as possible. It was projecting a laughing, lighthearted Italian comic making his mother's favorite pasta dish. I gave the set the evil eye.

As I expected, Sal's front man was in the kitchen at three minutes past nine, trying to smooth things over.

"You know, performers get jittery before they go on the air. They do and say things they don't mean. I'm sure you all understand. Sal wanted you all to have autographed copies of his latest cookbook." He took some copies out of a grocery bag and put them down on Romeo.

"I think you better go up to medical to check on our set designer. Sal physically assaulted him," I said.

He made a little "pshaw" sound. "People often mistake Italian enthusiasm for more than it is. I'll go see him." As soon as he left, we threw the books in the trash.

By noon, we had all of our prep tucked away in the refrigerator, clearly marked DO NOT TOUCH. If we didn't mark the food, the night staff would have eaten it all before dawn.

"That's it for today, guys. See you tomorrow," I said.

"What time do you want me here?" asked Mae.

"We better start right at five o'clock."

"You got it. I'm outta here. See ya, boys. Thanks for the hand." I didn't know if she meant the food prep or the celebrity bashing, but they gave her big, toothy smiles.

Before I left the studio, I went up to medical to check on Jonathan, but they had sent him home to see his family doctor. I knew his neck wasn't broken; still, he was pretty shaken up. I made a mental note to call him later, not just because I was concerned about him but because I knew that the studio would give us a replacement tomorrow who would know nothing about styling food. It would make the shooting more difficult. Oofah. What a day.

When I got home around four o'clock, my Uncle Tony's car was parked in the driveway and I could smell the cannoli the minute I opened the back door. This was definitely a situation. A good china plate with a dozen or so filled cannoli was sitting on the counter, and my mother, Aunt Maria, and Nonna were standing with their ears pressed against the closed dining room door.

"Hey! What's up?"

The three of them turned together and whispered for me to shush. Then Mom tiptoed over to me and pulled me into the pantry.

"Uncle Tony is here with Mrs. Alfano and Father Joseph. She's been taking money from the candle donation boxes and he caught her."

"What? Why's she taking money?"

"It sounds like she's been playing bingo a little too much."

"Come on! How much can bingo cost?"

"Uncle Tony is trying now to get to the bottom of it."

"How'd she get caught?"

"Well, she's on the Altar Guild, so it was her job to bring the money to Father Joseph. He noticed that each week there was less and less and finally none. That's when he confronted her on the altar. She panicked, said she didn't deserve to live, and then threw herself on top of the votive lights. I suppose she planned to burn herself to death with the candles, but being so big and all she just snuffed out those that were burning and broke a few more. That's when Father Joseph called your Uncle Tony."

I couldn't help but laugh, and as hard as she tried, my mother couldn't keep a straight face. "Do you think she'll go to jail?" I asked between chortles.

"I don't think so. But she'll surely go to hell."

"That would be redundant."

"Come on. I have to hear the rest of this." My mother resumed her position next to Nonna and Aunt Maria, and I easily fit my ear at the door above their three heads. I'd never heard Uncle Tony so mad or heard him speak to his mother like this.

"You're telling me you spent your social security *and* the allowance I give you, a total of over *nine hundred dollars a month,* in a bingo hall and you needed to pinch pennies from the poor box? How could bingo cost that much? Jesus, it was only a dollar a card the last time I played."

"I played more than one card, Anthony."

"How many cards can you play? Five? Ten? That still doesn't account for all that money."

"*Aiuda, Jazzugeet.*" I thought it was an inappropriate time for Mrs. A to be asking Jesus for help since they were his pennies she'd swiped, but she was probably not in a rational frame of mind.

Uncle Tony's tone became gentler. "*I'm* trying to help you, Ma. But I can't help unless you tell me what's going on."

"It wasn't just Bingo, Anthony," she admitted. "Mrs. Colasanto won this big amount of money playing the horses. She told her nephew what horses she liked and he played them for her. She said he'd do it for me if I wanted. So sometimes he'd come to the church on bingo night and I'd give him some money. When he didn't come, I'd tell my picks to Mrs. Colasanto and she'd tell him. Sometimes I'd call him on the phone. He'd play the horse and then collect the money later if I lost. I didn't realize I was losing so much, and sometimes he wouldn't wait for his money. I didn't always have enough to pay him back."

There was a frightening pause and then Uncle Tony absolutely exploded, sending the four of us cowering away from the door. "Colasanto? *Carmen* Colasanto? For Christ's sake, Ma. Carmen Colasanto's a bookie. What the hell were you thinking?"

"Watch your mouth, Anthony. Forgive him, Father. He isn't really a bookie. He just loaned me money as a favor to his aunt."

"*That's* what a bookie, does, Ma! *Mannaggia a l'America. Mannaggia.* How much did she take, Father?"

"Well, it's not really about the money, it's—"

"*How much?*" Uncle Tony was really steaming.

"About two hundred dollars. It will have to be paid back. And Mrs. Alfano is not allowed back in St. Michael's."

I would have thought that was exactly where she should be, on her knees. You know, purging her soul of sin and all that. But what did I know?

"Maria! Bring me the checkbook." We stepped back from the door so Aunt Maria could take the checkbook to Uncle Tony. My mother whispered to her to leave the door open so we could get a look at what was going on. Mrs. Alfano, head bowed, was sitting at the table. Her black dress was singed in several spots. Uncle Tony, his face beet red, was pacing and muttering behind her. Old Father Joseph, pale and washed out as usual, was standing—or, I should say, swaying, since he does drink a little—a few feet from the side of Mrs. A, with his hands folded so the tips covered his mouth as if in solemn prayer, or perhaps to cover any odor of the Jack Daniel's he preferred.

"Do you intend to press charges, Father?" Uncle Tony asked before he signed the check.

"I've been thinking about that and don't know what to do. Perhaps I have to speak to my superiors. Nothing like this has ever happened before."

"Oh, come on, Father. Don't you remember guys tipping over the baptismal font, trying to get into the poor box with a penknife, drawing dirty pictures in the Mass books?" Uncle Tony was never a fan of Father Joseph's; now he seemed to be as put out with him as he obviously was with his mother.

"No. I don't remember any of that."

"Well, then you don't remember Frankie DeCesare and Vinny Guccione."

"I never liked that Vinny Guccione." Mrs. Alfano was probably hoping the conversation was now turning to someone else's sins.

"I'm going to have to think and pray about this," Father Joseph said without uncovering his mouth.

Probably seeing this as an opportune moment, my mother picked up the plate of cannoli and went into the room. "Would you care for one, Father?" Her attempt at a bribe was totally blatant, but the priest took a cannoli anyway. I thought that was in poor taste. He really should just have left without eating pastry as though this were a christening celebration instead of a robbery-and-candle-snuffing confrontation.

In the end, it was Nonna who put a stop to any talk of pressing charges. "Oh, she's just an old woman, Father. And how do we know that money would have gone to the poor and not for a little bourbon for the rectory? Now eat your cannoli and let's forget this ever happened." Father Joseph ate his cannoli.

BEFORE I WENT TO bed that night, I called Jonathan. There was no answer, so I left a message on his machine saying that I hoped he was okay. As difficult as he could be, I wouldn't want to do the show without him. I didn't know how to make brown beautiful with parsley.

Chapter 14

Who's foolin' who?
—*Delbert McClinton*

The next morning, even with a stop at the buffet, I was the first one in the kitchen. Danny was second. He poked his head in the door. "Is this late enough? I've been hiding around the corner for twenty minutes so everyone would see that you got here first."

"Never happened," I said.

"Sure it did. I saw you come in with your Danish and coffee."

I held up my empty plate. "They were muffins."

He came into the room. "I thought you only took muffins on your second buffet run."

"I mix it up to confuse anyone spying on me."

"You just can't count on people anymore," he said, sitting down across from me. "By the way, I got my first Ella delivery. The chicken came wrapped prettier than a present from Clery & Co."

"From where?"

"Clery & Co. One of Ireland's oldest department stores. The chickens were wrapped individually and laid out neatly in the box. I think I got Ella, Ella, Ella, and Ella." That made me laugh. "He also sent me some of his eggs to taste. You should have seen the yolks. They were almost orange. He must give the chickens some leafy greens with their feed. "

I squinted at him. "Do you know that because you spent summers on your grandparents' farm?"

"It's the truth," he said, putting his hand over his heart. "I swear."

"Okay. I believe you." I looked at the clock. It was almost a quarter of six. "We should get started."

"Where do we begin?"

"First of all, did you bring a change of shirts?" He was wearing black jeans and a faded blue chambray shirt, which would be fine, but he needed a different shirt for each of his three shows.

"Oh! I left them on a chair around the corner." He walked out the door and came back in carrying several hangers. "Sonya said I could wear a chef's coat or street clothes. I decided to go with the street clothes, but I wasn't sure what would be best, so I brought a few choices. Should I try them on for you?" He laid the selection of shirts on Romeo and began to unbutton the one he was wearing.

"No!" I said a little too emphatically. "Sonya will be the one to decide."

"So you don't want me to undress?" he asked, grinning at me.

"No. I do not. I want you to cook." I took two aprons from the linen draw and handed him one. "Here. And you should keep the bib up in case you need that shirt for the show."

"Yes, Chef." Most male chefs fold the bib of a chef's apron under and tie the apron around their waists, which leaves their tops unprotected. I don't have linen service, so I keep the bib up. I slipped my apron over my head without realizing that the neck strap had a knot in it. Mae must have worn it last and knotted the strap so the apron would be the right size for her. The knot raised it too high for me to tie the straps at my waist, so I reached behind my head to undo it. It was stubborn, the way knots are after they go through the wash, and I was having a hard time with it.

"Here, let me do that." He stood close to me and reached behind me and began to work the knot. His knuckles kept brushing the back of my neck and I think my heart stopped, or at least my breathing did. I wondered if he could feel the little tiny hairs standing up. I bet he could. He was grinning that grin at me again.

"There," he said. "You seem to have a lot of trouble with your clothing."

"Only when you're around, but don't take it personally." If I didn't move away from him soon, I was afraid it would become more personal. Now that I had made it clear to him that I did not want to get involved, I actually enjoyed the flirting. I just wasn't certain that my body was clear on the message. I picked up my tote bag and dug out the scripts. "You want to work on the lamb?"

"I'll do anything you want, love. You know that. Just give me the word."

I pulled four racks of lamb out of the refrigerator. "This one we leave untrimmed so you can show what it looks like from the market. This one needs to be completely trimmed; that's the one we'll cook ahead of time. Trim all the bones but one rib on this one. That's the bone you'll clean on TV. And trim this one completely but do nothing with it."

"What's that one for? I didn't see it in the script." He had done his homework.

"That's in case you can't get the bone trimmed fast enough."

"I will," he said.

Mae walked in followed by two Tonys. Her hair tuft was sprayed kelly green and she wore a bright orange ruffled skirt and a white tank top. She looked like the Irish flag and I was glad for her that Danny picked up on it.

"Well, look at you, love, sporting the colors."

"I thought it'd be cool in your honor."

"Where did you ever find a skirt that color?" I asked. I meant for my question to sound more inquisitive and less incredulous, but Mae didn't seem to notice.

"I dyed it. I have more of the dye at home if you want me to dye something for you."

"Thanks. It *is* an absolutely amazing color."

She smiled in acknowledgment that it was amazing and then asked, "Where should I begin?"

"With the tuna tartare, and let's go over it first." Because the tuna spot was essentially two separate recipes, the tartare and the wonton cups, we had to lay out the ingredients carefully. The cameras would shoot the tuna from one angle, then swing over as Danny moved to another spot on the set. We had to make sure that he had what he needed in each position, so he wouldn't be moving back and forth. We'd need salt in both places so he wouldn't have to reach. We'd decided that he should make the tartare and leave it in the bowl where it was made. Then he could move to the wontons, assemble them, pop them in the oven, and return to a third spot on the counter with a twin bowl of tartare and already baked wontons. He would then fill one and put it on a plate with the triangles. Danny knew what he was going to do at each spot; we had to make sure that what he needed to do it was in the proper place.

Mae marked trays according to position on the set and then began to make the wonton cups. It was still too early for Jonathan to be there, if he was coming, but I began to worry a bit since I knew a substitute designer would not have a key to his cabinet. We had some dishes and platters in the kitchen but nothing like what was in Jonathan's private stash. I began to rummage through cabinets to see what I could find.

Danny finished trimming the lamb and I set him to work on cooking shallots and mushrooms for his swap. I gave him a Tony all to himself so he wouldn't have to hunt for equipment or peel his own shallots or wipe his own mushrooms.

A little after six-thirty, Sonya came into the kitchen, greeted us all, and then said, "Casey, I have to fill in as line producer today, so I won't be around much. Can you manage here?"

"Not a problem. I *was* wondering about Jonathan, though. Have you heard from him?"

"No. But if he doesn't show up, let Lisa know and she'll stand in as stylist." Lisa was primarily responsible for keeping the living room set seasonal: pumpkins and leaves in fall, holly and red candles in December, tulips in April—that kind of thing. I knew her answer to styling the food would be to scatter blossoms around it.

Once Sonya left, the first thing I had to deal with was Danny's wardrobe. "Okay, O'Shea. Looks like you're going to have to take your clothes off for me after all."

He laughed and put down his knife. "You first."

Mae looked up from her capers and said, "Did I miss something?"

"Since Sonya won't be around, we're going to have to decide what he should wear for the three spots." I crossed my arms over my chest, grinned, and said to him, "Let's see what you've got."

He grinned right back at me, took off the apron, and began unbuttoning his shirt.

"Not here. Around the corner." I picked up his hangers and led him out the door and around the corner to a small alcove at the right of the kitchen door. It was secluded enough for a quick change, and we all used it in a pinch. Otherwise, he would have to use the bathrooms, which are upstairs, or change in the kitchen. A few years ago, we had a chef change in the kitchen. He was so proud of his upper body that he kept his shirt off longer than necessary, and it was extremely distracting. I wasn't sure how distracting a bare-chested Danny would be to me, but I wasn't willing to take any chances.

I hung the shirts on some wiring hanging from the wall and started to walk back to the kitchen.

"You leaving?"

"It's not a two-person job. Come into the kitchen when you've changed."

"Feel free to peek if you want!"

He returned shortly in the black polo shirt he had worn the first day we'd met.

"I like that for the salmon spot. The contrast will be good. What do you think, Mae?"

"Definitely.' "

"Next," I said to him.

Danny tried on three more shirts. We decided on the faded chambray shirt for the lamb and a bright blue polo shirt that made his eyes seem even bluer for the tuna tartare with fried wontons.

"Okay, Danny, don't put any of those three back on until shooting."

It was great having the extra set of hands, especially his. He knew his own recipes by heart and worked through them more quickly than either Mae or I could have. A little after seven, Jonathan arrived in a neck brace.

"Jonathan. How are you?" I said with real concern.

"Don't ask. I'm lucky to be alive. If that brute ever comes on the show again, I am definitely quitting."

"Did his front man see you after the show?"

"*Please!* That asshole! He tried to give me a cookbook. What nerve! I told him my lawyer doesn't cook."

"I'm glad you're well enough to be here," I said.

"I'm not well enough," he said, touching the brace, "I'm dedicated." He reached into his pocket for the key to his cupboard.

"What happened to you?" Danny asked.

The question was music to Jonathan's ears. He leaned on the counter next to Danny and gave him a blow-by-blow description of his ordeal. Danny listened and commented but never stopped working. When he'd finished his medical analysis, Jonathan switched topics. "I'm *so* glad that we are going to put potatoes and vegetables on the plate with the lamb. You have no idea how difficult it is to make brown appealing. But," he said, throwing his chin in the air, "no one listens to me."

Even with Jonathan drawing out the details of his near-death experience and making his color point yet again, Danny's help moved us along a lot faster than I had expected, and we finished well ahead of time. By seven forty-five we were done. I sent Danny up to makeup and returned to the buffet alone.

DANNY WAS AS RELAXED with the cameras rolling as he was working in the kitchen. He trimmed the last bone on the lamb rack, explained what he was doing, smiled for the cameras, and charmed the pants off Karen all at the same time. Still smiling and explaining what he was doing, he put the lamb in

a hot skillet—we could hear the sizzle—chopped some shallots, turned the lamb, and chopped mushrooms. He transferred
the lamb to the oven, drained the excess fat from the pan,
added a few tablespoons of butter, and then tossed in the shallots and mushrooms. A little salt, pepper, and an explanation
that it should cook until the mushrooms released their liquid,
and then he switched to the pan that held the already cooked
shallots and mushrooms and added some stock. When he
poured the Madeira into the pan, he put his arm across Karen's
chest, said, "Step back, love," and tilted the pan so that the
Madeira exploded in a burst of flames. It was a great piece of
food television and totally ad-libbed. He removed an already
cooked rack of lamb from the oven, sliced one rib chop from
it, put it on a plate that already held cooked asparagus and
mashed potatoes, and napped it with the Madeira sauce. A star
is born! Danny sailed through his two taped spots with equal
ease, in one take.

Sonya came into the kitchen to congratulate him. "You're a
natural, Danny." She beamed. "That was terrific. And, all of
you, the food looked fabulous. Thank you." She turned back
to Danny. "I'd love to have you back sometime."

"Brilliant. I'd love to do it again."

"I'll be in touch," Sonya said as she left.

We all went on about him in the kitchen until I had to leave.
I still had so much to do before I was ready to leave for Italy tomorrow. "I'll walk out with you," Danny said.

Out on the street, he said, "I was wondering. Are you expecting a long mourning period?"

"Mourning period?"

"You know, from your breakup."

"I'm not mourning. That's not why I don't want to go out
with you."

"Oh," he said. "Because I was going to tell you that the accepted wisdom is that you're supposed to get right back on the horse when you're thrown."

"Danny, when I get back on the horse, it can't be a wild one. It's not what I want."

"I'm not that wild, Casey. I can get you good letters of recommendation from old girlfriends, if you like."

"Is it a very large stack? I don't have much free time to read."

Before he could answer, a car pulled up and Kim the greeter rolled down her window and chirped, "Sorry, Danny. The traffic was horrifying. Am I very late?"

"Your timing is perfect," I said and walked away.

Chapter 15

On the road again.
— *Willie Nelson*

Thursday evening, I met Sonya at JFK for our flight to Milan. If Sally had been with us, there would have been a strong possibility of being upgraded to first class, but she had left for London on Saturday, so I resigned myself to coach. I had packed little sandwiches of brown bread and tequila-cured salmon, and when the drink cart stopped at our seats, we each ordered some white wine and unwrapped the sandwiches.

"Where are we meeting Sally?" I asked between mouthfuls.

"In Parma. Tomorrow." Sonya reached for another sandwich.

I hated to risk acid reflux, but I had to ask. "And George?"

"I don't know. When he called to say he would be in Italy, he asked me to fax him our itinerary but didn't say when he was coming. I asked Sally but she didn't know, either."

"Wouldn't it be cool if he didn't show at all?"

"A blessing." She pulled an apple and a pear out of her carry-on and gave me a choice. The pear looked deliciously ripe and I took it.

I bit into the pear and put my head back for a moment, overwhelmed with thoughts of all that Sally had going on. It seemed that she would soon be dealing with a new publisher and, God forbid, maybe a new television network. She was giving up her London flat, which had been such a part of her life with Peter. That was another thing—Peter. She'd learned something about him that hurt. And worst of all, it seemed to me, was having to deal with George. I knew she thought she could tough it all out, but I wasn't so sure.

"Do you think having George around will affect Sally's performance?" I asked.

"I thought about that, but I've seen Sally go through some tough times and never show it on camera. She's such a professional. I'm betting that she'll be okay. He'll just ruin life for the rest of us."

Ain't that the truth?

WE LANDED IN MILAN early in the morning, and after *grazie*-ing and *prego*-ing our way through customs we met Giuseppe, who was waiting for us with a sign that said BUON GIORNO IN AMERICA. Giuseppe would be our driver for the entire trip. He was a man in his sixties, perfectly groomed and wearing a tweed jacket, pale yellow sweater vest, and a necktie. He was courteous and protective and immediately took us under his Harris tweed wing.

He packed our luggage and our jet-lagged bodies into his impeccably clean Mercedes-Benz and headed for the *autostrada*. "Ah, la Parma," he said. "He is the queen of cities. City of art, of music, food—*incredibile,* the food." It turned out that Giuseppe was from Parma and, like most Italians, suffered from a chronic case of *campanilismo,* extreme partiality to one's own city.

About three hours later, we arrived at the Palace Maria Luigia, in the center of Parma, and while Sonya was checking us in, I called Sally from the house phone.

"Hi, there," I said when she picked up.

"Is that Signorina Casey Costello?"

"*Sì, Signora Woods. Come stai?*"

"Wait a minute. I have to look that up." I could hear pages turning. "*Molte bene. Grazie.*"

"*Brava.* What are you up to?"

"Just going over the scripts. Why don't you and Sonya come up to my room?"

"Perfect! We'll drop our bags and be right there."

"*Arrivederci,*" she said.

"*Ciao.*"

"That's right. *Ciao.*"

Sally had a knockout penthouse room with huge windows that framed the city center. The three of us stood looking out and I was totally blown away by the reality that here I was in Italy, with my people. I was feeling really connected and wished that my mother and Nonna could have been here with me.

None of us had eaten lunch, so we found a nearby trattoria where the menu was only in Italian, a good sign. Just about every item listed was a specialty of the area. We knew this because the name of the dish was followed by the words *di Parma.* That meant that it contained either Parmesan cheese or Parma ham or, if you were lucky, both. Sonya ordered *tortelli d'erbetta di Parma,* a kind of elongated ravioli filled with cooked beet greens, ricotta, and Parmesan cheeses and served swimming in butter and more Parmesan. Sally and I ordered *tagliatelle di Parma,* thin ribbons of egg pasta with a sauce of butter, Parma ham, a little tomato, and lots of cream and

Parmesan cheese. It doesn't get much better. For our second course, we each ordered *rollatini di vitello di Parma,* thin slices of veal rolled around Parma ham and Parmesan cheese and braised in Marsala.

We spent the next two hours eating our food di Parma, sipping local wine, and practicing our limited Italian on the waiters. Sonya knew only "good day," "please," "thank you," and "where's the WC?" but Sally had been studying and knew a lot of useful phrases, such as *una bottiglia di vino rosso, subito,* and *il conto, per favore.* I could understand most of what was said to me and with enough red wine was able to respond to anything. Sally and Sonya said I sounded just like a native. It's in the genes.

Sally never mentioned London, and neither did we. It didn't seem like a happy subject. After dessert and espresso, Sonya paid *il conto,* courtesy of the network, and we walked back to the hotel through the Parco Ducale. We were immediately blown away by the expanse of green right in the center of the city. That was probably the way tourists felt about New York's Central Park.

"Look at the size of those trees," Sally said.

"Many of them were actually planted in the fifteen hundreds, when the ruling Farnese family established it as a park," Sonya explained. "Then, in the mid–seventeen hundreds, a Frenchman named Petitot redesigned the gardens for the French Bourbon rulers of Parma. That's why they're in the French style." Sonya knew these things because she'd had to research as much as possible about each city we'd visit in order to decide what she wanted for B-roll. B-roll consists of hours of tape a cameraman records around the city without the talent; an editor then cuts it down into seconds of footage. The edited tape is used to introduce a scene, establish the location, and provide atmosphere. Sally will provide the voice-over that tells the audience what they are seeing.

"Well, they are perfectly lovely," Sally said. "And I love seeing all these Italian women walking arm in arm. It just seems like the right thing to do with friends." She linked her arms in ours. "You know any Italian songs, Casey?"

"Is the pope Catholic?" I asked, and I taught them "Funicoli, Funicola," which Nonna had taught us as kids. I don't think I had the words quite right, but who would know? One meal in Italy and we were already feeling totally Italian. Tomorrow, I'd have to teach them the tarantella. We were a giddy, jolly threesome when we arrived back at the hotel. We made plans to meet for dinner and then crashed for a siesta. What a country!

IN SPITE OF THE fact that my body was still on New York middle-of-the-night time, I was wide awake and psyched to get going when Giuseppe picked us up at seven the next morning. Our routine in each of the cities would be the same. Mornings, Sonya, Sally, the director, and the camera crew would go out in the field to tape Sally at a place of culinary interest. I would go to the restaurant to work with the talent and get things prepped for the afternoon cooking shoot. I realized that this schedule gave me very little time alone with Sally, and I wanted so much to talk to her about the land mines she was trying to avoid. Then again, maybe it was best to skirt them altogether while we were in Italy.

Giuseppe dropped me off first and then drove Sally and Sonya to meet the crew on location. Among other culinary marvels, they were going to tape Sally stirring curds and whey with a parmigiano-reggiano cheesemaker and then patting the little pigs that ate the whey and wound up as Parma hams.

My stop was a restaurant located in a converted farmhouse, but one that must have been occupied by a rich *padrone* and not the likes of my farmer ancestors, who, according to Nonna, had been lucky to have a mud floor under their feet. It was a two-story stone farmhouse with a terra-cotta roof and a thick, ancient front door, to which was taped a sign that said APERTO OGGI PER TV AMERICANO. The restaurant was a family-run business with the seventy-five-year-old *nonna,* the talent, at the helm. Anna Maria reminded me of my own Nonna. She was short, round, and grandmotherly. I guessed that she had been to the beauty parlor that morning, because each strand of her gray hair was twisted into a perfect curl and I could smell hairspray; her fingernails were newly painted a bright pink. Her pale pink housedress was starched and ironed. I *loved* her. She was going to demonstrate *tagliatelle di Parma,* the same dish Sally and I had drooled over at lunch yesterday.

We finished the setup just before noon, when our *TV americano* group pulled up in the Mercedes and a van. Sonya introduced me to the crew: Nicole, responsible for makeup, was Italian. The camera, sound, and lighting crew were English. Sonya had worked with them before and she told me that they worked hard and played hard. The playing part didn't surprise me; they looked a lot like a seventies heavy-metal band, and the head cameraman's name was Rocket. You don't get a nickname like that by being captain of the chess club. The director, John, was American; I had met him a few times before on location. He was easygoing, and he and Sonya worked well together.

While the crew was setting up cameras and equipment and Nicole was attending to Anna Maria's makeup, one of her daughters made us lunch, *fritti di Parma.* She took pieces of pasta dough, rolled them paper-thin, and deep-fried them in vegetable oil until they puffed up like fat little pillows. She drained them on paper towels, split them open, and filled them with thin slices of Parma ham and Parmesan cheese. They were insanely delicious.

By the time we were ready to shoot, assorted sizes of children, grandchildren, spouses, and more than a few neighbors had formed a small crowd in the kitchen. The room was sufficiently large to hold them all, and after warning them not to make a sound, John called for a run-through and then for action. Using some Italian and some English, Anna Maria and Sally walked us, and eventually millions of viewers, through *tagliatelle di Parma*.

"*Primo, la pasta*," Anna Maria said, scooping flour from a large crockery bowl onto the counter and shaping it into a mound.

"Looks like about three cups," Sally said.

"*Sì*. Now you make *una fontana*." She used her hand to form a well, which she called a fountain, in the center of the flour and broke three eggs into it.

"Those are three large eggs." Anna Maria had collected them from her chicken coop so there was no egg carton marked "large," but Sally knew a large egg when she saw one.

"*Battate con una forchetta*." Anna Maria beat the eggs rapidly with a fork until they were a deep, orange-yellow mass, supporting the outside of the flour well with one hand as she replaced the beating with a swirling motion.

"Her fork is gradually drawing in bits of flour from the inside wall," Sally explained. When the eggs were no longer runny, Anna Maria put down the fork and used both hands to cave her wall in over the doughy mass. Then she pushed and squeezed the mass until it resembled a pasta-dough wannabe. Sally pinched it and said that it was still crumbly but held together.

"Now you must first clean the surface," said Anna Maria, setting aside the paste she had made and scraping the counter clean. "Then you knead *la pasta*." She pushed the crumbly paste with the heel of her hand, several times, then folded it, turned it over, and pushed, folded, and turned several more times.

"How long do you knead it?" Sally asked.

Anna Maria shrugged. "Until it is smooth and feels like pasta dough. Perhaps *dieci minuti*." She lifted a kitchen towel off the ball of dough we had made that morning and handed it to Sally. "Like this," she said.

Sally patted the dough and declared it "as smooth as a baby's bottom." She asked, "What's next?"

"Now we stretch it." Anna Maria shifted the pasta machine from the end of the counter to the center, as we had gone over that morning. She broke off a piece of the dough and rolled it several times through the machine, letting Sally pick up the sheet as it came through. When it was as thin as Anna Maria wanted, Sally held the long strip up, draping an end over each hand. "This is perfectly lovely, Anna Maria. It's so thin I can see through it. How do we cut the *tagliatelle*?"

Anna Maria, God bless her, had remembered all our stage directions and was in the process of changing the head on the pasta machine. When she had the cutting attachment in place, she took the pasta from Sally, sliced it into three pieces, then let Sally roll a piece through so that it came out the other end as ribbons of *tagliatelle*. "That's wonderful!" Sally said, admiring her perfect strands of *tagliatelle*. Anna Maria scooped up the strands and deftly twisted them into little nests that she set on a floured towel with the other nests we had made that morning.

We had to break there so that the camera could move to the

stove, where we had a large pot of boiling water for the pasta and a good-sized sauté pan for the sauce. We put butter in the pan, and when it was almost completely melted, the cameras began to roll again.

"You have about six tablespoons of butter melting, Anna Maria. Now what?" Sally asked.

"Adesso, il prosciutto di Parma," said Anna Maria, picking up a plate that held narrow strips of prosciutto. Sally popped one in her mouth and said, "About a cup of Parma ham cut into julienne pieces." Anna Maria offered the plate to Sally to see if she wanted more. Sally held up her hand and shook her head no, so Anna Maria tipped them into the pan and stirred them around a bit. Then she poured heavy cream from a pitcher into the pan.

"That's about two cups of *real* heavy cream. And that has to boil and reduce." That was the cue for John to stop tape while the cream reduced. When it had, they picked up again on a close-up of the reduced cream.

"The cream is reduced to about a cup," Sally said before asking Anna Maria what came next.

"I pomodori." Anna Maria spooned a few tablespoons of tomato puree into the pan, immediately turning the white sauce into a pale pink about the color of her dress. She stirred in some salt, pepper, and nutmeg, and said, *"Basta,"* then turned to the boiling water. She dropped a couple of tablespoons of salt and several strands of *tagliatelle* into the water. After a few minutes that would eventually be edited out, she retrieved the plump strands with a long-handled, weathered pasta scoop, tossed them in the sauce, and then transferred them to a pasta dish and grated a snowy mound of Parmesan on top. She handed it to Sally, who already had a fork in her hand. *"Mangia,"* said Anna Maria, and Sally did as she was

told and declared it *delizioso*. John declared the spot *delizioso*. With hugs, grazies, and arrivedercis, we packed up and left for Bologna, the Fat.

Bologna is called "the Fat" because of its good food, and we arrived just in time to head out for dinner. We quickly checked into the hotel, left our luggage for the bellman to deliver to our rooms, and set out in search of the restaurant Sonya said had been highly recommended to her. Our hotel was in the old part of the city near the main piazza, Piazza Maggiore, and we soon found ourselves walking along the miles of sidewalks protected by arched roofs. Sally remarked on what a good idea it was to build "arcade umbrellas" in case it rained.

"They have an interesting story," said Sonya. Boy, it was nice having her along. "In the eleventh century, Bologna was a wealthy city but very crowded. People from all over were immigrating here because it had the first university in Europe—built in 1088. There was no room to build more living space, so people began to expand their houses out over the sidewalks, and that made these porticos. The first one was built in 1211, I think it was. Before long it became a city law that if you built a house, you had to build a portico. These go on for miles."

"That's fascinating," said Sally.

"Wow. I love my people," I said.

We continued under the porticos stopping every now and then to admire the architecture and to look in shop windows, until we came to Sonya's restaurant. It served traditional Bolognese food, so we decided to order the *bollito misto*. *Bollito misto* means "mixed boil," and the mix seems to include every four-legged farm creature known to man. Our waiter wheeled an elaborate cart up to our table and began to lift ingredient after ingredient out of simmering broth. He carved and placed on our plates calf's tongue, veal breast, chicken, beef brisket, a sausage he told us was a local *cotechino,* and sausages that looked like the sweet Italian sausage from home. In case we might feel we weren't getting our money's worth, he added some small whole potatoes. He placed two different tangy, cold sauces, mustard and a pickle relish called *mostardo,* on the table and left us to eat ourselves to death. I really regretted having let Mary talk me out of clothes with elastic waistbands.

When we finally cried uncle and refused the dessert he wiggled under our noses, he told us to *"fate una passeggiata."* That means "take a walk," but he wasn't kicking us out. That's what the Bolognese do after dinner under all those porticos; they take a stroll. With food like this, I understand the law requiring those passages to be built.

I walked Sally to her room, wondering if she was up for talking, but when we got to her door she said, "I am going right to sleep. That dinner wore me out. Good night, honey."

In spite of the long day, I wasn't ready to sleep. I had finished the book I was reading on the plane and foolishly hadn't brought another one, so I tried to watch a little television. After an episode of *Friends,* dubbed in Italian, and a little CNN news I was getting antsy. Since we'd be in Bologna for two nights, I decided to wash out some underwear. That's when I noticed that Sally's carry-on had been delivered to my room by mistake. She'd have the latest food magazines; she always traveled with an adequate supply of reading material. She was probably asleep by this time, so I unzipped it and found several cooking CDs. *Great.* I'd wanted to look them over since Sally had mentioned them in New York. There were five of them, but only one was open, so I picked that one and got out my laptop. When I opened the CD case, I saw that there were two discs inside—one marked, the other not. I slipped the unmarked one into my laptop.

It was blank for a minute, and then I was looking at Peter Woods. He was sitting at a table in a small, unfamiliar kitchen, speaking to a man who was sitting to the side of him. I was confused for a moment, because Peter was not speaking English, and I thought maybe this was some type of comedy-show spoof. They were always doing takeoffs on Sally. But there was nothing funny about it, especially when the other man began to pound his fist on the table and rant at Peter.

"Boris. Speak English," Peter interrupted in English. "You know I can't follow your Russian when you rave like that."

"I have told you," Boris said, pounding the table again. "I will only pay the amount we agreed to. Not one dollar more."

"We agreed to that amount before I had this new material. What I have now is worth more." Peter rested his arms on the table and leaned toward the other man. "If you would just let me speak to whoever is in charge, I know I could convince him. I don't think you understand how big this is. You'll get five, ten times the money I'm asking from the Iranians alone. North Korea will pay even more. Why don't you set up a meeting for me with the guy in charge?"

"*I* am in charge. Me. Boris Davinsky. I am my own leader."

"We both know that's not true."

At that point, Boris stood up and tipped the table over. I saw Peter's arms fly up, and then the CD went blank. I stared at it with my heart racing so fast that I had to take huge, deep breaths to slow it down. "Oh my God!" I said out loud. "Oh my God!" This is what Sally had found out about Peter. "Oh my God." He was selling some kind of material to a Russian thug who was selling it to people who were not our friends. Peter worked in nuclear physics, so I could guess what kind of information. I began to pace the room, actually wringing my hands.

I thought about this man whom I had adored, with whom I had shared so many good times, and I felt sick to my stomach. I could only imagine the horror Sally must have felt when she'd found out such a thing about the man she had married. I ejected the CD and put it back in its case, regretting ever having seen it. Not only did I not want to know what I now knew, I didn't know whether I should tell Sally I knew. Would she be grateful to have someone to share the hurt or would someone else knowing make it harder for her? I turned off the lights, and tossed and turned for a long time before falling asleep without an answer.

Chapter 16

Postpone the pain.

—*Mark Chesnutt*

The next morning, I knocked on Sally's door on my way to the lobby. I handed her the carry-on and explained that it had been delivered to my room by mistake. I watched for any reaction that might open up a dialogue about Peter, but she simply thanked me and said she hadn't even missed it. I had decided that if she didn't mention it when I returned the carry-on, I would wait until we were back home to discuss it. I would visit her in Washington, so we would be away from the public. Until then, I was going to pull a Sally and just bull it through.

We met the others in the lobby, and Sally and Sonya took off to shoot balsamic vinegar, tortellini, and a 180-pound mortadella. I took off to a local restaurant to meet a 180-pound *buffone*. Gino Baffoni, the talent, was shorter than me, but his hair was a lot taller and died jet black. He was wearing an open-collared shirt with a red silk kerchief tied around his neck, and I swear he had on eye makeup. He was Italy's *primo, numero uno* cookbook author and television personality; that's what he told me the minute we met.

"Tell me," he said standing so close I could smell salami breath, "how do I make my own show on American television." He handed me his six very thin paperback cookbooks and three DVDs, all marked with his name.

Reincarnate yourself as another person, I thought. "I really don't have anything to do with that," I told him. "I'm just a prep cook." He immediately took back his books and DVDs and gave me a look that combined disdain with dismissal. I knew the look; it was a Mrs. Alfano standard.

"*Allora*, then who is in charge? Who is able to put my show on television in the United States?"

Sonya would kill me if I said her name, so I improvised. "No one who is traveling with us can do that, but there is a man in New York who does it all the time. George Davis. Yeah, he's the one. I'll get you his number."

This seemed to satisfy Gino, and he led me into the restaurant kitchen and dropped me off. Gino was not a restaurant chef, and this was not his restaurant. We were borrowing it for the shoot. The meat sauce we'd be featuring, *ragù alla bolognese,* was his recipe, and he'd be the one on television, but beyond that he didn't seem to want any involvement. Fine with me. The restaurant chefs were much more fun.

None of them spoke much English, but I understood enough of their Italian to learn that I was the first female ever to work in their kitchen. They thought it was a riot. They also seemed to think that I was too delicate to lift anything, get close to the stove, or play with knives, so they outdid themselves in helping me. I liked that and was seriously thinking of taking them home with me. We finished prepping and making lunch well ahead of time, then made *cappuccini* and went outside to the patio so we could continue to bond.

When the crew arrived, they found us still on the patio, drinking *cappuccini* and telling Italian jokes.

"Are we ready, Casey?" Sonya asked, stretching out the words so they insinuated that I had gone bonkers and abandoned my job to hang out with Italian macho men who didn't have a good intention among them.

"Absolutely. We also have lunch prepared. Do you want to eat first?"

"We certainly do," said Sally.

"Where's Gino?" Sonya asked.

Jeez. I'd forgotten all about him. "I'm not exactly sure." I turned my head just in time to see him running across the street toward us, waving for the traffic to stop and let him pass. He rushed right up to Sally.

"Signora Woods," he gushed, kissing her hand, "it is so very good to meet finally my American colleague. We have so much in common, do we not?"

Not.

"What would that be?" asked Sally.

"We are the best! *Numero uno.*" He made a fist with his index finger extended and lifted it up in the air above his head as he said it.

"Let's eat," said Sally.

After lunch, it was time to face the inevitable: Gino in front of a camera. John had to ask him three times to stop trying to watch himself in the monitor. They finally moved the monitor, and we were ready to roll.

Sally started. "I am here with Gino Baffoni, who is going to show us how to make an authentic Bolognese sauce. Where do we begin, Gino?"

Gino gave the camera a toothy grin and began. "Here we have some chop-ped meat." He made the word two syllables. "Some chop-ped carrots, some chop-ped celery, some chop-ped . . ."

John turned to me and whispered in my ear, "What's he saying?"

"Chopped," I whispered back.

"Cut, please," said John aloud. Sally had to tell Gino to shush because he was going on to the chop-ped garlic.

"Uh, Gino. Could you say 'chopped' instead?" John asked.

"Chop-ped," said Gino.

"No, *chopped*," John said.

"Chopped-ed" said Gino.

"Uh. Chopped. One word."

"Chop," said Gino, and Sally screamed, "CHOPPED!" right in Gino's face. He took a moment to regain his composure, but he got it right on the next take and finally began to make the Bolognese sauce. The pan on the stove had butter that we had already partially melted, and he poured in some olive oil. Then he stirred in the previously identified chopped vegetables, and after several minutes (which would later be edited out), the vegetables were translucent. When he added the finely chopped beef, Sally told the viewers, "You could also use a very good grade of hamburger." He poured in some milk, let it evaporate, and then added crushed tomatoes, red wine, and broth. "Now you must cook the sauce two, three hours until it is done," he said. The cameras stopped and we swapped the pan for an identical one with a finished sauce. We also poured boiling water and cooked spaghetti into the pot that had been sitting empty on the stove. When the cameras started to roll again, Gino scooped the spaghetti out of the pot and into a pasta bowl, and Sally spooned sauce on top. He sprinkled grated Parmesan over the spaghetti and Sally ate, raved over it, thanked

Gino, and said *arrivederci* to the camera and, more emphatically, to Gino. John called it a wrap and Sally turned to leave, but Gino took her arm.

"Signora Woods. This night I give a special cooking demonstration at Il Teatro. I expect there will be no seats left, but if you would do me the honor to come, I can get you in."

Yeah. But, who'd get her out?

Sonya, Sally, and I met the crew in the hotel lobby at seven that night to go to dinner. While out shooting B-roll, Rocket had discovered a simple, family-style restaurant that he thought we should try.

The restaurant resembled the Costello dining room on a Sunday, times twenty. That's how many long community tables were set in rows the length of the room. Most of them were already occupied with parents and their children, groups of college-age kids, singles reading newspapers, and couples giving each other "the look." The room was alive with happy sounds, delicious smells, and a mandolin player in the corner. It was perfect.

As soon as we sat down, a waitress wished us *Buona sera* and put two carafes of red wine down on the table. That freed up her hands to remove the two loaves of bread from under her arm, and she put those on the table as well. She left and returned a minute later with plates that held cubed mortadella and thin slices of Parma ham. In Italian, she told us there were no menus but we had a choice of pasta: *tagliatelle alla bolognese* or *tortelloni di biete al burro e formaggio*. Everyone looked at me to translate.

"There are only two pasta choices. You can have *tagliatelle*—those are the noodles that Anna Maria made—with a Bolognese sauce. You all know what that is. Chop-ped meat and chop-ped vegetables."

"I'm going to jump over this table and chop-ped your head off," John said.

"Okay. Okay. Or you can have *tortelloni*—think ravioli—filled with Swiss chard and ricotta cheese and served with butter and Parmesan cheese. Okay, *tagliatelles* raise your hands."

I got a count for the waitress and asked in Italian if there were choices for the main course.

"*No, signora,*" she said. "*Il secondo è maiale al latte.*"

"*Molto bene!*" I said with enthusiasm, and she seemed pleased that I was happy with the lone entrée.

"What are we eating?" Rocket asked.

I was familiar with the dish, not from home but from culinary school. "It's a Bolognese specialty, pork loin braised in milk."

"Oh, that does not appeal." John had his nose all scrunched up.

"It sounds like English food. Meat all boiled to death," Rocket said.

"Just wait until you taste it. The meat gets incredibly tender and juicy and the milk reduces down to this delicious, nutty sauce. It is so good." I tried to make the dish sound as delicious as it really was, but they didn't look convinced. Hey, they had no choice.

John turned his attention away from the pork and to today's shoot. "So, Sonya, how'd you find that Gino character?"

"I didn't. We had a local cooking-school teacher lined up, but her mother died last week and she couldn't do it. The research people at the studio came up with his name right before I was leaving, and we had no tapes to watch. What a major piece of work he was!"

"Well, don't get your knickers in a knot over him," Rocket said. "We took mostly close-ups of his hands."

"Hard to believe that such a delicious sauce could be made by such an irritating man," said Sally.

"We ran into a pompous bloke like that at the airport a few months ago," Rocket said. "We were in line for one of the nine-seater planes that fly to Dublin. They were all backed up on account of weather, and when they began to fly again, they took us in order. There was this Bond Street–type guy who insisted that he had to get on the first flight because he had to be in Dublin before noon. Well, we *all* had to be in Dublin before noon. He was mouthing off to the counter clerk, who was losing patience with him. So, when he said to her, 'Do you know who I am? Have you any idea who I am?' she picked up the loudspeaker and said, 'Could I get some help here at the counter? We have a man who doesn't know who he is and would like help in identifying himself.'"

Rocket's story started the crew on a round of telling battle stories and eventually led to jokes that would have made my father blush. It was like having a front-row seat at an uncensored comedy club. Many of the jokes involved the wearing of napkins formed into nun's wimples, little-old-lady babushkas, and nappies, which I figured out were diapers when Rocket ran the napkin through his crotch. The guys in the crew were very naughty and outrageously amusing and they had us in stitches.

Rocket had just finished telling a joke about an old man and his nubile young bride when Sally said, "I have one. The chicken and the egg are in bed. The egg looks grumpy and the chicken is smoking, so the egg says, 'I guess that answers the question of who came first.'" The joke was all the funnier for Sally telling it, and the crew wolf-whistled and clapped for her.

Rocket put his arm around her and said, "So how about it, Sal. You and me have a little slap and tickle later." Sally and my father are the only two people I know who laugh so hard that tears really do roll out of their eyes. Sally's were pouring.

We were still laughing when we got back to the hotel. "I haven't laughed that hard in years," Sally said. "Aren't we lucky to have them with us?"

"They're the best. I just love it. Ouch. Do you have a nail file, Sally? I broke a nail this morning and I keep scratching myself with it." We were just outside her room.

"Sure do. Come on in. We can have a little nightcap."

When Sally opened the door, there was an envelope on the floor. "You've got mail," I said mimicking the AOL mail-call sound.

"See what it is. I'll get the nail file."

I opened the envelope, which had the hotel's logo on it, and scanned the note.

"I am here in the hotel, room 321. Call. George."

Mannaggia.

Chapter 17

What's he doing in my world?
—*Eddy Arnold*

I woke up Monday morning with a strange sense of dread. At first I thought I might have had a bad dream, and I tried to remember what it was. Then I remembered that it was worse than a bad dream: it was a nightmare. Last night, when I had handed the note to Sally, it was as if I'd thrown a bucket of cold water at her. She'd read it and said, "I'll have to call him. I'll see you tomorrow, honey." And that was it. No nightcap. No more laughing. No more Sally. Talk about rotten timing. Today was my birthday, and I wondered if George was someone's sick idea of a present.

I rolled over and looked at the clock. Seven. This was a travel day; we were scheduled to leave for Florence at nine. I knew Sonya was an early riser, so I showered, dressed, packed, and knocked on her door at seven-thirty. As I guessed, she'd already been up for hours.

"Happy Birthday, kiddo," she said, giving me a big hug.

"Thanks," I said. "But it's not going to be so happy. Guess who's here."

"Who . . . oh, damn it, no?"

"Yep." I told her about the note.

"Well, there's nothing we can do about it. I wonder if he expects to ride with us to Florence." Sonya looked as though she was trying to figure something out—probably where the train station was in case George decided to ride with us. "Have you spoken to Sally this morning?" she asked.

"Not yet. I wanted to tell you about George so you wouldn't be surprised. I'm going to her room when I leave here."

"I just don't get it. It's not as though he's such a great agent. I mean, have you ever heard Sally say anything like, 'Wow, did you see that commercial I did? Wasn't it brilliant?' I haven't. Not once." She sat down on the corner of her bed and kind of sank into it. She looked so defeated, and I couldn't make it better by telling her he was only a temporary problem. She took a deep breath and clapped her hands on her thighs. "Well, as Sally says, let's keep our eye on the target. We have a lot of shows to do and we have to keep things moving along in spite of what's going on behind the scenes." She had no idea how much that was. I left Sonya's room before I could break down and tell her that Sally was dealing with a hell of a lot more than lousy commercials.

"Come in. Door's open," Sally called out when I knocked on her door. I wished she wouldn't always leave her door unlocked like that, but she got so many visitors she hated to keep getting up to open it. She was sitting at a room-service table eating breakfast, and she opened up her arms to hug me.

"Happy Birthday. How do you say that in Italian?"

"*Buon compleanno.*"

"*Buon compleanno, mia amica.* You don't look a day older."

Funny. I felt years older than yesterday. "*Mille grazie, mia buon' amica.*"

"Sit down. Do you want to share my breakfast?"

I poured some coffee into a water glass and nibbled on a less-than-satisfying Italian version of a croissant.

"Casey, will you tell Sonya that I won't be traveling to Florence with you today? I'll meet you there tonight. I need to spend the day with George."

"Doing what?"

"I told you he has something I want. He's taking me to get it."

I bowed my head down and ran my hands through my hair. "I want this to all go away, Sally."

"It will, Casey, and I'll be in Florence tonight in time for your party." Sonya and the crew had arranged to take me out for my birthday. They had reserved a small private room at one of Florence's better restaurants, and they all kept telling me it was going to be more than just dinner—"just you wait." Now I thought about George being at the party as well and felt anything but in a party mood.

"This is crazy, don't go with him. Tell him to give you what he has and then fuck off. He'll go off with his rodent tail between his legs." I was beginning to work myself up into an Italian frenzy, but Sally stopped me.

"Casey, if I'm not stewing over this, you shouldn't be. I told you. It will be over soon."

Soon was just too far away.

I MET SONYA IN the lobby just before nine and told her about Sally.

"Well, at least we don't have to spend the next hour or so in a closed car with him. I would have killed him for sure."

"Not if I got to him first." We climbed into the Mercedes and Giuseppe told us that we would now sadly be leaving the region of Emilia-Romagna and going south. I guess anything south of where you live in Italy is considered the land of the *banditi*.

Since Mrs. Alfano's Italian roots were more southern than mine, I could understand the reasoning. Sonya told Giuseppe that we wanted to speak only Italian on the way down. Mine was getting better every day and Sonya was learning a lot of single words, but I think she said that so I'd have to do most of the talking and she could put her head back and contemplate murder options.

When we arrived in Florence, Giuseppe gave us a brief tour around the city before delivering us to the hotel. He explained that although it was no Parma, Firenze was an incredible city. He was right; it was an incredibly beautiful city.

I checked into the hotel and then followed the bellman to my room. My parents had sent me off with birthday money for the trip, and I planned to buy something special with it. Once in the room, the bellman systematically showed me how everything worked.

"This is for the heat and the cool," he said with his hand on the thermostat. "And to open the curtains, you push and pull the stick. *Spinga, tira. Spinga, tira.*" He had hold of a plastic bar attached to the curtain rod and he was repeatedly pushing the curtains back and forth. I expected that next he would show me how to turn on and off the lights and the shower and then how to pick up and put down the phone. I took some euros out of my purse and handed them to him. End of lessons. He told me to enjoy my stay and left.

I quickly slipped on a comfortable pair of clogs and headed out into the city to try to shop my way to a happy birthday. The expensive shops along Via Tornabuoni were tempting, but unless the sales that Signors and Signoras Gucci, Armani, Versace, Prada, and Escada were proclaiming in their windows were ninety percent off, they were out of my range. I walked down a cobblestoned street that ran off Tournabuoni and found tiny shops that sold great items made by Signor Nobody and were affordable by Signorina Costello. Three hours later, I clogged back to the hotel laden down with gifts for myself, as well as some for my family. George was slithering out the hotel door just as I approached it, and I stopped him on the sidewalk. He was wearing what looked like new shoes and had somehow succeeded in finding the only ugly pair in Florence. A long scarf with black fringe and an exposed Ferragamo label was wrapped around his neck. I was having trouble shaking my image of tightening it.

"Hello, George. Is Sally back?" I asked.

He sneered at me, and I wondered which package held the Swiss Army knife I'd bought for my father. "For the moment," he said.

I gritted my teeth and met his snide stare with my own. "And just which moment would that be?"

"The last moments you'll be working with her," he said, smirking, and then scurried away, rodentlike.

"*Vaffanculo!*" I called after him, but he was too far away to hear me. Unfortunately, the woman coming out of the hotel with her little girl was not. She covered the child's ears and gave me a piercing look.

My mother would crucify me if she were here. "*Mi dispiace,*" I apologized, but she ignored me.

I asked for my room key at the front desk, and the clerk said, "Ah, yes, Signorina Costello. There is a message for you." He handed me a hotel envelope, and I recognized Sally's writing. The note said that she was back and for me to call. I spent several minutes calming my anger from my encounter with George, then went to her room instead of calling.

"Door's open. Come in." She was sitting up in bed reading.

It looked as though she had dozed off and was just waking up. She patted the bed, inviting me to sit.

I sat at the foot of the bed. "I got your note."

"Yes. I just wanted you to know that I was back." She looked at the packages I had set down on the floor. "You've been shopping. What did you get?"

"Everything I could afford." I opened the bags and unwrapped several layers of tissue paper to show her my haul. She wanted me to try on the sweater I'd bought, and she inspected the inside of a small leather purse I'd chosen for my mother. As I was rewrapping everything, I told her that I'd run into George outside. "He said you were only back for a moment. Does that mean you didn't get what you wanted?"

"No, it was a wasted trip." There was an edge to her voice, but she still sounded as though she could be discussing something as inane as the items in my shopping bags, although it was costing her a hell of a lot more than my birthday check.

"When *do* you get it?"

"I'm going with him on Saturday. When the shoot is over."

A picture of George sneering at me outside popped into my head. It made my blood boil to think of Sally going anywhere with him. This has gone too far, I thought. I can't sit by quietly while she throws away a life's work on a scumbag like George Davis. I wasn't positive about the connection, but it was a safe bet.

"Sally," I said, moving forward on the bed so I was close enough to put my hand on hers. "I have to tell you something. It's not easy, but well, I know about Peter." I said it very gently, but her eyes shot open and she took a quick, deep breath anyway. I went on: "I accidentally watched the CD when we were in Bologna—the night the hotel left your carry-on in my room. I was looking for something to read and I thought it was a cooking tape."

Her eyes teared up, and I felt like scum. "Upsetting, isn't it? How could I live with someone all those years and not see him for the traitor he was?"

I just didn't know how to respond to that. I handed her a box of tissues and said, "The CD is what George had that you wanted."

"Yes."

"But now you have it. Why is he still around?"

"There are more. George said that man Boris had all their meetings on tape and he was willing to sell them to me for a lot of money. We were supposed to meet him today, but he failed to show up, so we're going to see him on Saturday."

"Where?"

"Yugoslavia."

"*Yugoslavia?* Why Yugoslavia?"

"I don't know. That's where he is."

"Jesus, Sally. How did this all start in the first place?"

"Out of the blue. George approached me about a year ago and said he had something I might want. At first he told me a lot of details about the times Peter was in Russia. You know, he went there often as part of the Russian-American science team. I was surprised that George knew so much about him, but I didn't take it as proof that Peter was doing anything like what he claimed. Then he showed me that CD. The one you saw. It was clear that Peter was negotiating to sell some formulas. He worked in nuclear physics, so I could guess what kind of formulas. George said if I didn't pay, he would take the information to the press." I thought about George appearing on all the talk shows. I could see him on *Morning in America* in his red smoking jacket, and a new wave of nausea hit me.

"How did George know about the tapes in the first place?"
Sally frowned. "You know, I don't know that. I never asked."

"Sally, George is bottom-feeder, a weasel. He'll probably sell the information to the press anyway."

"That's why the contracts. That was my idea. I agreed to pay him huge commissions on all the royalties from all my work. I knew no matter what I'd pay him, he'd always ask for more. So I made a deal that would keep on paying anyway. I wanted him out of my life."

"But Peter is dead, Sally. I know you loved him, but he's gone and you can't do this to yourself to protect someone who's not here."

"I'm not doing it for Peter or for me. It's his sister, Ruth. The dear old thing practically raised Peter after their mother died. She never married so she could be there for him. She's so proud of him, brags constantly about him to everyone. If she knew this it would kill her."

"Jesus, Sally. This is a crime. George has to go to jail. He's not only the dregs of humanity, he's a criminal. Extortion is a crime. You have to put a stop to it. And you probably have a better chance of keeping this quiet by going to the FBI or CIA. I don't know which one handles this stuff. But whatever, I doubt that they would want this to get to the press. You have to let the authorities deal with it."

"If I had found this out when Peter was alive, I would have immediately gone to his superiors to stop it." She fell silent, and I imagined by her expression that she was struggling with the horrible thought of turning her husband in to be jailed or worse. "Peter is dead and can do no more harm. But I want to see the rest of the tapes. To see if he had actually sold anything to that Boris. In that case, I'll go to the authorities."

"And if not? What? You'll just pay George for the rest of your life?"

She lifted her chin and spoke with vengeance. "Ruth is eighty-two and not in great health. The minute she passes on, I plan to turn George in."

"Can I watch?"

She laughed. "I'm sorry that you have to be around him at all, honey."

"Me too. When I passed him outside the hotel, he said that I would be out of the picture soon."

Sally looked away for a minute. When she turned back to me, her voice was stern. "He is trying to include that awful Carol Hanger in the contracts. I've told him I won't go for it."

"Are you sure you can call that shot?"

Her voice became small. "No." She went on, "But I'm doing all I can." She gave me a positive look. "I did tell him he was not welcome this evening at your party." I mustered the best smile I could. You have to be grateful for small favors.

THAT NIGHT, I WORE a dress that Mary had picked out for my trip. I had told her that I wouldn't need anything that dressy, but she'd convinced me otherwise. "You don't know who you'll meet, since you'll be with Sally and American TV. It could be a count or a prince or Marcello from *Under the Tuscan Sun*." As soon as she'd mentioned Marcello, I'd put the dress in my "take it" pile. The pinkish-brown dress was a very thin, satiny silk weave that Mary said was "charmeuse" and I said was the next best thing to foie gras and white truffles. The neckline plunged into a deep V, revealing nothing but suggesting everything. The skirt ended midcalf and would have totally met Nonna's approval were it not for the slit to my thigh.

We all piled into the van, scrunching ourselves so we would fit. Sally had a method for making this work. "Alternate: one person sit forward, the next back, and so on." I was in the forward group, trying to keep Rocket, in the back group, from parting my slit with his knee. I was losing.

When we got to the restaurant, the maître d' said, "There is a problem. There is couple who will not leave the room."

We all looked through the main dining room into a smaller room off to the side and could see two people sitting alone at the sole, large table. The woman had her back to us and was wearing a floppy purple hat over her long, straight black hair. She had a pleated pink chiffon scarf wrapped around her neck in such a way that from the back it looked as though it must be covering her mouth. The man sat to her side with his face visible. He had a mop of blond curls, thick black-rimmed glasses, and an incongruous bushy black mustache.

Rocket asked the maître d' if he had told the couple that the room was reserved for the night. He said he had but that they still refused to leave.

"I'll handle this," Rocket said, and he walked into the room and up to the table. At first, he spoke quietly to the couple; then his voice grew louder and angrier. I glanced into the main part of the restaurant to see if other customers had noticed. If they had, they weren't reacting. I should know by now that loud angry voices are nothing to Italians. I looked back into our room just in time to see the woman raise a hot-pink gloved hand in a rude gesture.

"Maybe I should go in," I told John. "Rocket's Italian is not all that good, and he may have said something other than what he thought he said."

"No, I'll go," John said, walking into the room. Within

seconds, he too was speaking in an angry voice to the couple. I couldn't hear if either the man or woman said anything back, but I could see that she was still making rude gestures.

"Maybe we should just go someplace else," I suggested to Sonya. "This is uncomfortable." Looking around, however, I noticed that I seemed to be the only uncomfortable one. The rest of the crew was chatting quietly, the people in the dining room were scarfing down soup and pasta without so much as a glance our way, and the maître d' was gone.

"I'll take care of it." Sonya stormed into the room in a take-charge manner. If anyone could take a situation in hand, it was Sonya, but before I could express that opinion to anyone else, she too was arguing with the couple. Worse, she'd grabbed hold of the woman's hair and would have pulled her up out of the chair by it had the woman not held herself down by gripping her hat with both hands. "I'm going to find the maître d'," I exclaimed to Sally and the rest of the crew. "This is ridiculous."

"Don't bother, Casey," Sally said. "We'll speak to them. You wait here in case he comes back." And the rest of my group walked into the room, leaving me alone looking in at this mad scene of all my friends yelling at some weird couple who didn't know when to leave but did know a lot of Italian hand swearing. It took about a half a minute for me to realize that I had been had. I began to laugh. As they saw me laugh, they yelled, "Happy Birthday" and the couple at the table stood up, removed hats, wigs, mustache, scarves, and glasses and I was looking at my cousin Mary and Danny O'Shea.

"Oh my God!" I said, rushing into the room. "What are you doing here?"

"We're here to celebrate your big thirtieth birthday," Mary answered, hugging me.

"But how?"

"I planned my trip to Paris so I'd be there when you were in Italy. We've celebrated twenty-nine birthdays together. I wasn't about to miss this one. When Danny said he'd be in Ireland this week, I asked if he was game to fly over."

"I've been wanting to go into Chianti country to taste some new wines and products anyway, so this was perfect." He kissed me on the cheek. "Happy Birthday, Casey."

"This is so great. I can't believe it!" I looked at the rest of the group. "So, you were all in on this?"

"Who do you think wrote and directed the scene?" John said. "Danny and Mary were easy, but the maître d' took some major directing skill."

"I made the—how you say *travestimenti*?" Nicole said.

"Disguises," I translated for her. "I'm blown away. I don't know what to say."

"Don't say. Sit, so we can eat. I have to catch a ten-fifteen plane back to Paris."

Danny sat down next to me, and waiters immediately appeared with platters of antipasti and several bottles of wine, which they left on the table.

The antipasti led to baked pasta with porcini and cream and several bottles of big Tuscan red wine, which led to Tuscan pork roast with garlic and rosemary, and more bottles of an even bigger Tuscan red, which led to salad, then cheese, and a really big Tuscan red. The crew all made toasts and as the wine flowed, the toasts got funnier. John ended his by saying, "And remember: a day without wine is like a day without sunshine."

"And what's a bloody day without sunshine?" Rocket asked, raising his glass.

"Night," said Danny sending us into more fits of laughter.

Between courses, we passed the disguises around the table,

and took several rolls of very funny, potentially incriminating photographs. I figured that the show was picking up the tab for the meal and if they saw the pictures, they would wonder if any one of us were competent to be out on our own.

When Sally put on the pink gloves, black mustache, and yellow curls, Rocket jumped up to get a clearer shot and pulled the tablecloth with him. It sent two glasses of water flying into my lap and Danny's.

"Whoa," Danny said in a falsetto voice. "You got me where the sun don't shine."

"Does charmeuse shrink?" I asked Mary, standing up to wipe the water off my skirt.

"I like it better when you wet the top," Danny said.

"How's that?" Rocket asked, leaning by him to get a closer look at my dress.

"Casey has had a few run-ins with water lately," Danny explained.

Rocket leaned back and said in an exaggerated whisper, "Well, in case you hadn't noticed, mate, there's not much of that top to wet."

"Oh, I noticed," he said, grinning at me. It would have taken a lot more than cold water to dampen our spirits. We were all ready to party, and we did. We laughed our way right through dessert and on to chilled glasses of *limoncello*. I had never had the sweet, thick lemon liqueur, and after one sip I declared that I would never let another liquid cross my lips.

"It's like the absolute perfect lemonade. Not too sweet. Not too tart. No, not lemonade; more like a melted lemon sorbet," I said.

"Be careful," Danny said. "It's lethal. The alcohol content is quite high."

• • •

By the time we dropped Mary at her plane and got back to the hotel, John had curly blond hair, Rocket wore the purple hat and pink chiffon scarf, and a Sally with long black hair had convinced Danny to come to Ravenna with us when he got back from Chianti. It just seemed like the best idea to all of us. John had his arm around Danny and told him he could bunk in with him and they'd show the Brits how to have a good time. Seemed to me the Brits had figured it out fairly well on their own. We agreed that Danny would meet us back here on Thursday so we could travel to Ravenna together.

Danny walked me to my room and I leaned back against the closed door; leaning was easier than walking or standing. He rested his hand on the door next to my head. "You okay?"

"I'm great. I still can't believe you came all this way for my party."

"Why not? You came to mine."

"That was across town. This was across England and France and . . . did you have to cross Spain as well?"

"No. But I would have."

"That's because you're sweet." I slurred it slightly.

With his one hand still on the door and the other by his side, he leaned in toward me and rested his cheek against the side of my head. "Mmm. Casey. Casey. What is it about you that attracts me so?"

"My knife skills?"

I could feel him take a deep breath, and then he leaned back so he could look at me. If he found my comment amusing, he wasn't laughing. He was looking at me in a way easy to recognize, and I took a deep breath of my own. He lifted his hand from his side, slid it around the back of my neck, and drew my face to his. At first, his kiss was light and then it became deep and demanding. I could taste *limoncello* on his tongue and I ran my tongue over it hungrily. He wrapped both arms around me and his kisses became so wanting that they sent a quivering warm sensation to the spot that an hour ago was cold and damp from Rocket's spilled water. Or maybe it was my own wanting of him that was making my nipples tighten and that spot feel warm. My arms were around him and my hands had a life of their own as they caressed his strong, firm back. He felt so unbelievably good that I let myself simply melt into him. I was close enough to feel that his own watered-down body part was reacting, and I slid my hands down to his hips to pull him closer. He moaned softly and ran his hands the length of my body, then stopped and concentrated in the area of the slit.

"Wait," I said breaking from his kiss so I could reach into my bag for the room key. He took the key from me and unlocked the door. I walked to the center of the room and sensed that he wasn't walking with me. I turned to see him leaning with both hands against the doorjamb, looking pained. He wasn't moving into the room, and a Bill Anderson song rudely pushed its way into my head: "Walk Out Backwards (So I'll Think You're Walking In)."

"No, Casey."

"*No what?*"

"Not like this, though Lord knows I want you." I really wished he hadn't brought the Lord into a situation in which I was so willingly eager to sin. "You've had more than a little to drink, love, and if I come in, you might regret it in the morning."

"I won't. I won't. I double-swear I won't."

He reached around the door and put my key on the dresser. "I don't want to take that chance, because if you do regret it, you'll hate me tomorrow. Sleep well. I'll see you Thursday," he said and closed the door.

"I hate you now," I screamed at the closed door.

Chapter 18

An empty bottle, a broken heart, and you're still
on my mind. —*Emmylou Harris*

The next morning there was a note under my
door and a pain in my head so intense it made
it impossible to focus on the words. I needed
coffee and a hot shower. I put the unopened note on the dresser
and called room service. "*Caffè in abbondanza, per favore.
Quattro caffè. Caffè italiano, non caffè americano.*" I had
found that American-style coffee in Italy was little more than
colored water. I needed coffee with substance, but the thimble-
ful the Italians serve was not going to do the trick, so I'd ordered a lot of it, along with dry toast.

"*Subito, signora.*"

"Immediately" meant I had the twenty minutes I needed to
stand in the shower and defog my head. My breakfast was
delivered ten minutes after I stepped out of the water. Still
wrapped in the hotel's terry robe, I sat down with my four
small pots of Italian coffee, dry toast, and the note, which I had
already guessed was from Danny. I opened the envelope and
pulled out the piece of hotel stationery. "Dear Casey. It's not
nice to tell people you hate them. I'll see you Thursday morning

at eight-thirty in front of the hotel. Don't be late. I have your birthday present. Danny."

Well, if he planned to give me what I had wanted last night for my birthday in front of the hotel at eight-thirty in the morning, we'd be arrested.

HALF AN HOUR LATER, I was dressed and in the lobby. Sally arrived next.

"*Buon giorno,*" she said.

"Not so *buon,*" I groaned. "I guess *limoncello* is not exactly just melted sorbet."

"You feel okay?"

"Better now, but I wouldn't have given odds on my survival an hour ago."

Ten minutes later, Sonya came running up, out of breath and apologizing for keeping us waiting, and the three of us got into the Mercedes. I wasn't exactly happy when she said she felt as lousy as I did, but I was glad to know that I wasn't the only one who had misjudged my dinner wine.

Once we were under way, Sonya took a small pile of papers out of her tote and handed them to us. "Michelle, my new assistant, sent me an e-mail with these attached. They're messages that viewers sent after Danny's live show. The response has been utterly overwhelming. Viewers absolutely *loved* him! We haven't had a response like that since your first shows, Sally. They want to see more of him."

"Why that's wonderful," said Sally. "You should grab him for more shows now."

"I've thought about that, and I think I have a great idea. I wanted to run it by you first. Since you're going to be in the studio to do the voice-overs a week from next Monday, how about doing a show together with Danny?"

"Why not?" said Sally. "I think that would be great fun."

"Fantastic. I'll ask him on Thursday when he gets back from Chianti."

"If he says yes," Sally said, "we can go over what we'll do when we're in Ravenna. That's perfect. Did you tell him already about his fan mail?"

"Not yet. He'd left by the time I called his room this morning."

Sally looked at me and raised her eyebrows. She had that glint in her eye. "Unless he slept elsewhere?"

"He didn't," I said.

"Oh?" she said. "Last I saw you two were walking off together."

Sonya looked over the tops of her reading glasses at me. "Do you and Danny have something going on that I don't know about?"

I looked down at the pile of love letters to Danny Everyone's-Vole-But-Mine O'Shea. "Do you mind? I'm pretending to read here."

GIUSEPPE DROVE INTO THE hills north of the city and dropped me off at a restaurant known for its Florentine specialties, particularly its *bistecca alla fiorentina*. The classic dish is not just any steak. The beef is cut from the very large, white Chianina breed of cattle, and the *bistecca* is a two-pound or more T-bone served blood rare. The crew had already taken B-roll of the cattle, Sally was on her way to the *macelleria*, the butcher, to see the beef being cut into steaks, and I was on my way to slaughter.

Chef Mario Ponti, the talent, was about five foot ten, with curly brown hair, a rounded belly, and wandering hands. When they weren't busy with the food they were busy with me. The first time he pinched me I gave a little scream and wagged my finger at him. I probably should have punched him, because he obviously took my reaction as encouragement. The next time he grabbed a whole cheek and squeezed. I pushed his hand away and told him not to do that again.

"*Mama mia.* You American girls are too tight up." I didn't know if he meant my butt or my attitude, but it made no difference. I was going to have to set some rules here. The problem was, I didn't want to make him mad. I've known Italians who'll kick you out of their places for a lot less than rejecting their manhood. He grabbed his crotch—or, as my mother would say, "adjusted himself"—and gave me "the look." "*Ah, che corpo!* " he said, looking the body he was admiring up and down. This guy took flirting to a whole new level, which was freaking me out.

"Mario, you're a nice man," I lied. He adjusted himself again and grinned at me. I continued: "But I'm . . ." I tried to remember the right vegetable from episodes of *The Sopranos.* Not eggplant—that's a black guy; not squash or cucumber—those are dopes; fennel. Yes, fennel. "*Una finocchia!*"

He removed his hand from his crotch, looked me up and down once more, and said, "What a waste!" I guess I had it right. A female fennel is a lesbian.

"Not to my lover," I said.

From that point on it was all business. By the time the others arrived, by putting his hands to their proper use, Mario had a wood fire going in the fireplace for the *bistecca* and had made six pots of *ribollita,* a Tuscan vegetable, bean, and bread soup, in various stages of boiling and reboiling. We set up for the *bistecca* first.

The *bistecca* was not a demonstration but the final scene in the segment on Chianina beef. The segment would open with

B-roll of the cattle with Sally's voice-over describing what they were, then proceed to the butcher showing how to determine if the cut was authentic, and finish with Sally eating one in the restaurant.

Sonya directed the cameras to set up by the fireplace, and the opening shot showed the red-hot wood coals burning under the footed Tuscan grill and the raw steak sitting on a board on the fireplace hearth. "Action," said John. Mario salted the meat, drizzled it with olive oil, and transferred it to the grill. After a few minutes, which would be edited out, he turned the steak and John let a few more disposable minutes pass before directing Mario to transfer the steak to a plate. The meat was so large it completely covered the plate and hung over the sides a bit. After a long close-up of the plate, John said, "Cut" and the cameras set up by the table where Sally was sitting. The next shot was of Mario putting the steak in front of Sally. Sally said a few words about how big and gorgeous it was and then sliced into it. There was a close-up to show how red it was; then Sally took a bite and, once she'd swallowed, said, "Now, that's a steak!" She wished us all a good appetite and John said, "Cut. Nice job."

We threw a couple more steaks on the fire and cut them up for lunch before we went on to Mario and Sally demonstrating the soup. I kept my eyes on his hands to make sure they were on the soup and not Sally's butt.

We stayed in Florence that night and the next morning drove a few hours south to wine country. Today's shoot would take place completely at one location, but what a location. The Fontana al Sole vineyard and winery was set in the rolling hills of Chianti, overlooking miles of the Tuscan landscape. The property was a large fifteenth-century villa that had been restored to an extraordinarily beautiful working estate. As well as producing their own wines, the owners, Carlo Pina and his wife, Michaela, our talent of the day, pressed their own olive oil, made pecorino cheese, produced chestnut honey, grew all their own vegetables, and raised their own chickens and pigs. It was idyllic, or so I thought when Giuseppe dropped me off at the front door.

A uniformed maid answered the bell, and I could hear the ruckus coming from the kitchen in the back of the house. At least, I surmised that it was the kitchen from the sound of dishes breaking against a wall. I hoped that wasn't our set. There was a lot of yelling, and I could hear a female voice say, *"Un sacco di merda."* That's a sack of stuff you step in if you don't watch where you're going.

The maid disappeared, and a few minutes later Carlo appeared. He was a dashing man, in a Marcello-Mastroianni-when-he-was-forty sort of way.

"Come in. Come in. My wife, she is a little upset right now."

"I'm sorry. Did something happen?"

He turned his palms up and assumed a look of exasperation. "She seems to think so but, well, you know how these things are."

Unfortunately, I did know how "these things" were. I figured I'd better find our talent and begin damage control. I asked Carlo to show me the way, but I could have just followed the sobs. They were coming from a shapely blond woman who was sitting at the long wooden kitchen table with her head down on her folded arms. When she heard us come in, she looked up and screamed at Carlo, *"Va via. Sei una montagna di merda."* In less than two minutes, he had gone from a sack to a mountain of the stuff. This was so not looking good.

Carlo left me alone with the sobbing Michaela, who was

about forty and, if you looked past the mascara running down her face and the swollen, red eyes, very pretty. I didn't have a clue where to begin. She was obviously not thinking about making *panzanella,* and we needed a finished one for the opening shot.

"I'm awfully sorry. I guess I've come at a bad time." How observant am I? I was standing in the remains of six place settings of Ginori china, some with food still attached. "Did you remember about the television show today? You know, you're going to show us how to make the Tuscan bread salad, the *panzanella.*"

She stopped sobbing and looked at me. For a moment, I thought the gentle, rational sound of my voice had brought her back to the task at hand. But she'd only been gathering her strength to bring her sobs to a whole new decibel level. Now Sally, Sonya, John, Rocket, the crew, and I all knew that no matter what, "the show must go on," but I wasn't so sure that Michaela grasped the concept. I needed a better point of reference to get her moving. And I had it—my kitchen at home, my mother, my aunts, my cousins, my Nonna—anyone who was having a "situation." Cook and talk. Bitch about men.

I moved around the kitchen and opened closets until I found a broom, then I began to sweep up the mess and start a diatribe about the worthlessness of the male species. She jumped right in, calling them all lying, cheating bastards. This was good. She got a dustpan and held it for me and said Carlo was a pig. I found the stale bread for the salad and said none of them could be trusted. She pulled down a large salad bowl and said Carlo was a snake in the grass. I put the stale bread in a bowl of cold water and said men were all scum. She reached for the olive oil and red wine vinegar and said she should never have married him. I reached into baskets on the counter, took out red onions and garlic, and said we'd all be better off without them. She chopped some tomatoes and basil and said—well, my Italian is a bit limited in this area, but I think she said Carlo had a limp, undersized penis. I sliced the onions and garlic, put them in the salad bowl, and said men were useless. She put the tomatoes and basil in the bowl with the onions and garlic and said she hoped he went to hell with a broken back. I squeezed the water out of the bread, broke it up into the salad bowl, and said men were dickheads. I doubted that she understood "dickheads," but I was running out of insults in English and Italian. She added salt, pepper, oil, and vinegar to the salad, I tossed it, and we vowed together never again to have anything to do with men.

By the time we'd finished preparing the salad, Michaela was no longer sobbing and I was beginning to think we just might make it through the demonstration. I wasn't so sure about the footage we needed of Carlo and Michaela touring the grounds together.

Michaela pulled through for the demonstration, but the tour of the estate was a completely different state of affairs. *Affair* is probably a poor choice of words, considering the circumstances. It was a horror show. There were occasional outbursts, with Michaela trying to kick Carlo in his undersized, limp penis and Carlo telling her to back off. Sally was beginning to look like a boxing-match referee, standing between them and telling Michaela repeatedly to stay on her side. Poor Nicole was constantly repairing Michaela's makeup and telling her, "There. There. It will be fine." When we set up the cameras for shots of the olive oil press, the alleged site of Carlo's alleged sin, Michaela's emotional dam burst anew. Sonya had reached the limit of her patience. *"Basta!"* she yelled at the startled Michaela, using her favorite new Italian word. "Pull yourself together or all of America will think you are a whining, whimpering *stunad*." I'd taught her that word. That did it. We finished the shoot, packed up our gear, and gratefully headed back to Florence.

THAT NIGHT, SALLY, SONYA, and I agreed to have an early, light meal and go to bed at a decent hour. The day's shoot had left us all drained. We stopped at the first restaurant we found and ordered pasta.

"Boy, I didn't think we were going to make it through that disaster this afternoon," Sonya groaned, shaking her head. "I have never seen anyone that emotional."

"You should come to my house more often," I said.

"I thought the husband was a real twerp," Sally remarked emphatically, making me laugh at her choice of words. "I was kind of hoping she'd get him where she was aiming to kick."

Over espresso, Sonya mentioned that we had to work out the travel details for tomorrow's drive to Ravenna. "Rocket and the crew are driving the van there tonight so they can shoot B-roll early tomorrow morning. He wants to get a sunrise on the Adriatic. So we have to take John and Nicole in the Mercedes. That makes it kind of crowded, and I thought you could ride with Danny, Casey."

Oh God. I knew I was going to have to face Danny on Thursday, but I wasn't planning on spending a whole lot of time alone with him. The tables had taken a very ugly turn from him hitting on me to me looking like a desperate, sex-starved predator throwing myself at him. He'd probably think I'd asked—no, begged—to ride with him, and the last thing I wanted to resemble was another woman panting over him. I had planned to collect my birthday present at eight-thirty, thank him politely, and then get in the car with Giuseppe at nine. "Why don't I go with you and Sally in the Mercedes and let John ride with Danny? They were very buddy-buddy the other night and would probably love the time together."

"That won't work because I need the time to talk to John. Now that we're close to the end of shooting, we need to go over editing details."

"Nicole?" I pleaded.

"I know she'd love having Giuseppe to talk to in Italian. She's spent so much of this trip trying to keep up with the crew's English that it would be nice for her not to have to work at talking."

I raised my eyebrows at Sally, hoping she would offer up her spot, but instead she raised her eyebrows back at me. "I think it will be good for you to get to know Danny better." She smiled and added, "If he does more shows, you'll be seeing a lot more of him."

I didn't mention that my attempt to get to know him better the other night had not resulted in my seeing the particular more of him I had anticipated.

Chapter 19

I hope that I don't fall in love with you.
　　　　　　　　　　　　　　—*Tom Waits*

By the time I walked through the front door of the hotel the next morning, I had rehearsed enough lines to put two weeks' worth of a sitcom in the can. I couldn't not mention the other night, but I wasn't sure which way to play it. Maybe an alcohol-induced memory lapse: "What a night! I don't remember a thing after Sally put on the wig. How'd I get home, anyway?" Or I could be brazen: "You have no idea what a good time you missed by closing that door, gorgeous." Penitent and professional: "I apologize for putting you in that position. I acted foolishly. It won't happen again." I hadn't quite decided which way to go when I stepped outside and saw Danny. He was sitting on a bench facing me, and he was not holding a present. That would eliminate "Look, I don't want a present from you. I don't want anything from you." He stood and smiled. "Audrey. Right on time."

"Excuse me?" I stared at him blankly, confusion clouding all my carefully rehearsed lines.

"It's me, Gregory. And for the next several hours"—he took me by the hand and led me to the curb—"this is our Vespa scooter."

"Oh my God! Danny! What's going on?"

"That movie you told me about when we went to McLaughlin's place. Remember?"

"*Roman Holiday,*" I said in a warm, fuzzy tone I had not rehearsed.

"When Mary asked if I'd come over for your birthday, I tried to think of a present but I couldn't come up with anything. Then I remembered what you'd said about touring the city on a Vespa scooter and thought you might like this. It's Florence, not Rome, but I didn't think that was a crucial component."

"Not at all! Oh my God, I wish my mother were here."

"I'm afraid it's just a two-person scooter, love. We can take photos." He nudged the kickstand and righted the scooter, then sat on the seat and stretched his long legs out to either side to keep it upright. "Okay, Audrey. Hop on."

"Wait. I told Sonya we'd meet them in Ravenna by lunchtime." I turned toward the door of the hotel. "I'd better let her know we won't be there."

"She knows. I checked it out with her first. She told me to have you back by tomorrow morning in time for the shoot and mentioned that you should check your e-mail in case there are any scheduling changes."

I beamed at him and slid onto the seat behind him. "I can't believe you've done this," I said.

"I'm curious about something," he said.

"What's that?"

"Was the scooter red in the movie?"

"I don't know. The movie was in black and white, but I bet it was."

"Had to be, and you said the movie was old, so this one's the oldest I could find. A 'sixty-three. Not much torque, but fun to ride." He started the engine. "So where does this holiday begin?"

"Well, first I have to sneak away from the palazzo by climbing out of a third-floor window, running downstairs, and stowing away on a catering truck. Since I'm already out here, we can skip that part."

"Good idea. What's next?"

"I sleep in the street for a while, you find me and take me to your bedroom, I start to undress, and you leave. We've done that scene already." There. I'd mentioned the other night.

He turned his body and grinned at me. "Maybe we need a retake." And that was all that needed saying about the other night. Sometimes ad-libbing is the way to go. "What happens next?" he asked.

"I buy shoes, cut my hair . . ."

"How many times have you seen this movie?"

"You don't want to know. I had to buy a second copy because Mom and I wore the first one out."

"Okay, shoes, hair. Where does the Vespa come in?"

"Now."

"Thank God. I thought we were going to spend the day shopping and primping."

"No. We drink champagne and smoke cigarettes at an outdoor café and then we zip around the city and you show me all the touristy spots in a way a princess never gets to see them."

"That I can do. Let's go. We'll make one stop before the outdoor café."

DANNY OBVIOUSLY KNEW THE city well since he navigated it easily, zigzagging around to avoid the many areas where no vehicle traffic was allowed. We scootered on the outskirts of the city, ascended a hill, and stopped at the Piazza Michelangelo.

"I wanted you to see all of Florence from up here first," he said as we looked down at the rooftops, domes, and towers of the city.

"Wow. It didn't seem so large from down there. It's a lot to take in."

"I'll do my best, but we're only going to get a quick look at most of it and we'll have to walk a lot of it since you can't drive everywhere. But we have the whole day. I figure we should leave here at sundown, turn the Vespa in for a car, and drive to Ravenna tonight. Hop back on. Time for champagne and cigarettes." He drove back down to the city, parked the scooter, and led me to a small café in the Piazza della Repubblica, where he ordered champagne and asked for two straws.

"You're going to drink champagne through a straw?" I asked.

"They're props. Cigarettes. Unless you want the real thing. I can go across the square and get you some."

"No thanks. I'll smoke the straw."

From there we walked to the nearby Piazza del Duomo, where Dante Alighieri was born, and then to the Cathedral of Santa Maria del Fiore, and the green-and-white-marbled baptistry, and the Duomo with its Brunelleschi Dome, which had dominated my view wherever I had been in Florence. He insisted that we climb up the 414 steps to the top of Giotti's Campanile and just as we got there, the tower's bells and bells all over Florence erupted into waves of ringing.

"It's for your birthday," he announced over the din.

I opened my eyes wide. "Are you serious?"

"No. Even I'm not arrogant enough to think you'd believe me." He took my hand and hurried me down the stairs. "Okay, back to the Vespa."

We parked the scooter, walked to the San Lorenzo food market, and tasted our way through as much of the two stories of stalls as we could. Back outside, we walked a bit and then he led me through a narrow side street that opened out onto the Piazza della Signoria, the center of Florentine political life since the fourteenth century. "There's Michelangelo's *David*," I exclaimed, walking ahead to get a closer look.

"Not even close," he replied. "It's a copy. The real one will be our next stop."

When we walked through the hall of the Galleria dell'Accademia and I saw the real *David*, I knew what he meant by "not even close." The real *David* loomed so large over us, and was so breathtakingly magnificent, that I got goose bumps.

"Okay," he said. "A change of scenery." He drove to the other side of the Arno River. "This area is called the Oltrano," he said, and then parked and paid some euros so we could walk through the Pitti Palace and into the manicured Boboli Gardens. My feet hurt and I was glad to sit for a while and take in the plantings, sculptures, fountains, and looming cypress trees.

"God, Florence is such a beautiful city!"

"You're getting a real whirlwind tour, Casey. Florence is a city meant for slow, meandering walks. It would take days to do justice to the museums alone. It's a crime to be here and not go through the Uffizi Gallery, but we just don't have time."

"How do you know Florence so well?"

"My aunt. My mother's sister is an art teacher in Dublin. Four times a year she brings classes here to go to the museums, churches, and all. When we were young, my cousin and I would go with her. At first, we'd try to lose the group and find anything we weren't supposed to. But after a while, I realized she had something interesting to say, so I stayed with her. It didn't take long to fall in love with the city seeing it with her. I come over anytime I can." We sat quietly for a little while, absorbing the magic of the gardens, and then he said, "You ready, Audrey?"

"Anya."

"Hmm?"

"Audrey's name was Princess Anya in the movie."

"So what's mine?"

"Joe."

"You get a name like Princess Anya and I'm just plain old Joe?" I shrugged. "Hey, it's my movie."

"Where to next, Joe?" I asked once we were back on the scooter.

"Lunch. And it's at a plain old Joe place."

The "plain old Joe place" was through a tiny door that opened onto a narrow, stone alley. The only color on the street came from the flowers that cascaded from a window box below a small, iron-grated window. I asked how he'd found such a hidden place and he told me that his aunt always brought her groups there. The family knew Danny well, and when we walked in, Mama saw him right away. *"Daniele! Mio caro."* She beamed, putting her hands on his face just as Nonna does to me. Then she frowned and told him he was too thin. "Don't they have food in America?"

"Not like here, Mama." Danny laughed and introduced me.

Mama took both my hands in hers and scrutinized me. Italian girls are used to being scrutinized by Italian mamas, so I smiled and let her look me over. She tilted her head to the side, squinted, and then asked Danny if I was his girl.

"You bet." He grinned at me.

"*Bellissima!*" she said. "A little thin, but better to be that way before all the *bambini* come. Then you don't get too fat."

I was beginning to squirm. Danny grinned and let me squirm. When Mama finished with my wedding plans, she led us the few feet through the restaurant and out the back door. A small overgrown garden with an overhead pergola of grape vines was set with five small tables. She sat us down at one of them and left, saying she would feed us properly.

"Properly" meant starting with an antipasto of a variety of *crostini* topped with chicken livers, tomatoes, and olive paste accompanied by plate-sized slices of fennel-and-garlic-laced salami. I was eating more than my share of salami and told Danny I had never had one that tasted quite like it.

"It's a local specialty called *finocchiona*. It's made with wild fennel. That's what gives it the subtle flavor."

"Do you want that last piece?" I was trying to be generous.

He laughed. "You take it. But beware. Mama's on a mission."

Mama's mission was *pappardelle al sugo di lepre,* wide pasta noodles with a deep, rich rabbit sauce, followed by *arista,* a boneless pork roast larded with rosemary and garlic and served with *fagioli all'uccelletto,* white beans stewed with sage, garlic, and tomato.

"Why are the beans *uccelletto?*" I asked.

"Because they're cooked in the same way as little birds are," Danny told me.

The pork and little-bird beans were followed by salad and then wedges of local sheep's milk cheese and Mama was back in the kitchen rounding up dessert.

Danny stood up and said, "I'm going to break her heart and tell her we're going to pass on dessert."

"Why would we want to do that?"

"Because we wouldn't have room for gelato and I know the best place not far from here to get it. Surely Joe bought the princess a gelato in the movie?"

"No. She bought one for herself before they hooked up."

"So she wouldn't have to share."

"You got it."

Mama sent us off with hugs, pinches to the cheeks, and a scolding to Danny not to be gone so long and to bring his girl back again.

We walked, with our *gelati* and a crowd of people, back and forth over the Ponte Vecchio, looking in the jewelry-store windows and marveling at the bridge itself, which had miraculously survived World War II. Danny told me it was the only bridge over the Arno that hadn't been destroyed.

"Now we're going to one of the coolest places in Florence."

"Where's that?"

"A pharmacy."

"You're taking the princess to a drugstore?"

"I said a pharmacy. Climb on."

Profumo Farmaceutica di Santa Maria Novella is a pharmacy only in the ancient sense of the word. As soon as I saw and smelled what "pharmacy" it was, I recognized it as the origin of the exquisitely wrapped, handcrafted soaps, colognes, potpourris, and creams I had seen in their shop on New York's Lower East Side. But nothing could compare with seeing them in the frescoed chapel where thirteenth-century Dominican friars had first experimented with elixirs and potions. Centuries-old apothecary jars and bottles sat on the shelves of carved wooden cupboards that swept almost to the top of a high, vaulted ceiling. I walked slowly around the room, taking it all in, as Danny spoke to a smartly dressed salesgirl.

"What an incredible place!" I sighed, walking over to stand beside him. "It's so beautiful."

"Pretty special," he agreed, putting his hand high on my back and turning to the salesperson. "I think mimosa," he told her.

"A very good choice, I think," she said, dabbing a small amount of mimosa eau de cologne on my wrist and then my neck with a delicate applicator.

Danny bent forward so he could smell my neck, then stood back. He drew his eyebrows together and put his hands on his hips. "I definitely think that's you. First, you get this oddly enticing tart kick, then you detect the sweetness. It's a subtle sweetness—not overpowering, but definitely there."

"Hilarious," I said sarcastically and kicked him playfully in the shin.

"Then you get the kick again," he winced, rubbing his leg.

I lifted my wrist to my nose. "Hmm. That's actually pretty nice."

"I don't know if it's in the movie," he said, reaching for his wallet, "but I'd like to buy it for you."

"Well, thanks, Joe." I smiled at him and thought, This is how he does it. Not by the bold flirtation, but by being so damn charming you're ready to follow him anywhere.

I bought several bars of pomegranate hand soap for gifts. The salesgirl explained that the soap was made with aged milk and all-natural ingredients. Much of it was still done by hand and always with great care. She could have been talking about food.

As the sun was beginning to set, Danny said we had time for one more stop. We parked the scooter and walked to the Straw

Market, a bustling semienclosed bazaar under a loggia. He took my hand and led me past tables of cheap leather goods and overpriced touristy trinkets, racks of tangled hanging belts and scarves, and the occasional straw good of the type that had given the market its name.

"So, did we miss any scenes?" he asked while shaking his head no to a vender who was holding up a leather jacket for him to try.

"Well, there was the one in which Anya drove the Vespa."

"I never thought to ask you if you wanted to drive. Have you ever driven a scooter or a motorcycle?"

"No. But neither had she."

"How'd she do?"

"She went out of control, drove through a crowded outdoor café, upturned a fountain, sending a shower of water over them, knocked down an art exhibit, and crashed into a vendor's cart. Then she and Joe got arrested."

"Jeez, Casey. That sounds like the best part. How could you leave that out? What else did we miss?"

"They go to a dance on a boat, and then they get into a wild brawl, she hits a royal plainclothesman over the head with a guitar, and they jump off the boat into the Tiber River."

"You're making this up."

"I'll loan you the videotape. You can see for yourself."

"And in the end they fall in love."

"Well, they fall in love but they can't be together because she has to go back to being a princess and he has to pretend he doesn't know her."

"That ending sucks. Does he at least get to keep the Vespa?"

He had stopped in front of a bronze statue of a boar. The bronze on the animal's body was weathered beyond recognition, but its nose was bright and shiny. "The legend is, if you rub the boar's nose and toss a coin in the water, you will return one day to Florence." He handed me a coin. I looked at him and couldn't bring myself to say what I was thinking. No return trip could ever compare with this one, and I couldn't imagine coming back without him and letting some lackluster visit cloud the joy I felt about the day. "You've made this day very special, Danny. Thank you," I said, toning down the intensity of my feeling. "As Princess Anya said, 'A day I will cherish in memory, as long as I live.' Something like that."

Danny and I both threw our coins, and then he put his finger under my chin. "I think the legend also says that if you kiss the person you are with when you rub the boar's nose, you'll return to Florence with that same person."

"You made that up."

"Yup."

I kissed him anyway. In my family, you don't fool around with legends.

WE ARRIVED AT THE hotel in Ravenna, and while Danny looked for a place to park, I checked myself in and then went to call Sonya and Sally from the house phone. There was no answer in either room; I guessed they were at dinner. I went to the ladies' room, and when I came back out Danny was all checked in and waiting for me. "Do you mind going right out? I'm really hungry."

"Me too. Let's go. Do you have any place in mind?"

"The backyard," he said, leading me out the back door of the hotel. "I don't know Ravenna at all, but I said, 'Seafood, outdoors, near the water' to the desk clerk and he pointed this way."

"What? You didn't ask for a moon as well?" I asked, following him out the door.

The outdoor restaurant was practically in the water in our backyard. We sat at a simple wooden table next to a stone fireplace where the chef, a large man with a deep baritone voice, was tending to several small whole fish on the fire and singing Italian songs about the sad lot of fishermen. A waiter brought an unlabeled bottle of local sparkling white wine to our table and left menus. Danny was watching the chef, and I was watching Danny and wondering when I had let myself go from "Not interested" to "No problem—I've always wanted a fling with a meadow vole." It was Italy. I was letting it cloud my judgment. I should tell him again, now, that I don't want to get involved. Let him know that the other night, it was the *limoncello* talking. Tell him that today was fabulous, but, as I said, I'm not looking for a relationship. I'll offer a good friendship.

He turned to look at me, then gazed up at the full moon in the sky. "I guess you ordered the moon, because I forgot to ask for it." He lowered his head and his amazing blue eyes smiled into mine. "Thanks."

Then I thought about Mary and all the money she had spent on the lacy French underwear she'd brought me for my birthday. I was wearing it, and I knew it would hurt her deeply were I not to take advantage of it. "You're welcome," I said with the best come-hither smile I could manage.

In the corridor outside my room, I stopped, closed my eyes, stood on one foot, and put my finger on my nose.

"What in all creation are you doing?"

"This is the test the police use to determine if you are sober enough to drive or engage in other activities that require a clear mind. I wanted you to see that I am in good condition for the other activities part."

He put his hands on his hips and gave me a shocked look. "Are you hitting on me, Casey Costello?"

"All that Irish charm and you have to ask? I just don't want you to use my wine consumption as an excuse to walk away again."

He slipped his arm around my waist and opened the door. "There isn't enough wine in Italy to make that happen tonight."

When we walked into the room, I saw that his bags were there as well as mine. I had been curious about how he'd planned to handle sleeping arrangements. Now I knew.

"Well, you were very sure of yourself," I said, pointing to his luggage.

"Not *very*. That's why I bought you the perfume."

"I wish I'd known. I would have held out for the body cream as well."

He stepped close to me, and ran his hands under my T-shirt. "If I remember correctly from the slit in your skirt, you don't need body cream."

"Want and need are not the same thing," I mumbled against his neck.

He unhooked my bra and caressed my breasts. "You're dead wrong there," he said, gently stroking my nipples with his thumbs to prove his point. Okay, so there were exceptions, and if he pulled another "No, Casey" exit, I would have no choice but to dismember him.

But there were no *no*s from either of us. Not when he lifted off my T-shirt and slipped off my expensive French bra; not when I unbuttoned his shirt and ran my hands over his chest;

not when he slipped his hand into my pants and I undid his. Not once from the moment he lay me on the bed and his hands wandered over my body the way he had said one should tour Florence, slow and meandering, or when his mouth lingered at the high spots. Every aroused inch of me craved him, and he covered my body with his and gave me what I wanted and needed.

Chapter 20

Didn't expect it to go down this way.

—*KT Oslin*

When I opened my eyes the next morning, the first thing I saw was Danny coming out of the shower, wrapped in a towel. "Good morning, Princess," he said, smiling at me.

"Anya should have been so lucky," I said.

"There are advantages to being a commoner." He walked over to the bed and kissed me. "How much time do we have before we have to leave?"

"A couple of hours. Enough time for breakfast . . ."

"And if we skip breakfast?"

"Enough time for me to take a quick shower and then whatever you have in mind."

I was in and out of the shower and back in the room, wrapped in a terry robe, in no time. He was on the bed, leaning back against the pillows. I snuggled up next to him.

"That was such an incredible day yesterday, Danny. Thank you."

"You're welcome," he said, untying my bathrobe belt and slipping his hand inside. "I thought the night was pretty incredible," he added, leaning over to kiss the top of my breast.

I put my hands on his face, encouraging him to breast center. "I mean, I can't believe you even found the old Vespa."

"I told you. I can do anything," he said doing anything with my other breast.

The anything was sending warm sensations everywhere. I cooed, "You just didn't tell me you could do it so well."

He looked up from anything and grinned at me. Then his expression changed. "Oh, I meant to tell you. When I went in to arrange for the scooter, I saw that friend of yours from the party at Oran Mor."

"Who's that?"

"What's his name? That guy with the red pajama top who was at your table."

"*George Davis!* Believe me, he's no friend."

"No, not Davis. What *is* his name?"

"It's George Davis. The obnoxious, ugly guy in the red pajama top and ascot. He was sitting next to Sally."

"That's who I mean, but the clerk in the rental place called him by a different name. What was it? I should remember. The pajama guy kept complaining and complaining, and the poor clerk was frazzled. There were these long lines of people waiting to be helped and the clerk would look up at them, then back at the guy, and say, I'm so sorry, Signor . . . what was it? Signor . . ." Danny tapped his forehead and then had a eureka moment. "Signor Davinsky. That's it. Davinsky. I can't believe I couldn't remember. The clerk must have said it a hundred times."

My brain began to shuffle information like an electronic mail-sorting machine. It tossed data into different slots, trying to find the one where that name fit. Not there, not there. It took less than a minute for the mail to land in the right box, and when it did, my blood ran cold. I sat up, and I spoke only when my heart had stopped racing and I was sure I could control my voice.

"Are you sure?"

"Yeah. The clerk was holding his passport, and he looked down at it every time he said it."

"But his name is Davis."

"A lot of people shorten their names for business so they're easier to remember." He began to fondle my breast again, obviously finished with any conversation about George. But I wanted to know more.

"Did you speak to him?"

"No. I was going to when I first saw him, but then he was making such an ass out of himself and annoying all the people lined up waiting to get cars that I didn't want to let on I knew him. I turned my back so he wouldn't see me." He began to kiss the places he had been fondling, and it was hard for me to avoid the sensations his touch aroused. But the information he was giving me was arousing concern.

"What was he complaining about?"

"*Everything,* and in two languages. He complained in English that the car wasn't what he'd ordered, then he started mouthing off in Russian that he was going to call the authorities. Then back . . ."

I interrupted him. "You speak Russian?"

"Yeah. I guess I didn't tell you this. My father's brother was one of a group of entrepreneurs who went to Russia after perestroika. He opened a catering business that was going gangbusters and he wanted me to join him in it after culinary school. He asked me to study Russian because he said the Russian lowlife would rob you blind if you didn't understand the language. I worked with him for about a year before going back to Ireland. My Russian got very good, but my food was going to hell."

"What's the Russian lowlife?" Besides George Davis-Davinsky, I was tempted to add.

"Russia has a black market like you wouldn't believe. People steal and sell anything illegal of any market value. There are huge profits being made, and the Russian Mafia is involved in the biggest."

"There's a Russian Mafia?"

"Sure is, and it's every bit as powerful and frightening as the Italian Mafia in the movies."

My cold blood ran even colder. I knew that Sally couldn't possibly know what she was dealing with. "What types of things do they sell?"

"You name it. If it's illegal and there's a market for it, the Mafia will make the deal."

"Weapons?" I asked.

"That's a very big item. Weapons and formulas for making nuclear bombs. Lots of that goes on. There's a guy, Vladimir Chomsky, on trial now for attempting to sell nuclear information to the North Koreans. He hasn't been convicted, but the government has a pretty tight case."

"How do you know all this?"

"It's in the American papers. Small articles, but I notice them because I'm interested. Mostly my uncle keeps me up to date on what's happening. He took a real beating from a Mafia type before he learned how to deal with them."

"How *do* you deal with them?"

"You pay. One way or another." He was slipping the robe off my shoulders and I stood up quickly, leaving him with a handful of terry robe and a questioning look. I had to stop Sally from going off with George tomorrow.

I began to get dressed. "Danny, I just remembered that I made some changes in the recipes for today and I never gave them to Sally or Sonya," I said, improvising. "They have to have them this morning, and I have to take them to them. It shouldn't take long."

He looked puzzled. "Well, I'm disappointed by the sudden change in plans, but I do appreciate the work ethic."

"I'll be back soon." I kissed him.

"This doesn't have anything to do with my not buying you the body cream, does it?"

"No. Honestly." I started to leave.

"Shouldn't you take the recipes with you?" he asked when I started toward the door empty-handed.

"Yes, of course," I said, picking up my tote bag.

SALLY WAS NOT IN her room. I hurried to the dining room. She was not there either, but Sonya was.

"Hey, good morning, Casey," she said, smiling at me. "How was your Roman holiday?"

The one a million years ago? I thought. "It was so incredible!" I tried not to rush the details about the day, but I needed to talk to Sally, so I gave her a brief, enthusiastic description and then said, "Sonya, I was looking for Sally. Have you seen her?"

"She's not back yet."

"Back from where?"

"Her business with George."

My eyes shot open wide. "That's tomorrow, Sonya. Saturday. Sally said Saturday."

"George changed it to yesterday. Sally said they'd be gone overnight."

My heartbeat quickened. I was on the brink of hyperventilating. I took a sip of Sonya's water. "Do you know where she was going with George?" Maybe they weren't going to Yugoslavia to see Boris. Maybe it was something else.

Sonya pursed her lips and then said, "Please. Do we know anything about George?"

More than I'd like to, I thought. "Is she coming here to the hotel when she gets back?"

"No. She's going to meet us in Comacchio."

I wasn't going to Comacchio. The restaurant where I would be prepping was totally in the other direction. "How do you know she'll get there?"

Sonya gave me a matter-of-fact look. "Sally's never missed a deadline or a show. She's never canceled on me. She'll be there."

I tried hard not to show my panic. "I just have this uncomfortable feeling that George will, will . . . I don't know, like not bring her back or something."

She leaned toward me. "Casey. George is an A-number-one asshole, but I doubt that he's a kidnapper."

I let out my breath so I could speak. "Listen. Will you call me at my restaurant and let me know she's there?"

She put down her cup and gave me a puzzled look. "What's up, Casey? Is there something I should know?"

"I just feel weird when she's with him. Humor me, please. Call when she gets there." I said "when," but my head was screaming "if."

"All right. We'll be in Comacchio before you're at the restaurant. I'll call there and let you know."

"Thanks, Sonya."

WHEN I GOT BACK to the room, Danny was sitting at a small desk drinking coffee and looking over a map. He was wearing jeans but no shirt, shoes, or socks. Not only did I hate

George for what he was doing to Sally, I hated him for interfering with what could have been a rather nice morning.

I dropped my tote next to the desk. "Danny, I'm going to need your help."

"No problem. I'm a real pro at backups and swaps now."

I pulled a chair up next to him. "I wish that were what this is about." I knew Sally expected me to keep quiet about it, but I was sure she was in trouble, and right now, he was the only person who might be able to help.

"Whoa," he said when I'd finished. "That does not sound good."

"Did you ever hear the name Davinsky when you were in Russia?"

"No, but my uncle may have. Do you want me to call him?"

"Would you, please?"

He looked at the clock. "Yeah. I should be able to get him now." Danny called while I paced, fretted, and tried hard not to think of Sally in the same thought with cement shoes. After speaking Russian for a few minutes, Danny hung up and said, "He's out for about three hours. I left this number for him to call." I was still pacing and wringing my hands, and he stood me still by placing his hands on my shoulders. "Come here," he said, putting his arms around me. "I'm sure it's going to be fine, Casey. Try to relax."

"I'm afraid that's no longer an option."

"Can you fake it? You're going to have to go to the restaurant and get set up. You can't assume the worst." I knew he was right, but it seemed absurd in light of the fact that, for all I knew, Sally could already be swimming with the fishes. "Why don't you take the car to the restaurant and I'll call you or come there when I hear from my uncle."

"How will you get there?"

"I'll get there. Don't worry about it." He kissed me and then said, "Now go. And let me handle it."

I DIDN'T DO MUCH driving in the United States, and I discovered that Italy was not the ideal place to practice one's skills, or lack thereof. Italians blasted their horns to move me out of their way and then zoomed by me with nasty stares. After just barely escaping being obliterated by an Alfa Romeo, I parked in front of the small seaside Ristorante da Rosa. I took several deep breaths, told myself the show must go on, and walked up to the building. The restaurant structure itself was simple and unremarkable, but the outdoor dining terrace was magical. It was off to the side of the building and framed above by a vine-covered pergola. I could see tiny Christmas-tree lights attached to the deep green vine. Large terra-cotta pots were scattered throughout the space, and they all held white flowering plants with lush, deep green leaves. The tables were covered with starched white linen cloths and all had glass-enclosed candles and small vases with fresh flowers. The view from the terrace was the seductive blue of the Adriatic Sea.

"*È bella, no?*"

I turned and recognized the woman from the tape I'd watched a few weeks ago in Sonya's office. She was wearing the same flowered housedress and frilly apron.

"*Bellissima!* It must be so romantic at night, with the little lights and the moon over the water," I said.

"*Paradiso.* I am Rosa," she said extending her hand. "You are American. Are you the television people?"

"Yes. I'm Casey Costello. I'll be helping you get the food ready."

"Ah, yes. Your producer called and left a message for you. 'Sally is here.'"

I looked up to where God was and said, "Oh, that is so good." Rosa gave me a questioning look. "Just scheduling difficulties," I said to cover.

"But they are fixed. No?"

"Yes."

"Good, then. Come in. We'll have espresso, first, no?"

"Yes. That sounds terrific." I hadn't had time for breakfast, and I could feel my energy level sagging. "Could I use your phone first?"

"*Certo.*"

I called Danny, told him that Sally was back, and asked if he had heard from his uncle.

"Not yet. I'll call as soon as I do."

"You have the number here?"

"You mean the one you wrote on the pad on the desk, the pads on both bedstands, and left on a piece of paper in my pocket?"

"Check the bathroom. I taped it to the mirror."

I could hear the hissing of the espresso machine, and soon Rosa was carrying a tray with two small cups of deep brown espresso and a plate of biscotti that she had made herself. "Sit. Sit," she said, nodding toward a table in the center of the kitchen. It was the same one as in the tape.

Rosa spoke to me a little in Italian and when I answered her in Italian, she seemed pleased that I knew her language. I told her that my Nonna's family was from Naples.

"Ah, then do you know how to make the *brodetto,* the fish soup?"

"Yes. But we call it *zuppa di pesce.*"

"And you add toasted bread, no?"

"That's right. And, of course, our fish are different. We use ocean fish, and most of those are a lot bigger than the Adriatic fish you use."

Rosa put down her coffee, went to the refrigerator, and pulled out several packages wrapped in newspaper. She opened them one by one. Each held a different species of fish, and all looked as though they had been swimming in the sea a few minutes ago. "Look how beautiful they are," she said as she unwrapped each package. Seeing all those whole fish made me realize how much prep there was. We had to get enough of that fish trimmed and ready for a completed fish soup and three backups.

"They are *incredibile*," I said, then stood up. "I think we'd better get started and clean and trim them."

"Not this fish. This is for show. Come, I'll show you what I've done." She led me to the walk-in, where several trays marked *uno, due, tre* and so on were lined up on shelves. She had the entire setup all ready to go, complete with backups.

"That's amazing," I said. "It's perfect."

"*Grazie.* Now, shall we make *piadine* for lunch?"

"Absolutely. I'd love to see how they are made."

"*Buon.* We start with the dough." She took a large crockery bowl off the shelf and put some yeast, warm water, and a couple of tablespoons of flour into it. She stirred it around and said, "Now you let that sit until it is foamy, about five minutes. Do you make pizza dough?"

"Yes."

"This is the same thing. Very easy." When the yeast was foamy, she added flour, olive oil, and salt and handed me a large wooden spoon. "Now you stir it hard until it comes together. Then we knead." She floured the counter and I stirred until the ingredients came together and then turned the dough mass out onto the flour. Rosa divided it in half and we each kneaded a piece until it was smooth. We shaped them into balls, and Rosa covered them with a kitchen towel. "Now we prepare the fillings," she said.

She went into a large pantry and returned with a basket filled with Italian salamis, ham, cheeses, red bell peppers, broccoli rabe, and fresh arugula. Just as Sally had said on the promotion show, "Casey Costello was cooking right in the kitchen with a real Italian," but it was no different from cooking with Mom or Nonna. The ingredients were the same, and Rosa, like my mother and grandmother, used no recipes. She knew her way around her ingredients and seemed pleased that I did as well. I realized that more than the country, more than the language, the food connected me to my heritage. I oiled the peppers and put them in a hot oven to roast. When they were charred, I removed the stems and seeds and cut them into thin stripes. I laid them on a dish and put a little olive oil, salt, and vinegar on them. She peeled the stems of the broccoli rabe then cut it into two-inch pieces before blanching if for a minute and then sautéing it with olive oil, garlic, and hot pepper. I washed the arugula, removed the tough stems, and dried it. We put the fillings on platters. The colors were dynamite.

"Now we make the *piadine*." She lifted the towel and exposed the yeast-inflated balls. She punched them down and gave me one. "Tear it into six pieces," she said as she divided the other one. She handed me a rolling pin. "Now roll, as big as this." She made about an eight-inch circle with her hands. "It should be thin, like this." She picked up an edge of the dough she had just rolled to show me that it was about a quarter of an inch thick. When all the dough was rolled out, she put two griddles on the stove, saying that they must be very hot before we put in the dough. "Now you watch me and do what I do." No problem. I'd been raised on the "watch me and do what I do" method of teaching cooking. She dipped her hand in a small bowl of water and flicked it at the griddle. I did the same. The water immediately sizzled and fizzled into air. "The pan is hot enough," she said.

She pricked one of the dough circles with the tines of a fork and put it on the hot griddle, and then I did what she did. After a few minutes she turned it over, cooked it a few more minutes, then removed it and brushed it with olive oil. I removed and brushed mine with oil. "Now you put the filling you want on top and fold it over, like this," she instructed, putting some salami and cheese on hers and folding it. I put broccoli rabe on mine, folded it, and bit into heaven.

"Save a bite for me, will you?"

I looked up and saw Danny. He was smiling, and I figured that people don't smile if the world is coming to an end. Maybe I had overreacted to everything. I introduced him to Rosa and he sat at the table and ate two *piadine* before telling Rosa he needed to talk to me. We went outside and walked as he told me what his uncle knew. "He's heard of Boris Davinsky. He was a small player, an outsider really, in the Russian Mafia, but supposedly he was the one who made the contact with an American who was willing to sell nuclear secrets. He didn't know the American's name, but I guess it could be Sally's husband." Danny made the American's identity seem uncertain, probably because he had witnessed how upsetting it had been for me to tell him about Peter on the CD. "Boris was just a go-between, and when the American disappeared, Boris lost his only contact and his value to the Mafia. The Mafia thinks he turned Vladimir Chomsky in to the authorities and then agreed to be a witness against him and the mob. Then he disappeared.

He probably panicked. The government is looking for him so he can testify at the trial. The Mafia is looking hard for him to make sure he doesn't. I'm guessing that he's bleeding Sally to get enough money to go into long, permanent hiding."

"What about George?"

"My uncle never heard of him. He said that Boris didn't have a son. He has a daughter, but she lives somewhere in the U.S. George could be related, but I don't know how."

"Do you think the Mafia knows about George?"

Danny stopped walking for a minute and looked at me. "I know what you're thinking, Casey. If the Mafia knows about George, and uses him to find Boris, are they going to stumble on Sally as well?"

I shook my head yes. "Is Sally in danger?"

He put his hands on my arms. "She could be, Casey. It would be good if you could convince her to speak to the authorities in the United States."

"What about here? Is she in danger here?"

"We shouldn't let her be alone."

"Is that what your uncle said?"

"Yes."

"I have to tell Sally right away, and then I'll tie her up and carry her to the authorities if she won't listen to me."

"I'll help, but don't do anything until you finish this afternoon's shoot."

"No, you're right. I'll wait."

Waiting was not easy on my nerves. When the crew arrived, we fed them *piadine*. I watched Sally carefully for any signs that she might have had to fight off a mad mob of Russian thugs, but she seemed to be in good spirits. I did notice that she ate only half a *piadina;* a waning appetite is never a good sign.

If anything was bothering her, the camera would never see

it. Sally and Rosa were delightful together. From the first *buona sera*, they were like young girls sharing confidences. The cameras captured two good friends chatting, enjoying each other's company, and making *brodetto*. When we cut to swap a finished soup for the one they had assembled, they continued to talk to each other as though they were in the room alone. The cameras rolled again and Rosa ladled some of the soup into a bowl. She picked up two spoons, handed Sally one, and told her to *mangia*. They each ate a spoonful and then looked at each other, pressed their index fingers into their cheeks, and said, *"Squisito!"*

When John said, "That's a wrap," it hit me that it was a total wrap. We were finished, and after spending all this time together, it was hard to think of saying good-bye. Rosa invited us to stay for a while and enjoy the view from the terrace. It was dusk and she put on the tiny vine lights and opened several bottles of prosecco. We stayed long enough to eat the *brodetto* and see the moon come up and for me finally to teach everyone to dance the tarantella.

It was late when Danny and I drove Sally back to the hotel. "Don't discuss it tonight," he said while we were walking alone to get the car. "Wait until morning, when you can sit down with her fresh. Tell her you want to have breakfast with her in her room first thing in the morning, but don't alarm her now." I agreed, but when we walked Sally to her room, I couldn't help but tell her to be sure and lock her door, and I waited to hear the safety catch fall into place.

As soon as Danny opened the door to our room, I headed into the shower and scrubbed away the smell of fish, wishing I could scrub away the smell of George Davis as easily. Ten minutes later, dressed only in a few dabs of Santa Novella mimosa eau de cologne, I slipped into bed next to Danny. He wasn't even wearing the mimosa.

"Mmm. You smell so good," he said tickling my neck with his nose and then moving his head lower to see where else I was mimosa-dabbed. He found the spot between my breasts, kissed it, and asked, "Are you too tired? It's been quite a day."

I ran my hand through his hair. "Not at all," I said and fell asleep.

Chapter 21

I stepped from eggshells to pins and needles, from burning
coals to shards of glass. —*Nathan Moore*

I arrived at Sally's room at seven the next morning.
She already had a room-service breakfast for two
set up and was sitting at the table studying a packet
of papers that appeared to have come out of an open express-
mail envelope that was on the floor.

"What's that, Sally?"

She grimaced. "These are the new publishing and television
contracts." She looked up at me apologetically. "It's the new
network. I had no choice."

I put my hand on top of them. "*Don't* sign them," I said.

She pushed my hand away. "Casey, I don't like this any more
than you do. I'm doing what I have to do."

I raised my voice. "Sally. Shut up and listen to me."

She must have noted the determined look on my face and
sound in my voice, because she opened her mouth and then
closed it again. When she closed it, I sat down across from her
and took a deep breath. "Please just hear me out. The man in
the tape, Boris Davinsky, is a Russian mafioso. He ratted out
a Mafia bigwig by the name of Vladimir Chomsky, who is in

jail waiting to go to trial. Then Boris disappeared. The Mafia is looking everywhere for him, and my guess would be that they don't plan to chat with him when they find him. The Russian government is looking for him because he is supposed to testify at Vladimir's trial."

"My God," she said in a small voice. "I never thought about anything dangerous like the Mafia."

"That's only half the danger, Sally." I sighed the next word. "George. His name is not Davis; it's Davinsky, as in Boris Davinsky." She gasped. "If I could find that out, so can the Mafia; so can the Russians, and they'll go through George to find Boris—and they could find you in the middle. If the Mafia finds you, they won't ask any questions to see if you are just an innocent bystander. They won't care. If the Russian government finds you, it's probably Siberia."

I saw an expression in her eyes that I had never seen there before—raw fear. "How do you know all this?" she asked.

"Danny."

"You told Danny?"

"Actually, he told me." I told her about the incident in the car rental place and about Danny and his uncle in Russia. "I didn't say anything to Danny at first, but when I tried to warn you, you had gone off with George. I knew you were in over your head, and I was in a panic."

She reached over and squeezed my hand. "You must have been. You did the right thing. What else did Danny say? Should we get him in here to talk about this?"

I'd been hoping she'd want to talk to him, and I quickly called the room and asked him to come in. The first thing he did was put his arms around Sally and tell her not to fret about what she'd done, that innocent people in Russia often got caught up in this type of mess. Then he sat down and said that we needed to discuss the immediate situation and how to deal with it.

"I called my uncle this morning, and so far there is no word about Davinsky being murdered or picked up, so that means everyone is still looking for him. Tell me, did George cross the border with you to see Boris?"

"No. He took me to the border and I went alone to a seedy hotel nearby and met Boris. I crossed back over early the next morning and met up again with George."

"That's good. George probably knew that his name would send up red flags if he crossed the border. That's why Boris wouldn't leave Yugoslavia. Neither of them probably dared even to try to get false passports with so many people looking for Boris."

"So that means no one would know that Sally was with Boris?" It was more a prayer than a question.

"Most likely not," Danny said. I frowned, because I didn't want a "most likely." I was looking for a "definitely not." Then something else crossed my mind, and I turned to Sally. "Did you see the tapes?" I asked.

She first looked at Danny, as though apologizing for Peter. "Yes. And it seemed clear that nothing had changed hands and I agreed to pay money and sign the contracts."

"I'm afraid you're dealing with someone bigger than you bargained for, Sally," Danny said. "You're going to have to go to the authorities."

She bent her head. "I know. You're right. I should have done that in the first place, but I thought I could just pay for the tapes and be done with this. It never crossed my mind that this man was involved in anything like a Mafia."

"I'm sure it didn't," Danny said. "I think it would be best to speak to the authorities in the United States. I just feel you would be safer there. When are you supposed to see George again?"

"He's coming for the contracts at noon."

"You should be gone when he does. You should get back to America as soon as possible."

"Do you know anyone in the FBI or CIA?" I asked.

She answered right away. "Yes. Our good friend John Long is FBI. He knew Peter from college." She grimaced and looked out the window. "I hate for him to learn about this."

"He can't feel any worse than you do, Sally. And perhaps he can help."

She nodded, and Danny asked me when we were scheduled to leave Ravenna.

"Giuseppe is supposed to pick us up at four o'clock and drive us to Milan. Our plane leaves tomorrow morning."

"Go online, Casey, and see if there are any flights out tonight," Danny said.

I turned on Sally's laptop and logged on. "The last flight for Washington leaves Milan at three-thirty."

Danny looked at his watch. "We can make it. I'll drive you. Any seats available?"

I checked for an available seat, then changed my mind and asked for two. I couldn't let Sally travel alone. If she did get kidnapped, at least I'd know about it and could get help or— I gulped—be taken with her. "Done," I said.

"Pack up, Sally," Danny said.

"I'll tell Sonya we're leaving," I said.

"What are you going to tell her?" Sally asked.

"That there's a risotto Milanese waiting for us and we don't want to miss it. Pack!"

We were in the lobby twenty minutes later. Sonya didn't question our early departure. She was working with John and buried in details. "And, Sonya," I added, "I've decided to go to Washington with Sally for a few days, so I won't be flying back to New York with you."

"That will be nice," she said distracted by whatever she was working on.

"What an unbelievable start of a day," I said to Danny in the lobby once we had checked out and were waiting for Sally to do the same.

"Looks like his was worse," he said, cocking his head toward a man sitting nearby reading a newspaper. I looked over and then back at Danny. "What?" I asked.

"Look at his feet."

I looked and saw that he was wearing one blue sock and one brown. I laughed. "I never know how people can do that. Don't they look at their feet when they put their socks on?"

The man's face was hidden by the newspaper. Danny said, "Maybe he wears thick glasses and didn't have them on when he dressed." He reached up and touched my hair. "Or maybe he had a beautiful woman in his room and couldn't take his eyes off her as she dressed."

I smiled. "That makes more sense." I raised my eyebrows. "Then why do yours match?"

"I only have white ones."

DANNY DROVE LIKE A maniac, meaning like the Italians, all the way to Milan. Incredibly, along the way he and Sally discussed what they would make on the show they were scheduled to do together. Sonya was right about Sally; no matter what she was going through, she took care of her work. I, on the other hand, was busy looking out all the windows for Mafia.

Sally and Danny decided on Baked Alaska. It could be assembled in the allotted time, was impressive to see, and allowed Sally to use her blowtorch. Danny agreed to follow the recipe in Sally's book, so we just had to work out what parts of it we should show.

"How do you beat your meringue, Danny, by machine or by hand?" Sally was always interested in other chefs' methods.

"Sweetie makes the desserts for the restaurant, so it's been a while since I've done it. But I've always preferred a copper bowl and balloon whisk."

"Me too. But maybe for the show we should use a standing mixer, because more people will have that."

"That works for me."

"What test do you use to see if they're ready?" Sally asked.

"The egg."

"Good. Me too." Meringue recipes usually say to beat the whites until they are stiff but not dry, but a lot of people don't know what that looks like, and it is easy to overbeat them. If you sit an egg, in its shell, on the meringue and it sinks in more than a couple of inches, the whites are not ready. If it doesn't sink at all, they are overbeaten and you should beat in another raw white to compensate.

Sally turned around to look at me. "Are you taking notes, Casey?" I was so busy keeping Mafia watch that I hadn't written anything down, and I would need it for the scripts.

"I'm starting now," I said, looking for my tote. Then I remembered that I had packed it in the trunk. "My tote's in the trunk."

"There's a pad in my backpack on the floor," Danny said, accelerating to pass three slower-moving cars; they were only doing ninety.

I unzipped his backpack and stretched the top open to look for the pad. It was clearly visible, right under the photo of Kim the greeter, greeting me from the beach, in a barely there bikini. I glanced up to see if Danny was looking in the mirror before turning the photo over. It was one of those make-your-own-postcard photos, and on the back she had written, "Wish you were here" followed by several *X*'s and *O*'s. Just in case that wasn't tacky enough, she'd planted a lipstick kiss in a totally hideous, cotton-candy shade of pink over the address. I could feel the heat of anger rising and bit my lip to stop the stream of Italian expletives begging to be released. Well, what had I expected? I knew what he was like. We had been together in completely unreal circumstances and I had had him all to myself. That would not be the case back in the real world. I would have to share, and I'm not a sharing kind of person. I decided to say nothing and slipped the photo back into the backpack before taking out the pad.

"Did you find the pad?" Danny asked without turning around.

"Got it," I said.

At the airport, Danny talked the young woman at the security gate into letting him take his dear old mother, Sally, to the gate. The guard actually began to bat her eyelashes. As I went through the gate, she was telling the monitor checker that *she'd* like to be his dear old mother.

When the plane was ready for boarding, Danny held me back while Sally went ahead. He took out a business card and asked me for a pen. "Here's my home number in Ireland. Call me. Anytime for anything. I fly from there to New York tomorrow night. Let me know you're okay."

"I will."

"And you'll make sure Sally calls her friend in the FBI right away?"

"Done."

He put his arms around me and pulled me close. "And you'll make sure you won't get on that plane and decide to downgrade me to 'nice' again?"

I kept my tone light. "You are nice." He tipped his head back and squinted at me. I continued, "And sweet and thoughtful. And helpful—"

"Stop! I sound like the Easter Bunny." He played with my hair. "You know, our schedules in New York will make it hard to find time to be together."

So that's how he plans to deal with it. Scheduling. I wondered which part of which day he planned to give me. I stepped back from him and said, "Look, Danny, I've had a great time with you. It was a blast. But I'm not thinking about going out with you in New York."

The frown he gave me made me wish I were facing a Mafia hit man instead. "And just what does that mean?" he asked.

I gave him a peck on the cheek, a cursory hug, and said, "Danny. It was great, but I have to run. The plane's finished boarding." And I started toward the runway.

"Wait a minute, Cascy."

"I have to go," I called over my shoulder. "I'll phone you from Washington."

Boy, I'd handled that well, I thought, and then concentrated on the more immediate issue: getting Sally home safely.

ONCE THE PLANE WAS in the air, Sally and I both fell sound asleep. For the first time that day, I felt safe. We were out of harm's way, and I slept soundly for two hours. When I woke up, Sally was still sleeping and I carefully climbed over her to go to the restroom. On my way back to my seat, I saw him. He was sitting in an aisle seat with his legs partially in the aisle. His socks were blue and brown. He was asleep with his hat pulled down over his eyes so I couldn't see much of his face, but he was young. Hit men are always young. I tried to remember the shoes, the pants; they seemed the same. I asked myself, what were the chances that two different men wearing mismatched blue and brown socks would be in our hotel in Ravenna and then on our plane to Washington? None. Sally was being followed. Correction: *we* were being followed.

I returned to my seat with my heart racing and not a clue about what to do. It was a long time before I could think beyond being hacked up and delivered to my parents in a trash bag. Okay, I told myself. Take it slow. Think it through. I figured he couldn't be armed on the plane, and if his goal was to get Sally, he'd wait until she left the airport. If Sally called the FBI from the airport, maybe they'd send someone to get us and we wouldn't have to leave the terminal alone. But what if they wouldn't send someone? Plan F, as in we're fucked. I decided not to tell Sally about the blue-and-brown-socked man but to convince her somehow to call her friend in the FBI from the airport. I stayed awake for the rest of the flight, enjoying the only comforting thought I had: George Davis getting to the hotel and finding Sally gone.

WHEN WE LANDED, JUST before six P.M., I tried to keep my eye on the two-socked man but lost him in the crowd. I had never gotten a really good look at his face and the floor was a sea of indistinguishable feet. I stayed close to Sally, and as soon as we cleared customs, I stopped her.

"Sally, call your friend John from here."

"I think we can wait until we get home."

"I'm not moving from this airport, Sally. Please call him."

"This is foolish, Casey. Let's go."

I sat down on the floor. "I'm not moving."

She tapped me with her size eleven foot. "Well, at least move out of the line of traffic. I'll call."

It took Sally a while to connect with John and when she finally did, she told him in an unsteady voice that she had learned some upsetting news about Peter and would like to talk to him about it. She listened a moment and then hung up the phone.

"He told me to wait here. He's coming to get us. He said he'd call when he's at the airport."

Twenty minutes later, Sally's cell rang and John met us at the exit door. He greeted Sally warmly, loaded our luggage into the trunk, and helped us into the back seat. I leaned back and sighed with relief. John slipped into the driver's seat and fastened his seatbelt—and then *he* got in. The man with two different socks. John started to drive, and I reached for the door. I knew I couldn't pull Sally out with me, but I could scream. There were plenty of people around to hear. If the car sped off, I could get the plate number and call the police. The door was locked from the inside. Oh God! Oh God! It would be the trash bag for us. I reached for my cell phone. But who would I call? Could 911 trace a moving car? Could I get out "We've been kidnapped from the airport by a make-believe FBI agent and a man with a blue and a brown sock" before they got out the hacksaws? "*Stop!*" I screamed. "*I have to pee!*" I was pretty sure I just had, in my pants.

John slammed on the brakes and turned to look at me. "Okay. But I'm going to have to send Agent Roark with you."

"Who?"

The man with two different socks turned around, and John introduced him. "This is Tom Roark, with the CIA. He's been following you since Ravenna."

"But how did he know to do that?" Sally asked.

"Let's wait until we get you home, Sally. We have lots to talk about. Meanwhile, let's find a bathroom for Casey."

"It went away," I said, having no desire whatsoever to get out of the car with or without Agent Roark's protection. "By the way, do you have another pair of socks like that at home, Agent Roark?"

He looked down at his feet. "Shit. I did it again."

Chapter 22

Ready for the times to get better.
— *Crystal Gayle*

Forty minutes later, we pulled up in front of Sally's house and she let us in. Sally lives in a quintessential Georgetown row house tucked away on a cul-de-sac just a block and a half from the stores and restaurants on Wisconsin Avenue. The three-story brick house had been Peter's before they married, and together they had renovated it into pure charm. The first floor had an entranceway, a den, and a guest bedroom that I would occupy for the next few days. It was the second floor that blew me away. There was a huge kitchen with a dining table that would seat twenty in a pinch. Sally and Peter had knocked down the wall between the kitchen and the dining room to make it that big. They said they had no need for a formal dining room; if you ate there, you hung out in the kitchen and either helped cook or enjoyed watching the show. At one end of the kitchen, French doors led to a small balcony overlooking the garden, and in the garden was a giant magnolia tree with branches that you could touch from the balcony. It was breathtaking to sit at the table and look out at that tree, especially when it was in bloom. The four of us sat there now, and it was hard to remember what it had been like to sit there and feel cozy and comfortable instead of panicked.

John asked Sally to start at the beginning and tell them what was going on. When she had finished explaining about Peter selling information to some guy named Boris, about George blackmailing her, about the tapes, and about the trip to Yugoslavia, she was visibly spent.

John turned to Agent Roark and said, "Tom?" Tom nodded, and John stood up and went over to Sally. He put his arm around her and said, "Sally, Peter was not a traitor. Not by a long shot. He was working for us."

"But I saw the tapes of him offering to sell some type of formula."

"That was part of the work he was doing. Undercover work. Let me try to clear things up for you." He sat back down and then turned to Agent Roark. "Tom, give me the photo of Davinsky." Tom removed a photo from the file he was holding and handed it to John. He showed it to Sally and asked if that was the man in Yugoslavia.

She said it looked like him but that he'd had a beard, glasses, and his hair had been darker. Tom handed John another photo, and John held it out for Sally to look at. "Is this him?"

"Yes. That's him. A hideously awful, awful—sleazeball." I guess John hadn't ever heard her use that expression, because he laughed. "You're right about that," he said. "We've known for a long time that there was an active black market in weapons operating out of Russia. We've been working with the Russians for some time to uncover it, but got nowhere until Peter came across Boris. But Boris was small potatoes and Peter was working him to try to get to the leaders."

"All those trips to Russia weren't for scientific meetings,

Mrs. Woods," Agent Roark added. "Peter was doing some very important, dangerous work for his country."

John continued. "Peter had just uncovered Vladimir Chomsky when, sadly for all of us, he died. The Russians picked Chomsky and Davinsky up and Boris agreed to testify against him in exchange for a lighter sentencing. Against our strong objections, the Russians let Davinsky out of jail until the trial, and he disappeared. He knew he was a dead man if the Mafia found him. We've been looking for him, the Russians have been looking for him, and several Mafia members are out to kill him. Thanks to you, we and the Russians learned that he was hiding in Yugoslavia and now have him under constant surveillance."

"I don't understand. How did Sally lead you to him?" I asked.

Tom answered. "When Sally crossed the border into Yugoslavia, the information on her passport was automatically sent to Washington headquarters with the fact that she was traveling to a former Soviet bloc country. That's standard procedure for anyone related to or associated with a person involved in an investigation, and Peter's name is still on the file." He turned to Sally. "I picked you up when you checked into the hotel and have been following you ever since. At first, it was just standard procedure, but when I discovered that you were meeting with Davinsky, the department went into red alert."

John took over. "Until you called me, Sally, we had no idea why you were there. We followed you and wired your house the same day. You know, we didn't know for sure that you weren't trying to sell him information that you might have learned from Peter. That's why we didn't immediately pick Boris up. If you were dealing with him, we wanted Boris's contacts."

"Oh, be real, John!" Sally said, putting her hands on her hips. "Me, a spy?"

He laughed at her. "Stranger things have happened."

"How does George Davinsky fit into this?" I asked.

It was Tom who responded. "We didn't know anything about him until he picked Sally up on the other side of the border. I got his name form the rental place and called it in to John. We're guessing he's a nephew. We're tailing him as we speak." He opened his file folder and held up another photo. "Does she look familiar?"

The hair was different and she wasn't as fat, but I recognized her and practically screamed, "That's Carol Hanger! What does she have to do with it?"

"Olga Davinsky. Boris's daughter." I remembered that Sully had thought that she and George looked alike. No wonder. They were probably cousins, and both lowlifes. "Boris sent her and her mother to live here when Olga was a child, so she was raised here, but she visited her father a few times every year. When Boris disappeared, she did too. We haven't seen her since."

I knew she was one of the bad guys. Just like my father said, you can't trust a woman with a bad hairdo. "I know where to find her," I said. "She has pink hair now."

John leaned forward and put his hand on Sally's. "You have been a great help in coming forward with this, Sally."

"Why didn't Peter tell me what he was doing? I wouldn't have told anyone."

"It's just not allowed, Mrs. Woods," Tom said. "You never know if couples are going to get divorced and one of them will decide to blow the cover for revenge."

"Did you know he was an agent, John?"

"Yes. Peter and I applied to the CIA together after college. I stayed in for a couple of years and then applied to the FBI."

"So Peter was already in the CIA when I met him."

"He was," said John. "He was one of their most effective agents."

Sally was quiet. I can only imagine all she was trying to digest. "What happens now?" I asked.

"Now that we know why you met with Boris, Sally, we'll pick him up. That will eliminate any of your worries about the Mafia."

"What about George?" I asked, relishing the thought of him being carted away in handcuffs.

"We'll stay on his tail for a while to locate Olga and determine if she's involved. My guess is she is, but we need some solid proof. With what Sally has told us, the FBI has enough evidence to convict George of extortion. He'll go away for a very long time."

I thought about George behind bars and couldn't help myself from singing out loud: "I've Been a Long Time Leaving (but I'll Be a Long Time Gone)."

"Gene Autry?" Sally turned to me and asked.

"Waylon Jennings," responded John, and I smiled at him.

He sat back and said, "I'm curious how Boris tied Sally to Peter. Peter always traveled under an alias. I'm hoping one of them will tell us. Meanwhile, I have to ask you both to tell no one until we've picked up George and Olga. We're guessing that once George finds out that Boris has been arrested, he'll return to the States and make contact with Olga."

Tom added, "If he calls you, Mrs. Woods, continue to deal with him. Tell him you left Italy early because of a relative's illness or death. We'll be watching your house and your phones are wired, so we'll know if he contacts you, and we won't let this drag on. My guess is we'll know all we need to know in a few days."

Tom looked down at the notes he had taken while Sally was telling her story. "Tell me about this Danny who filled you in on the Mafia connection."

I assumed he wasn't looking for the bedroom information, so I wouldn't be held accountable for holding back the personal stuff. I told him who Danny was and how he'd gotten involved.

Tom clicked open his pen. "I'll need his name, address, and phone number. You can let him know you're safe but you cannot tell him or anyone else what we have discussed. Not anyone. Do you understand?"

No problem. Who'd believe it anyway?

I DECIDED TO STAY with Sally at least until Tuesday. I had a live show Wednesday morning and would have to be back for it. I called my parents Sunday morning to tell them. I knew they were disappointed, since they were expecting me to be at Sunday dinner and tell everyone about Italy. Then I called Mae to ask her if she could handle the prep alone on Tuesday. She said she was cool with that and I told her that Sally and Danny would be doing a show together next Monday.

"That is so totally cool," she said. "Everyone I know who saw Danny on the show thought he was so hot."

"His show's been getting a ton of mail."

"I bet he and Sally will be great together. What are they going to make?"

"Baked Alaska. The recipe from Sally's book. I'll get the script to you in the next few days."

"Awesome," she said, and I hung up and called Sonya's office. I left a message saying that I was taking Monday and Tuesday off. If she had a problem with that, it would dissolve when she found out that Sally would be renewing her contract.

Now I had to let Danny know we were safe. By the time John and Tom had left last night, it was after midnight and Sally and I had simply crashed with exhaustion. I decided to ask Sally to make the call, and she was pleased to do it. I gave her his number and when she got him on the phone, she told him that we were safe and then told him how grateful she was for all he had done. They talked a little about Baked Alaska and then she handed the phone to me. "He wants to talk to you."

"You must be relieved that it's over," he said.

"Definitely! I mean there's still *some* unsettled business."

"There sure is. What was that all about when you left me at the airport?"

"I meant unsettled business with George."

"But as long as we're on the topic of our unsettled business—"

"We're not. Besides, I think our business is pretty much settled. I had a great time—"

"You said that already in Milan. And I believe you. What I don't believe is your sudden change in attitude. Is this all about that bloody vole thing?" He was almost yelling at me.

"Look, Danny. I can't really talk now. In fact, the phone lines are tapped and this is not even a private conversation." I didn't know if anyone was actually listening in, but it seemed like a good way to end a call I did not want to continue.

He was quiet for a minute and then in an even, cold tone said, "Let me know if there's anything I can do for Sally. I'll see you next Monday at the shoot. E-mail me the scripts. I think you have that address." He hung up before I could say goodbye. Sally was looking at me over the top of her glasses.

"Don't ask" was all I said, and she didn't.

• • •

MONDAY AFTERNOON WE HEARD the doorbell. It was John. When we opened the door, he said, "It's over" and stepped inside.

He accepted our offer of coffee and sat down at the kitchen table. "We've picked up George and Olga," he told us. "As soon as George found Sally missing in Ravenna, he tried to contact Boris. When he couldn't get him, he called Olga to see what he should do. She told him to fly back home and they would decide. We picked her right up and then picked George up when he landed in New York."

"Did you find out how he made the connection between Peter and me?" Sally asked.

"You're responsible for that, Sally."

"How so?"

"Olga visited her father in Russia often. When she was in culinary school, she brought books with her to study for tests. Your first book is required reading. Do you recall what picture is on the back flap?"

"Peter and me in this kitchen."

"Yep. Boris saw the picture and asked Olga about you. Found out you were famous and probably rich. They devised the plan and brought George in to make it work. George is Boris's late brother's son."

"Who made the tapes of Peter and Boris?" I asked.

"Boris did," John said. "We're pretty sure he was planning on blackmailing Peter once he'd made his money from the Mafia."

"So it's really over," Sally said.

"It is. And we've had the court slap both Davis and Olga with gag orders so they can't talk about it at all. I know that your friends who know some of the details may ask you both questions. You're free to discuss George's blackmail plans, but Peter's work with the CIA is still confidential and has to remain so until such time as it's declared declassified."

We both nodded our heads that we understood. Then there was just one more thing I wanted to know. "Did you handcuff George at the airport. In public?" I asked, mentally rubbing my hands together.

"We did," John said. "He looked affronted that we were doing it. He said to our agent, 'Do you know who I am? Have you any idea who I am?'" Sally and I looked at each other and burst into laughter. Lord, revenge is sweet.

WHEN JOHN LEFT, we called Sonya together to tell her that George was in jail and Sally would sign her contracts when she came in next Monday. Before we could say anything, she told us she had some great news.

"I just hung up with someone from the *New York Times*. They are doing an article about Danny for Wednesday's paper. It'll be on the cover of the food section. Earlier this morning, *People* magazine called. They want to come to the studio next Monday to take pictures of him on the show with Sally."

"Why that's just lovely," Sally said. "Perhaps Danny and I will do a great many shows together in the coming years." And then she told her that George was out of the picture and she was remaining at *Morning in America*.

"Bloody hell!" Sonya exclaimed. "I feel like I'm in a time warp. What happened?"

Sally was talking on the extension phone across the room and she raised her eyebrows conspiratorially at me as she spoke into the receiver, "We'll fill you in when we're in New York. Meanwhile, we are one happy family again."

"Amazing. Just amazing. You must have a song for that, Casey."

I started to sing into my extension. " 'Back in the saddle again . . .' "

"I know that one," Sally cried and then belted out in a yo-deling voice, "when a friend is a friend."

Chapter 23

Please don't tell me how the story ends.
— *Kris Kristofferson*

I flew back to New York Tuesday afternoon. My
father met me at the airport wearing a chauffeur's
hat and holding a sign that said SIGNORINA COS-
TELLO. He wrapped me in a big bear hug and said, *"Ciao
bologna."* This came from the same Dad foreign-speak that gave
us the Mexican send-off "Buenos snowshoes" and the bachelor-
party favorite "Arrivederci roaming." He said that Nonna was
waiting at the house and Mary was coming for dinner.

"Has Nonna been waiting since Sunday?"

"She wanted to, but we convinced her to go home and wait
for our call. So, my now truly world-class daughter, was it an
exciting trip?"

"You have no idea, Dad."

He raised his eyebrows. "You want to wait until we're home
to talk about the trip so you'll only have to tell it once?"

"Good plan," I said. "What's happened with the Conti clan
since I've been away? What's the latest with Mrs. A and her
bingo nights?"

"Well, Uncle Tony put her on Prozac."

"Why Prozac? Is she depressed?" I asked.

"How would we know? She hasn't smiled once in the thirty years I've known her. She's possessed with misery."

"Maybe we need an exorcism."

"Probably, but Father Joseph still won't have anything to do with her."

"So much for 'Father forgive them.' "

"Oh, and there's some really big news."

"What's that?"

"Your Aunt Connie is 'back from her trip.' " He used the euphemism the family had chosen and added his own mocking tone.

"No way. How did that happen?"

"Well, according to Russell, the girlfriend dumped Uncle Mike because he had strange eating habits and wouldn't take her to decent restaurants anymore."

"Russell probably made that up."

"Probably. But whatever the reason, it took Mike just two days before he was back at Aunt Connie's."

"And she took him back? Boy, Father Joseph could learn a thing or two about forgiveness from Aunt Connie."

"She did. And no one acted like it had been anything but a little vacation."

"Wow. I guess Aunt Connie missed out on the revenge gene. I would have made him suffer for a long time before taking him back, if I did at all."

"Not if you looked like Aunt Connie. She missed out on a lot of genes."

I glared at my father and imitated my mother's pretended annoyance. "Mike!"

He gave me the exaggerated naive look he'd perfected. "What. What'd I say?"

We laughed at how well we had it down and then he continued with the family saga.

"Raymond is supposedly turning over a new leaf."

"How so?"

"Well, Uncle Little Joey threatened to send him away to a rehabilitation place, so he agreed to go to one of those anonymous groups for—as your mother put it—for people with special problems. You know your mother—she couldn't bring herself to say 'drug addict' about one of her own. Anyway, your aunt Gina has been going with him every day since you left, and I guess it's working. Gina says he's a whole new person. He's cut his hair and is letting his pierced parts close up. I don't know what he'll do about that hideous tattoo."

As we were pulling into our driveway, my father said, "You might want to act as though you're hearing most of this for the first time when your mother tells you. She'll want to give you her interpretation of the situations."

"You got it."

No more than ten minutes from the time I walked in the back door, we were all sitting at the kitchen table drinking coffee and nibbling on Italian pastries. I told them briefly about Italy, knowing I'd have to repeat it all when Mary got there. I said nothing about George or Danny. I decided to withhold George until Mary got there and Danny altogether. Then I passed out presents, and after they had opened them and showed appropriate appreciation, Nonna said, "I have a present for you."

"You do?" I said.

"I'm making you eggplant parmigiana for your homecoming

dinner. Where you were in Italy, they don't know how to do it right." No one knew how to do it like Nonna. Hers was the best and the meal I craved most. I couldn't think of anything better.

"Would you like me to slice the eggplant?" Dad asked. The secret to a good eggplant parmigiana begins with the slicing. The pieces have to be very thin and even; thin so they will cook all the way through and melt into each other when they bake, and even so they will brown at the same time. My father has the steady hand of an artist and is the undisputed best eggplant slicer in the family. But Nonna still believed in caution.

"Okay, Michael," Nonna said. "But do it next to me so I can watch. Casey can help you, and I'll make the marinara. Paula, you make a salad and cook some sausages to go on the side." Marinara, a meatless tomato sauce, is secret number two of eggplant parmigiana. Meat sauce masks the flavor of the eggplant.

I washed the eggplants and gave them to my father to slice. Then, since we didn't have a sauna, I went to the garden to pick basil for Nonna's marinara. As soon as my father had several perfect, paper-thin slices in front of him, I gathered them up and put them in a colander with salt between the layers and a couple of paper towels on top. I placed a can of tomatoes on top of the towels to weight the slices so they would exude any bitter juices, and then beat up several eggs. Secret number three: don't coat the eggplant with bread crumbs; a thin coating of egg is all that is needed to protect the delicate slices while they fry. I poured olive oil into a large frying pan and then got out a large wedge of Parmesan cheese. That's the last secret: don't guck up the eggplant with a lot of different cheeses; just use freshly grated Parmesan.

As we stirred, sliced, and grated, Mom and Nonna gave me their versions of the family events. Mary arrived just as we were putting the eggplant in the oven, and after a few minutes of hugging everyone, she dragged me up to my room.

"So, tell me what happened after I left Florence."

"We went to Ravenna—"

"I'm going to strangle you. Tell me about Danny, and I want all the details."

So I told her about the Florence almost-making-it night, and then about the Florence holiday day, and then about the making-it-in-the-sexy-French-underwear night. I tried to make it sound like just one of those fling things.

She threw both hands over her heart and fell back on my bed. "Thank God. I can barely talk." Then she sat up and said, "See. What did I tell you?"

"What did you tell me?"

She held her hands guitar style. " 'I never mind getting burned if I can just stand near the flame.' "

"It doesn't go like that, but no matter because I do mind getting burned. It was a fling and now it's over."

"You're kidding, right?"

I shook my head.

"What? Are you crazy? If you're going to throw water on the fire, at least wait a while. You've just had a great time with a great guy. And, believe me, he *is* hot. Pul-lease tell me you haven't told him that it's over."

"I have."

"Oh shit, Casey. What'd he say?"

"He hung up on me."

She leaned back on the pillow and shook her head. "It's the Bobby Morgan syndrome all over again."

WE GOT BACK DOWNSTAIRS just as the eggplant was coming out of the oven. Everyone sat down to eat.

"Okay, now we are all here," my mother said, cutting the eggplant. "Tell us *everything* about the trip."

I began with the easy stuff, and they all had questions. Mary wanted to know in detail what the Italian women were wearing, which of the Calvin Klein outfits I had worn, and how on earth could I have not gone into Prada and Escada? Nonna wanted to know exactly what Rosa put in her *brodetto*, how Anna Maria made her pasta dough, and, again, why we hadn't gone to Naples. Mom asked if I'd spoken some Italian there, if I'd refrain from using my *goombah* garbage mouth, and if I'd gotten addresses to write thank-you notes. Dad had only one question, but he asked it more than once: "Where do I find this Mario bastard with the wandering hands?"

We were still sitting there two hours later, and fanny fatigue was beginning to set in. I had eaten three servings of eggplant, undone two inches of zipper on my pants, and had yet to tell them about George.

"Tell them about your Florence holiday, Casey," Mary said. I shot her the evil eye, which she ignored. I did want to tell my mother about the day, but I hadn't decided what I wanted to say about Danny, so I told them about the day and pretended it had ended as sweetly as the real *Roman Holiday,* with me and Danny going our separate ways.

Mary coughed but said nothing. We were working on coffee and Italian pastries when I finally brought up George. I told them as much as I could without getting into that classified area. They listened with their mouths open.

"It's so unbelievable!" Mary said. "George was blackmailing Sally and that's why she was pretending he was her agent? What was he using as bait?"

This is where it got tricky, but I had worked out an answer. "He made up lies but was able to convince Sally they were true.

I don't know what the lies were and, frankly, I don't want to know. Do you remember that girl Carol who was with him at the party at Oran Mor?"

"The one with the pink Marshmallow Peep hairdo who was shoveling the hors d'oeuvres into her purse?"

"That's her. Her real name is Olga Davinsky and she's George's cousin. They were in on this together. She's been arrested as well."

"Well, what will all the important chefs do for demonstration assistants with her out of the picture?" Mary said sarcastically. The stereo was on, and we could hear Louis Prima singing "I'll Be Glad When You're Dead, You Rascal You."

"My sentiments exactly," I said.

Nonna agreed and then asked me again about Danny. I wondered if Mary was feeding her information under the table.

THE REST OF THE week went by like a blur. I arrived at the studio Wednesday morning to find that Mae had things well in hand. I gave her the vintage boa-like wrap that I'd found in a flea market in Florence and she adored it. Then I took out my scripts and went to work.

Our celebrity chef, Allison Field, was an ex-sitcom star who had been fired from her show in a very public studio dispute. She was rumored to be difficult and demanding and was now television roadkill. But at the height of her popularity, she had given Sonya one of her first on-air interviews and so Sonya had said yes when Allison had asked if she could come on our show. Allison had just put out an exercise video that included a small booklet of low-fat, delicious recipes that, combined with the exercise, were guaranteed to keep one fit. By the looks of her, she was well qualified to tell the rest of us what to do with our bodies.

"Where do you want me to start?" I asked Mae, since she knew what still needed to be done.

"You set up the turkey meatloaf and I'll do the spaghetti-squash pasta," she said, grinning at the change of roles.

Jonathan, still in his neck brace, came into the kitchen and, ignoring the colors of the four peppers that went into the spaghetti squash dish, zeroed in on the brown meatloaf.

"It's not as brown as beef meatloaf, and it does have a nice red tomato salsa on top," I said hopefully.

"Brown is brown," he grumbled.

I gave him the colorful Deruta pitcher shaped like a chicken I had bought for him, and he actually smiled at me.

"By the way, how is your neck? Is it getting any better?"

"Not at all. I shouldn't even be here. The chiropractor said I'll probably have to see him for the rest of my life. He said I was a mess."

I grinned at him. "You sure he was talking about your neck?"

"I'm not in a funny mood, Casey."

So much for the smile. As for the mood, Jonathan had had funny-bypass surgery long before I'd met him.

Sonya brought Allison into the kitchen about half an hour before she was due on air. There was nothing about the star that even suggested she was difficult. She thought the food looked great, complimented us on the script breakdown, and even made Jonathan semihappy by ogling his cabinet collection of whatnots. Our collected opinion of her was that she was a kind, sweet person. She did a great show and finished by flexing several well-defined muscles for the audience.

Thursday we had an all-chocolate show, which had Jonathan close to apoplexy. The pastry chef was going to show how to temper chocolate and then make truffles and fancy decorations for cakes. I tried to convince Jonathan that the dark brown would be dynamite against a white background, but he pouted throughout the morning and I gave up trying to put him in a better mood. I wasn't in such a great mood myself. And I knew why. I had e-mailed the scripts to Sally and Danny, along with nice little notes. I didn't want to get involved with Danny, but I did have to work with him and wanted to remain friends. Sally had replied with "Sounds great! Can't wait to see you. :)." Danny had replied with nada

THURSDAY NIGHT, THERE WAS a different type of nada. Richard called.

"Casey, I'm sorry. I was an idiot. It was all so foolish. You and I weren't getting along and Lexi was letting me know she thought I was terrific. I just got crazy."

Welcome to the fold, I thought but said nothing, so he went on with his nada. "I miss you. I want you to come back to the apartment. Just so you know, Lexi no longer works for me."

"I'm sorry, Richard. But you're right. It wasn't working and there's no reason to believe that it will now."

"Casey, I love you."

"I'm sorry, Richard, but I don't love you. And I don't think you really love me. I think our relationship was just convenient."

"That's harsh."

"No. It's true."

"There's someone else, isn't there?"

"No. There *isn't*."

"Well, then you're still angry, and you have a right to be."

"Richard, if I were angry, I'd be swearing at you in Italian."

He was quiet for a moment and must have realized that what I'd said was true. "Is there anything I can do to change your mind?" he asked.

"Not about us, but I could use an appointment to get my teeth cleaned." Sometimes you have to be practical. Good dentists are hard to find.

FRIDAY MORNING WE HAD no live spot and we prepped for Monday's Baked Alaska. Mondays are always a tough day for live spots because none of us are there on Sunday. We baked the cakes, laid out the trays, molded and froze ice cream, and I mentally prepared myself for the deep-freeze treatment I expected from Danny.

Chapter 24

Maybe I didn't treat you quite as good as I should have.
— *Willie Nelson*

I couldn't remember ever going into the studio to work with Sally feeling as down as I did on Monday morning. I hadn't heard one word from Danny and I wondered if he planned to continue the silent treatment all morning. Maybe I hadn't handled it all that well after all. I hadn't expected this reaction from him, and I decided that if he was in the kitchen alone when I got there, I would act cheery, as though nothing unusual had gone on.

Danny was not in the kitchen when I arrived. In fact, he didn't come in until after everyone else was there. Obviously, he wanted to avoid having to be alone with me. At least he said hello to me—after he'd said hello to Sonya, Sally, Mae, Jonathan, and two Tonys. That "hello" was the extent of our exchange, and then we all went on with our work. Everyone but me seemed to be in great spirits. I made Jonathan look like a one-man comedy show.

With the eight of us crowded into the tiny kitchen, we were testing the limits of its capacity. We had the door open, since it was just about six o'clock and the show wasn't on the air yet, but I still felt like we were circus clowns ready to pop out of a Volkswagen or college kids cramming ourselves into a phone booth. I felt claustrophobic, but no one else complained. They were recounting stories about their first experiences with Baked Alaska, and Danny was telling us his.

"When the government gave me the scholarship, they held a fancy dinner for me and four others who had also been given money for school. It was held in the state dining room of the president's residence, and I was a bit nervous since I'd never been to such a posh affair. But my mother said just to watch the president and do what she did. So, that's what I did, and I made it to dessert without embarrassing myself. They served individual Baked Alaskas—flaming, mind you. Halfway through eating it, I realized that President Robinson had a doily on her plate and I didn't. Mine had been so frozen to the cake that I was eating it as well. Then I had to decide whether to eat the rest of it and make out that I'd never had one, or leave the half-eaten paper on the plate and give myself up for a fool."

"What did you do?" asked Mae. "Leave it?"

"No, I'm a proud son of a whore. I ate it."

Sally gave a great hoot. "That's wonderful," she said, wiping her eyes.

They were all trying to decide what they would have done with the half-eaten doily when the director called down for a beauty shot. Sonya said it would be a good idea for Sally and Danny to assemble the Baked Alaska so they could see how it would go on the air. They stood next to each other on one side of Romeo, Mae gave them a bowl of meringue, and Jonathan gave them a doily-lined glass plate with a génoise on it. "Take it from the point after the egg whites are ready," Sonya said.

Sally dipped a pastry brush in rum-flavored sugar syrup and spread it on the cake. "This is pig's blood. I think you'll find it very tasty."

Danny didn't miss a beat. He turned the bowl of ice cream upside down on the cake and said, "And here are the pureed snouts and tails. What's pig's blood without the rest of the pig?"

When they got to the point of swirling on the meringue, Sally thought they should have a race. Danny was faster and got to the top first. Sally said he'd cheated and she squirted meringue on his nose. Danny laughed and gave her a wicked grin as he went after her with his pastry bag. Sally tried to step back, but she stepped on Mae and had nowhere to go.

"Food fight, food fight!" yelled Jonathan.

"Stop. We need that meringue," Mae said, laughing so hard she dislodged several of her hair clips.

"Uncle, uncle," cried Sally, and the minute she opened her mouth Danny squirted meringue in it.

Sally licked her lips. "That's quite good," she said.

"I think you two need to work on that spot a bit," Sonya remarked.

We finished assembling the cake. Considering what it had been through, it looked very impressive. If Sally and Danny carried that same sense of fun on the air—minus the talk of pigs and the meringue fight—they would be equally impressive. It was obvious that Italy had cemented their relationship, which had already begun as a good one. He had been shamelessly flirting with her all morning, and she was flirting right back. My relationship with him, on the other hand, had obviously gone down the toilet. I missed the flirting.

• • •

WHEN OUR PREP WAS finished, and I decided not to do a pastry run and started to sit down at Romeo with my scripts, Sally took my arm and said, "Let's go to the buffet, Casey."

I hadn't had anything to eat that morning, but when I got there, nothing was appealing, so I just stood there and let Sally fill up her plate.

"Aren't you going to have anything to eat, Casey?"

"No. I'm not really hungry."

"Ah." She nodded. "Hell has frozen over." Then she looked at me and asked, "Could your loss of appetite have anything to do with the fact that you and Danny are acting like two children fighting over a shovel in a sandbox?"

"You noticed?"

"How could I miss it? You have never been very good at hiding your emotions. I don't know Danny as well, but I know when a person is in a snit."

"He was perfectly cheery in there."

She looked over the top of her glasses at me. "Do you want to tell me what this is all about?"

"You know the beginning: we had a fling in Italy. The end is that I didn't want to get involved here."

"I think you left out a lot in the middle. I think you care for him more than you want to admit, but I don't have time to talk about it now. I have to get up to makeup. Let's have lunch together after my voice-overs."

"Sure."

"Are you going to get muffins now?"

"No. I'm really not hungry." We started to walk back and I thought about what my father had said about being "lose-your-appetite in love." If that was what this was, it didn't feel so good.

THE MINUTE THE CAMERAS began to roll, they picked up that Sally and Danny were crazy about each other. She put her arm around him and said how pleased she was to be here with her good friend Danny O'Shea. She told the audience that they were going to make a fine old chestnut, Baked Alaska. "First you have to have a soft meringue, at just the perfect stage." The camera went in for a close-up of the meringue. "We have six egg whites, superfine sugar, and vanilla, with some cream of tartar to keep them stable. Are they ready, Danny?"

"Not quite," he said and ran the machine for a few seconds. "There." He removed the bowl and held it out for Sally to see.

"Stiff, but not dry," she said. "But we'd better be sure." And she rested an egg on the whites and told the audience that it should sink in exactly one inch. "Perfect. Let's put the Baked Alaska together."

Sally brushed the cake with rum-flavored sugar syrup while Danny explained what it was; then Danny turned the ice cream out on top of the cake and Sally pulled off the plastic wrap. They filled their pastry bags and swirled on the meringue. Sally beamed at Danny and said that everyone should cook with a friend. "It's so much more fun." Danny dusted the cake all over with powdered sugar and then reached under the counter and pulled out a blowtorch. Sally looked at it and said, "Huh," then pulled out a blowtorch twice the size and grinned at Danny.

"Yours is kind of small. Can it do the job?"

"We'll see," he said and together they torched the dessert.

When the show was over the *People* photographer began to take photos of Danny and Sally and a Baked Alaska that would be a Floating Island if he didn't work fast. Mae and Sonya stayed to watch the fun and I went back to the kitchen to help the Tonys clean up. I told them cake was on its way as soon as its modeling gig was up.

TEN MINUTES LATER, Danny came in. I was sweeping the floor. "Hey, Tony and Tony," he said. "There's Baked Alaska on the set that needs eating. Grab some before it's gone."

The Tonys looked at me for approval. "Go for it," I said. As soon as they left, Danny closed the door. He took the broom of out my hands and leaned it against the wall.

"Okay, Casey. It's taken some three thousand miles and eight days for my Irish temper to cool down, but now it's cool and I want to talk to you."

My heart was racing, and I hoped and prayed it was something positive. Bad news is never good on an empty stomach.

"You not only made me mad, Casey. You hurt me."

My empty stomach sank to the floor. "Hurt you? How did I hurt you?"

"You used me for a good time in Italy—a roll in the hay. Then, at the airport, you gobsmacked me. Let me know that I was nothing more than a little diversion."

My mouth flew open and I stood up straight. "Wait a minute. You've got it all wrong. That's not what I did at all."

"Oh really?" He was frowning at me and the blue of his eyes took on the color of a stormy ocean. "Then maybe you can tell me exactly what it was you *did* do."

I couldn't say anything for a minute because it struck me that what he said was exactly how it looked. I *was* the one who came on to him in Italy, after telling him repeatedly in New York that I wasn't interested. After Florence, I acted as though we were getting it on just fine, and then in Milan I iced him, without an explanation.

I owed him an explanation, so I told him about seeing the photo of Kim and told him I didn't think people went around with near-nude photos of casual acquaintances. "I just don't do well with relationships that aren't monogamous, Danny. I should have explained that to you at the airport, but I guess I didn't think it would matter to you."

My explanation did nothing in the way of removing the storm from his eyes. "That photo was in my backpack because it came in mail I received the day I left Ireland to go to your party in Florence. I opened all the mail on the plane and put it in my backpack. It's all still there. Kim was on vacation and sent everyone the same photo. The staff has it tacked it up in the kitchen."

"So you're saying that Kim means nothing to you."

"No, I'm not saying that. Kim means a lot to me. She's been with the restaurant since it opened and she's a great asset. She keeps all those young male businessmen coming in every day for lunch. But *I* am not involved with her and never have been.

"And, just so you'll know, I don't play around, Casey. Sure, I flirt, but that's just part of the blarney. For one thing, I don't have the time to fool around. I'm at the restaurant twenty-four/seven. And, for another, I've always been a one-girl-at-a-time guy. My past serious relationships, all two of them, have been long and monogamous."

"I didn't know" was all I could get out.

"No. You didn't. But you never even asked. Even if you had, I don't think you would have believed me anyway."

He was right. I wouldn't have. *Everything* he'd said was true. It did look as though I'd used him, and it must have felt like that—but only to someone who cared. And he had shown me a number of ways that he cared. But I had written them off. I felt absolutely horrible and couldn't think of a thing to say in my defense. So the emotions I was so poor at hiding took charge, and I started to cry.

"Oh, Jesus," he said. "Don't do that. That's hitting below the belt."

"I wasn't using you, Danny. I loved being with you. I wanted to be with you." And then I took a really bold move and looked directly in his eyes. "I want to be with you."

The storm went away and he reached up and wiped the tears from my face. "Apology accepted." Standing with his back against Romeo, he put his hands behind him, easily hoisting himself up to sit. He quickly stretched his legs out, wrapped them around my waist, and pulled me to him. He held me there with his knees and put his hands on my shoulders. "You know, I think you wanted to believe that I was that meadow vole because you were attracted to me from the first time you met me and couldn't deal with it."

"Well, that's an arrogant thing to say!" I tried to step back, but he tightened his legs around me.

"It's that. But it's true. Just as I was immediately attracted to you. I knew I wanted you the first time I saw you. Standing there in those wet, disheveled clothes, commenting on my ass."

"Hey. That was a very expensive silk Chloé shirt!"

He ran his hands over what he'd remembered seeing through the wet shirt. "I don't know what it looks like dry, but wet it's worth every penny."

I looked toward the door. "You *are* aware that we are in a studio with an awful lot of people who could walk in at any minute."

"Sally's standing guard. I told her not to let anyone in until I'd finished throttling you."

"And she agreed to do that?"

"Yep. She said if you didn't get the point by the time I finished with you, she'd have a go at you herself."

I smiled at that. Sally the yenta. "I guess she thinks I was acting like an idiot as well."

"In truth, the vote was unanimous. The Tonys held out for

a bit, but as soon as Mae came down on my side, they threw their lot in with the majority. Sally defended you by saying it's part of your charm." I leaned into him and he wrapped me in his arms and legs and kissed my neck. "You have no idea, in spite of how angry I was, how much I've missed touching you." Then he stopped kissing me and sniffed. "Umm. Do I smell mimosa?"

"Mm-hmm," I said.

He slid off the counter and kissed me at the bottom of the V on my V-neck T-shirt. "Where else is it?" he asked, coaxing the V away from center.

"No place I can show you here."

"I told you, no one will come in. Besides, isn't that why you all call this counter 'Romeo'?"

"Not exactly," I laughed and reached up to run my fingers through his hair. "Anyway, I think there are more appropriate places for you to inhale mimosa than the kitchen."

"You're right. My place. Tonight." He smiled. "Agreed?"

"Agreed."

"And the night after? And the night after that? And . . ."

I answered him by reaching my arms around his neck and kissing him while "When Irish Eyes Are Smiling" played loud and clear in my head.

"I'll take that as a yes," he said. "Okay, we can open the door. But do it slowly. My guess is there are at least six people leaning against it to see if I could do what I said I was coming in to do."

"What's that?

"Convince you that I want to be a prairie vole."

Recipes

THE CONTI FAMILY MEAT SAUCE

....

Italian Americans call this "gravy"; Italian Italians call it *ragù*. Everyone calls it ubiquitous in Italian cuisine. There are as many versions as there are towns in Italy, but once you have fallen in love with your version, all others will be forever lacking.

Makes about 2 quarts

*About 2 pounds inexpensive pork with bones
    (such as pieces of neck or shoulder)*

About ½ pound inexpensive beef

¼ cup extra-virgin olive oil

1 medium onion, coarsely chopped

*3 35-ounce cans Italian plum tomatoes (12 cups),
    with juices*

Salt and freshly ground black pepper

Braciole (optional, recipe below)

Meatballs (recipe below)

Rinse the pork and beef, pat dry, and cut into pieces roughly 4 inches square. Heat the oil in a deep, heavy pot and cook the onion until translucent. Push the onion aside, and working with a few pieces at a time, brown the meat on all sides. Push the tomatoes through a strainer to remove the seeds and pour them into the pot with all the meat. Season with salt and pepper and bring to a boil. Boil briskly for 15 minutes, then reduce the heat so that the sauce simmers gently and partially cover the pot. Cook, stirring occasionally, for 2½ hours. If the sauce becomes too thick, add small amounts of hot water. If using the *Braciole*, drop them into the pot after the sauce has cooked for 1 hour. Add the Meatballs for the last 45 minutes of cooking. Remove the meats from the sauce. Serve the sauce over pasta, and serve the meats separately.

Braciole

To be exact, these are *braciolini*, small meat rolls.
   Braciole is typically made in one large roll, but the
   small ones make serving easier.
Serves 6–8

1½ pounds beef top round (3 slices, ¼ inch thick)

½ pound prosciutto

½ cup fresh breadcrumbs

½ cup grated parmigiano-reggiano cheese

Salt and freshly ground black pepper

½ cup minced fresh parsley

Olive oil for frying

Cut the beef into pieces approximately 4 × 3 inches and pound each until it is about ⅛ inch thick. Cover each piece with a slice of prosciutto.

Toss together the breadcrumbs, cheese, salt, pepper, and parsley, and sprinkle the mixture over the slices, keeping it ¼ inch in from the edges. Roll the slices into sausage shapes and secure closed with toothpicks or tie with kitchen string. Heat the oil in a heavy frying pan and brown the *braciole* well on all sides. Transfer these to the meat sauce to finish cooking.

Meatballs

Serves 6–8

1 pound ground beef

4 large eggs, beaten

1 cup fresh breadcrumbs

¼ cup freshly grated parmigiano-reggiano cheese

Salt and pepper

⅓ cup dark raisins (optional)

Mix all the ingredients together and blend well. With wet hands, roll the mixture into balls about 1½ inches in diameter. Drop the balls into the simmering meat sauce.

NONNA CONTI'S EGGPLANT PARMESAN

....

S eem too simple? That's the beauty of this dish. The eggplant is the star of the show since it is not upstaged by an intrusive riot of other flavors.
Serves 6–8

1 medium eggplant, about 1¼ pounds

Salt and freshly ground black pepper

4 large eggs

Olive oil for frying

1½ cups Marinara Sauce (recipe below)

¼ cup freshly grated parmigiano-reggiano cheese

Peel the eggplant and cut it into paper-thin slices. Layer the slices in a colander, lightly salting each layer, and sit a plate on top, touching the eggplant. Put a heavy can on top of the plate and let the eggplant drain for about an hour, then rinse off the salt and pat the slices dry.

Preheat the oven to 400°F. Beat the eggs in a pie pan or shallow flat dish and season with salt and pepper. Pour enough olive oil into a 10- or 12-inch frying pan to reach a depth of ¼ inch and heat it over medium-high heat. Working with a few slices at a time, dip the eggplant into the egg, let the excess egg drip off, and then slide the pieces into the hot oil. Cook on each side just until golden brown then remove and drain on paper towels or brown paper bags. Watch the eggplant carefully; the thin slices will cook very quickly.

Layer the eggplant and Marinara Sauce in a shallow baking dish, ending with a film of sauce on top. Sprinkle the cheese evenly over the sauce and bake for 10 minutes. Serve hot or at room temperature.

Marinara Sauce

Makes about 1½ cups

3 tablespoons extra-virgin olive oil

2 large cloves garlic, peeled and thinly sliced

Small pinch hot pepper or ¼ teaspoon paprika

1 28-ounce can Italian plum tomatoes, with juices, chopped

Salt

About ¼ cup fresh basil leaves, torn

Heat the oil over medium-low heat in a nonreactive saucepan or skillet. Put the garlic in the pan, and taking care not to let it brown, cook it until it is soft. Stir in the pepper flakes or paprika, cook 15 seconds, and then pour in the tomatoes with their juices. Bring the sauce to a boil, reduce the heat so it bubbles in a few places, season with salt and basil, and let it simmer about 20 minutes until slightly thickened.

SAL VITO'S MACARONI
WITH CAULIFLOWER

....

This dish just begs for a large amount of garlic, but you can adjust the amount to your liking.
Serves 6

1 large head cauliflower, about 2 pounds

½ cup extra-virgin olive oil

5 large cloves garlic, minced

¼–½ teaspoon hot pepper flakes

1 pound penne or similar macaroni

6 anchovy fillets, rinsed, patted dry, and minced (optional)

Salt

Freshly grated pecorino-romano cheese or fresh breadcrumbs browned in olive oil

Remove the green leaves and cut out the stem of the cauliflower. Cut the head into 3-inch florets, and wash them in cold water. Drop the florets into boiling salted water and cook for 5 minutes. Lift the cauliflower out of the water with a strainer or slotted spoon and reserve the water on the stove. Chop the cauliflower very fine.

In a large sauté pan, heat the olive oil over medium heat, stir in the garlic and hot pepper, and cook gently until the garlic is golden. Meanwhile, return the cauliflower water to a boil and stir in the macaroni. If using the anchovies, stir them into the sauté pan with the garlic and cook for 1 minute. Put the cauliflower into the pan and toss the ingredients together well. Taste for salt and cook for 3–4 minutes until the cauliflower is hot. Drain the macaroni, transfer it to a warm pasta bowl, toss it with the cauliflower, and then sprinkle the cheese or breadcrumbs on top.

MICHAELA'S PANZANELLA

....

This is the perfect summer salad. It can be lunch all by itself or the side dish for cold chicken or barbecued meat or fish.

Serves 6

1 pound gutsy Italian bread, preferably whole wheat, several days old

2 medium red onions, peeled and thinly sliced

3 medium cloves garlic, minced (optional)

Salt and freshly ground black pepper

4 large, very ripe tomatoes, coarsely chopped into large pieces

½ cup fresh basil leaves, torn into large pieces

½ cup very good extra-virgin olive oil

2 tablespoons red-wine vinegar

Cut the bread into large pieces and put it into a bowl. Cover it with very cold water and let it soak for ½ hour. Put the onion slices into a smaller bowl, cover them with cold water, and let them soak for ½ hour, changing the water at least once. This will sweeten the onions.

Drain the bread and gently but thoroughly squeeze it dry, then break it up into a serving bowl. Use a fork to toss the garlic, salt, and pepper with the bread. Drain the onions and lay them over the bread. Toss the tomatoes with salt, pepper, and basil and scatter them over the onions. Cover with plastic wrap and refrigerate for at least ½ hour.

Pour the olive oil and vinegar over the salad, toss well. Garnish this dish with whole basil leaves if desired.

GINO BAFFONI'S RAGÙ ALLA BOLOGNESE

···

Bolognese sauce is not soupy like other tomato sauces. It cooks down to a thick, rich sauce that will sit well up on a dish of pasta. Spaghetti is the pasta favored for bolognese.

Makes about 6 cups

3 tablespoons unsalted butter

1 tablespoon extra-virgin olive oil

1 medium onion, minced (about 1 cup)

3 large cloves garlic, minced

1 small carrot, minced (about ¼ cup)

1 celery stalk, minced (about ½ cup)

Salt and freshly ground black pepper

1 pound finely minced stew beef or 1 pound ground beef

½ cup milk

1 35-ounce can Italian plum tomatoes (4 cups), with juices, chopped

¾ cup red wine

1 cup beef broth

3 tablespoons heavy cream (optional)

Melt the butter with the olive oil in a 12- or 14-inch skillet over medium-low heat. Stir in the onion, garlic, carrot, and celery. Season with salt and pepper and cook gently until the vegetables are softened, about 15 minutes. Turn the heat up slightly and crumble the meat into the pan. Sauté the meat until it is no longer pink, breaking it into small pieces. Season with salt, then pour in the milk and turn the heat to high so the milk evaporates. Pour in the tomatoes, wine, and broth, bring the sauce to a boil, and then reduce the heat and let it simmer for 2½–3 hours until most of the liquid is reduced. If desired, pour the heavy cream into the finished sauce and then reduce the sauce slightly.

ANNA MARIA'S TAGLIATELLE DI PARMA

....

F resh peas and/or tiny asparagus are a delicious addition to this pasta. Blanch the vegetables first and cut
the asparagus into small pieces. Sauté them with the
prosciutto and leave everything else as is.

Serves 6

6 tablespoons unsalted butter

¼ pound prosciutto, cut into narrow strips

2 cups heavy cream

Salt and freshly ground black pepper

Pinch grated nutmeg

*3 tablespoons tomato puree or Marinara Sauce
(recipe above)*

1¼ pounds homemade or storebought tagliatelle

Freshly grated parmigiano-reggiano cheese

Melt the butter in a large sauté pan over medium heat and
stir in the prosciutto. Cook gently for 3 minutes, then pour in
the cream and turn the heat up to high. Reduce the cream by
half, stirring often, and then season it with the salt, pepper,
and nutmeg. Stir the tomato puree into the sauce and cook for
1–2 minutes to blend the flavors. Toss the sauce with the
cooked tagliatelle in a warm pasta bowl, and sprinkle the dish
generously with cheese.